ANASSA

Also by Josh Martin:

Ariadnis

ANASSA

JOSH MARTIN

Quercus

QUERCUS CHILDREN'S BOOKS

First published in Great Britain in 2018 by Hodder and Stoughton

1 3 5 7 9 10 8 6 4 2

A CIP catalogue record for this book is available
from the British Library.

ISBN 978 1 78429 826 5

Printed and bound in Great Britain by Clays

MIX
Paper from
responsible sources
FSC® C104740

The paper and board used in this book are
made from wood from responsible sources.

Quercus Children's Books
An imprint of Hachette Children's Group
Part of Hodder and Stoughton
Carmelite House
50 Victoria Embankment
London EC4Y 0DZ

An Hachette UK Company
www.hachette.co.uk
www.hachettechildrens.co.uk

For Sally Graham and Stella Clarke.
Two mothers who, like Ashir, have passed on
but left great people in their wake.

Prologue

Etain

I keep coming back to this memory of you, Ma . . .

I was in the kitchen of the prophet house, clearing wooden plates stained dark with vinegar and oil, putting discarded tomato stems in the compost, rewrapping fruit in cloth. You were still frozen in your seat at the head of the table. The argument you'd just had with Aula hung in the air like the smell of burned bread. Aula had punched a hole through her ex-boyfriend's door or something like that. It was a fairly typical Aula mishap, and it was fairly typical of you to give her the old *you have a responsibility to control yourself* line.

What wasn't so typical was that you were still sitting there, like you were too tired to move. Like the argument had cleaned out all your energy. You treated Aula like she was one of your own, and she was. Aula was my best friend, more like my sister, so arguments between the three of us were always gonna happen. But this time was different.

Had you Seen something? I try to remember your face in that moment: the harassed lines around your mouth and eyes, the heaviness in your forehead, the grey streaks

1

worn into your tight black curls. Is that why you were sitting here – because you knew this was the last argument you'd ever have?

In a few hours you'd go over to Aula's palace rooms to make it up with her. There, you would have a vision that would weaken you enough to put you in the healing houses for the rest of your life.

How many times had you told me about the dangers of prophecy?

Most of the time, Etain, you'd say, *the future's just snatches and glances, like coordinates on a map. But sometimes a prophet will get a vision that will let her See not just coordinates but the whole winding route of someone's fate. And that's where the danger lies. Human eyes aren't well adapted to looking at the world that way, and delving too deep into visions can shatter your mind.*

And yet I *knew* you'd been trying to open yourself up to visions like that recently, to try to See something that would help Aula or Taurus or me.

The other prophets had gone to bed. It was just me and you now.

I finished wiping the table. 'Ma, what is it?'

You remained perfectly still, fist pressed against your mouth in thought. When you looked up, I had the sense that you were organising your thoughts and that the thoughts weren't getting put to bed without a fight.

'I'm just thinking,' you said.

'Worrying,' I corrected.

You wrinkled your nose in agreement.

'Aula will be all right, Ma,' I said. 'She just thinks no

2

one understands her. She still doesn't know there are *other people* who've got a prophecy about them besides her.'

Aula might have been born to *unite* the people of our city, Athenas, and its rival city, Metis, but I was born to *lead* both those peoples into a future that combined their seemingly antithetical cultures into one. You'd had me at that grindstone all my life. You had me learning all the leader tricks I could from Nadrik, and down in Metis you had Taurus absorbing everything he could from their leader, Mathilde, so he could report it all back to me later. I knew your life had been dedicated to getting those two things to work: our people united, and led by someone who you trusted. But I was still your girl, Ma. And I still just wanted your attention.

'Sorry, sweetheart, what did you say?'

I felt my face heat, annoyed at myself. I repeated, without embellishment this time: 'Aula will be all right, Ma.'

'Yes, yes, I know. You'll take care of her, Etain.'

For some reason that gave me a strange feeling in my stomach – because you didn't seem to be talking about the argument. You seemed to be talking about something that was way more long-term.

I guess I had you rumbled cos you jerked and stretched out your arms, yawning theatrically.

'What do you mean, Ma? Where are you going?'

You batted a hand at me. 'Darling, you know what I mean. I'm the mother figure. Sisters are much better at getting through to each other than mothers are.'

But you hadn't meant that, I knew you hadn't. I hesitated, wondering if I should be worried, hoping I didn't have to be. *You'll take care of her, Etain*.

'*When* will I take care of her, Ma? What did you mean? Like . . . when I'm leader?'

You massaged the skin around your eyes with your fingertips. 'Well, yes, I suppose so. But you'll have to take care of everyone when you're leader, not just Aula.'

I frowned. 'And . . . and where will you be?'

It had never occurred to me that you wouldn't be there. But at that moment it seemed like . . . like maybe you'd Seen that future already.

There was this horrible silence as you lowered your hands. You looked frightened. Like you really didn't know. But then you smiled. 'I'll be clearing up the mess,' you said. 'Now take that look off your face – don't be silly. What are you doing tonight?'

I sighed, thought about fighting against the subject change, and gave up when I caught your eye.

'Well, Aula's just had a nasty break-up.'

'So . . . ?'

'So, do you have the keys to the wine cellar?'

You sniffed. 'I would definitely *not* recommend looking above the lintel for it.'

'You're supposed to discourage me,' I said.

'I think you'll learn to discourage yourself from it sooner than I could persuade you to,' you replied.

I laughed.

I wish I'd known this was the last real conversation we'd get to have.

The next time I saw you, you were in Aula's arms, being

carried down to the Head Healer, Phythia. The networks of scars around your eyes were glowing.

In a matter of months, you'd be dead.

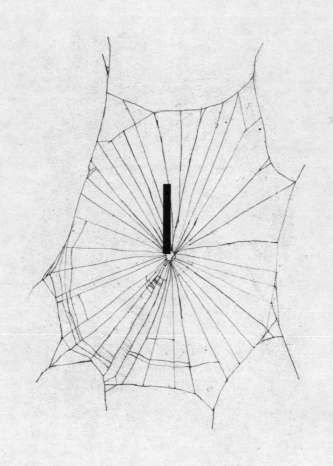

Etain

I am the Anassa: the leader of the only remaining humans on the last island on Erthe, and today I am leading us home. I am standing in the clearing into which I have poured all my people's energy for over a year. In front of me are the nine vishaal trees.

It's hard to describe their size: it takes me ten minutes to walk the full circumference of one of them. I can't approach the trunks without climbing on to their enormous, serpent-like roots that protrude above ground. The bark is smooth further up, but down here it's cracked like the floor of a desert, mottled with lichen.

The dawn isn't far off, and the warmth of the day with it: already I smell herbs wakening in thickets as the forest around creaks awake, shaking off its nightly coat of dew.

I look up. It's been nearly a year since my people called these trees home and they looked very different then. The *island* looked different. The vishaal trees – the same ones I'm looking at now – were shorter, growing only to tickle the underside of the cliff shelf that stretched out above them.

Before, the branches above me would have been home to a thousand people – each tree connected by a network of rope ladders and living-wood bridges, vines and natural magic.

My own city, Athenas, had rested on the cliff shelf above.

You couldn't tell that the nine pillars of Athenas used to

be trees – not when the trunks had been stripped of all their branches and covered top to root in metal casing. I used to ask Ma: 'Where did we *find* all the ore to make that metal?' I know the island is volcanic, obviously – that was how we could power the city with steam – but still, how did we mine it? She never had a satisfactory answer: no one did. No one had ever lived outside of the cities, bound there as they were by protective spells and stubbornness. Not until now. Not until *us*.

The first time I saw Athenas from a distance was strange – the pillars like nine sticks with plates sitting on top of them.

As I said, Athenas rested on that cliff shelf, but it was so strange to see how thin that rock was – how could it have supported a city with all those passages inside it? And that's not even mentioning Ariadnis – the place where Aula and Joomia, the Chosen One of Metis, had to go to get the Book of Wisdom and prove that one of them was more worthy of having it.

That was the beginning of the change. When Aula and Joomia caused the trees to grow up and merge with the pillars, the cliff crumbled. The plateaus that sat on top of the pillars fell. And both the Metisians and the Athenasians lost their homes. There was a hell of a lot of rubble to clean up around the base of the new mega-trees: rock, huge fragments of metal, rubble from buildings, books, old watermill structures, furniture, you name it. Around a month ago, the clean-up finally came to an end.

And today, finally, we're taking our first steps toward making ourselves a home again. I kiss my teeth in annoyance, because, before all that, there are rounds to do.

It's mainly me inspecting everyone's work around camp without looking like that's what I'm doing. It's an art form: I have to smile here, encourage there, suggest improvements, give direction. Deflect all the veiled criticism of me that people have stored like ammunition. Almost every adult in this camp has an idea that they'd do a better leadership job than me given the opportunity.

I pull in all my scattered thoughts as I walk, comb them down like flyaway hairs, braid them tightly into order so no one can see them reflecting off my face. I picked it up from Ma, and she was even better at it than I am.

This is the camp. It's where we live now. I think it's a pretty good spot: a few miles from the north-eastern beach. It rests on a slight hill, downwind of the river. It was easier to pitch here. The island hardly has a spot where it en't sprouting some kind of foliage, but at this end the earth is sandier, rockier and only populated by fynbos shrubs and a few angular cypress trees. Since we settled here, it's been a process of setting up water runs, latrine duties and cooking rotas.

I complete my circuit of the camp and roll back the flap to my tent. Head Healer Phythia's just inside the doorway, making tea. She took good care of Ma in those last couple of months before she died; now she looks out for me.

'Busy out there?' she asks.

'You try telling Ior his statue of the Wise One might be offensive to the Metisians,' I say. 'Or mentioning to *Sara* that the sleeping tents are leaking again. I thought she was going to shove a tent peg down my throat.'

11

'That old hag,' Phythia mutters, shoving some herb infusion at me as I fold myself stiffly on to the blankets on the floor. 'You look dreadful. Drink that.'

'En't healers supposed to be maternal and nurturing?' I yawn, nearly dropping the cup as it sloshes. It's moments like this when Ma's voice busies into my head. *What did I tell you about how to speak?*

I think to myself: *Well, you can count all your bullying on that subject as a success, Ma, cos even though I'd drop my King's-Scribe vernacular if I could, I've noticed that it gives me an authority that I wouldn't have without it. Are you happy? Of course you are.*

Phythia whacks her spoon on my clothes trunk. '*Stop* rubbing your eyes, you'll make them puffier!'

'I don't reckon it's gonna make much difference on two hours' sleep. You know, once in a while, you could lie and tell me I look radiant.'

She puts her hands on her hips. 'Well, how would you know if I meant it some other time?'

I give in to my quirking mouth and laugh. 'Fine. Forget I said anything,' I say. Phythia set up the healing tents herself on the day we decided to pitch here, and had her assistants recruited and half the herbs she needed picked by sundown. I'm glad we get on.

'How's your shoulder?' she asks, coming over to inspect it. I force myself not to flinch away from her, remembering the day it happened. The archer in Nadrik's army, the unreal *thunk* as I swivelled to take the arrow in my shoulder rather than my heart. That was the day Athenas fell—

'Still working, thanks to you,' I say.

12

'Stiff, then?' she says, gently probing the star-shaped scar.

I shrug (I *can* still shrug). 'It just doesn't like moving up and down. Or sideways. Or any direction.' I force out another laugh. 'My hand's fine . . . I can still *grip* things, but . . .'

'But nothing as heavy as a hammer,' Phythia says, giving me a knowing look.

I look away and shift my shoulder slightly out of her reach. 'I suppose I should start getting ready,' I say, 'Any tips?'

We hear the distinct clink of bangles outside and Phythia rolls her eyes. 'No need. Your brother's here.'

Taurus pulls open the flap of the tent with a grin, hooks Phythia into a hug and manages to throw me one of his loaves, all in the same movement.

I catch the bread and lift it to my nose. 'Rosemary,' I say appreciatively. 'I'm glad the herb garden's taking.'

Taurus raises his eyebrow and cups his hand around his ear. 'I'm sorry, what?' he says.

'I was about to say thank you,' I say as Phythia extricates herself from Taurus's arms and makes to leave.

'Stop wandering around in the middle of the night,' she tells me over her shoulder. 'That's my beauty tip.'

Taurus smirks and dumps himself in front of me, a tangle of long elegant limbs. *At least one of us looks like you, hey, Ma?* I think. *Would it sting you, to see Taurus now? You sent him to live in Metis when he was three years old, thinking there was no particular destiny for him. You got him to learn the culture of Metis and the leadership style of Mathilde and the Elders so he could relay it back to me. I wonder what it*

13

cost for you to send him there. I wonder what it cost him, and if he'd ever tell me about it if it did.

'What have you done to your braids?' he demands. 'I spent ages on those!' He shuffles over to me and begins to preen, giving me a closer look at his own meticulously kept dreads.

'You did them too tight,' I say. 'And I miss my *afro*.'

'Yeah, yeah, pardon me, my lady. Wait, are these . . . spider webs?' he asks absently, picking them out.

I shrug. I probably wouldn't have noticed anyway. Maybe they got there when I was fixing the tent canvas with Sara after it became clear she was going to dig her heels in if she had to do it by herself.

'Must've made a nice change from your nether regions,' he snorts, still pinching out the silks. I let out a cackle of outraged laughter and try to hit him, but he fends me off. Soberly, as if *I'm* the one misbehaving, he motions for me to close my eyes. He dabs kohl on the lids before mixing a little red ochre paste to paint three vertical lines on my forehead with a horizontal line underneath.

'What are they supposed to represent?' I ask. 'Earth, wind and fire?'

He squints. 'No. It's a crown.'

That word reminds me of being a kid, already with the knowledge that I would be leader, looking at pictures of royal leaders in an Old World book. In my mind I tried them all on: the heavily fletched war bonnet of a First Nations chief; a laurel wreath from a Roman Caesar; the gold-plated nemes of a pharaoh; or one of those fur-lined monstrosities worn by white-skinned Europeans.

I remember the twist in my stomach, trying to imagine it. *My head won't hold those up*, I remember thinking. *It will be too heavy*. That sure has me wishing for that time where I thought that the headgear would be the heavy part.

'You look very beautiful, by the way, Taurus,' I say. 'You don't even need to dress up. Come just as you are.'

His pleased smile disappears under worry. 'What was that Phythia was saying? You were up all night again?'

'Most of it,' I admit. He finishes painting, gives me a nod of approval and wipes his hands on my blankets. I decide to let that slide. He turns his back so I can change. 'This is gonna work.' I say it to myself, but it's a question too, and Taurus knows it.

'Course it is,' he says. 'Why couldn't you sleep? Was it the prophets?'

'No.'

'Was it . . . was it Ma?'

'Today's a big day, Taurus,' I say evasively.

'I haven't been able to stop thinking about her since I woke up,' he replies. 'It's like she's really . . . *present* today. Isn't that weird?'

Everything about that sentence annoys me. *Present?* You can't be *present* and *dead*, I manage to say. 'Uh huh.' But he doesn't seem to register anything amiss.

'Do you ever think about her?'

Wise One. I adjust the scarf around my waist. Silk won't stay tight over my hips.

'Etain?' he asks again. I carry on adjusting, and he sighs. 'You never want to talk about her.'

'No. I don't. So can you stop asking?'

15

There's the tiniest pause while he struggles not to look hurt. 'OK, sis,' he says brightly, and I immediately feel like a bitch. 'Anything you want me to do during the ceremony?' he asks. 'Anything you want me to *find*?'

He winks, and I give in and laugh.

A long time ago, a great magi named Lore predicted Taurus would be my compass. Ma and Ade might have Seen the prophecy about me being our people's leader, but Lore had Seen Taurus's future and many others hundreds of years ago.

She and her lover, Kreywar, brought us to this island after a comet triggered the Great Wave that flooded all other land masses.

Lore's and Kreywar's people were at war when they got here, but the two great magi stopped it. They took away their peoples' memories of the Old World and made them believe they had always been here. They invented the god that most of our people still worship to this day: the Wise One. And they created the Wise One's teaching of wisdom over all else. Only a handful of people, including Taurus and me, know the truth of it.

We only found out all this last year, through a memory preserved in Lore's journal. She'd kept it in a secret hollow in Metis, and Taurus had found it, all these years later.

The journal revealed that Aula and Joomia were really one person, split in two, and that they'd have to unite themselves in order to unite our cities. It also confirmed the prophecy Ma'd had about me becoming leader, and it gave us a new line on Taurus's destiny: *I Saw the boy who would be her compass.*

16

Ever since he'd heard those words, Taurus has had an uncanny knack for 'pointing' himself toward things. Like hearing the prophecy was enough to awaken the skill in him.

Not that he takes it very seriously. He says things like, *Now I'm me, but with added destiny.*

But maybe things would have been better the other way around: him as leader, me as compass. Let's be honest, Taurus is a much sweeter mouthful than me. At least people seem to *like* him. Most of the time I'm not sure if people respect me or if they're just scared that I'll give them extra latrine duty.

'Etain?' Taurus asks. 'You still with me?'

I shake myself. 'Sorry. What did you say?'

'I was asking you if I could *do* anything to help you at the ceremony later.'

'No. No . . . just . . . just make sure everyone's getting along. OK?'

'You bet,' he says.

Taurus

Six months ago, as Etain went to tell the council what had happened, I sat with Ade over the girl we'd found in the hollow of the tree. Occasionally, Phythia would come into the makeshift healing tent to see how she was doing. Except for the moment after the knot in the tree had parted and she'd opened her eyes, the girl hadn't moved.

I wanted to touch her so bad.

17

I wanted to know she was real.

She wasn't Aula. She wasn't Joomia. She was . . . somewhere in between.

Ade *did* touch her. She smoothed her hair back, stroked her cheek, sang for her to wake up in tones that were sometimes screechy, sometimes beautiful – Ade couldn't seem to tell the difference.

'Feel like the compass now, boy?' Ade said, after a while. 'Felt you, leading the memories. Felt you, fulfilling your destiny.'

'Yeah, Ade,' I mumbled. 'I led them.'

It seemed like a long time ago. Yet I could recall how excited I was when I saw them following me. I thought that feeling wouldn't ever leave, but it did. So what if I had brought the memories back? Was that it? *My one job?*

'*I saw the boy who would be her compass*,' Ade intoned.

I sighed. 'Yeah, I know, Ade. And I got to be the compass. But *Etain* doesn't need a compass. Have you seen her? She's their queen, and they all know it. It's in her blood.'

She laughs. 'Nah. It's in her making. But being compass?' She shakes her head. 'That's in your *blood*, boy.'

'Yeah, yeah.'

Sometimes Ade could be lucid like this. That didn't mean she'd be any better at getting her meaning across.

'No, *no*,' she snapped. 'You're not . . . not listening. You've *always* been compass. You brought your ma to me.'

'What?'

'When I was in labour . . . with her . . .' She strokes the girl's hair again. 'You brought your ma to me. Probably . . . don't remember. You were three.'

Kent Libraries,
Registration and Archives
www.kent.gov.uk/libraries
Tel: 03000 41 31 31

Items that you have borrowed

Title: A torch against the night
ID: C334604583
Due: 26 April 2022

Title: Anassa
ID: C334191472
Due: 26 April 2022

Title: Beyond the wall
ID: C334081378
Due: 26 April 2022

Title: Huntress
ID: C334016043
Due: 26 April 2022

Total items: 4
Account balance: £0.00
05/04/2022 10:37
Borrowed: 4
Overdue: 0
Reservation requests: 0
Ready for collection: 0

Thank you for using self service

'I remember,' I said. 'I just didn't think you—'

'You found Lore's study. Her journal. How did you do that? No one else did.'

'That was an accident. And technically Joomia stole the journal—'

'You knew when Lear came back. You was . . . you were rushing back from Athenas for that.'

'Some people have a sense for that kind of stuff.'

'You knew about the books when they got wiped clean.'

I opened my mouth to protest again, but she leaned across the girl's body and put a hand over my mouth. 'And you love this girl – my girl,' she said. There were no pauses in her voice then. 'You love one half of her like a sister, and you love the other' – Ade smiled – 'in a different way. And you put yourself in their paths. Doesn't matter if you were conscious of it or not.'

I sat back from her hand. 'So it was unconscious. That doesn't help me, doesn't help her. So why does it matter?'

Ade shrugged. 'Reckon it's time to take control of it. Reckon it's time for unconscious to become conscious.'

'How?'

'Talent needs one thing, boy. Practice.'

It's just before purple sky when everyone gathers around the nine trees. One thing everyone does agree on is that it's best to measure times by the sun, and the colour of the sky. There's a lot of fussing with clothes. It's mostly Metisians with Metisians and Athenasians with Athenasians. There's a vacillating mood in them, somewhere between excitement and nervousness, but no one's fighting. I guess that's good.

19

Some people have made lanterns with scraps of fabric and wire. The Athenasians bring incense on little copper dishes. Someone at some point decided that there should be songs, so we sing one from an Old World book of 'nursery rhymes' to a tune we've had to learn.

The Metisian magi have lit the trunks of the trees around us with strings of leaf lights. I'm keeping an eye on them. On all the Metisians really. It's taken me *months* to get them to trust Etain and get them involved in what's going to happen this evening. They're not always trying to be difficult, but everything they do is so steeped in tradition and respect of nature's slow courses that I'm beginning to see why the Athenasians see them as backward. I look around for the prophets and notice they're not here, which I'm worried is something to do with my people too. Metisians – they have the most pig-headed view of prophecy it's possible to have, and yet they *still* don't get the hypocrisy of believing in the prophecy that Aula and Joomia were involved in—

'Hey,' says Lear, at my shoulder.

'Hi,' I say, leaning over to kiss his cheek. His sleek hair is knotted elegantly on top of his head and he's painted a stripe across his eyes to emphasise their thin shape and slight angle for the occasion.

'Wise One, this song is terrible,' Lear murmurs to me and I grin. 'Have you seen the steps yet?'

'No,' I say.

'Come on,' he says, taking my hand, 'I'll give you a preview.'

The steps are what this whole ceremony is about.

We are putting up eighteen steps in total today – enough

to get us to the first branch of High Tree, the tallest of the nine new vishaal trees. We'll need *loads* more to go all the way up to where we'll be able to build proper homes, but at this stage we're just going far enough to symbolise a start.

Lear takes me a little way into the trees behind the crowd. The steps have been stacked here, anticipating the moment when they'll be carried to the base of High Tree. A few people are gathered around, waiting to do just that. They're stretching their arms and shoulders in preparation – the steps aren't light.

'What do you think, Taurus?' asks Mira, one of the carriers, as we come into view of them.

'They're beautiful,' I say.

The frames are made of recycled metal, gathered from scraps during the clean-up. Each step is curved, so it will fit properly against the trunk, and each one has been forged with a multitude of intricate marks by the hands of the Athenasian magi. This is not only for sturdiness and weathering, but also for growth and wisdom. On top of that, the Metisian magi have woven their own strange magic – a lattice of still-living vines that will also hold the steps securely against the tree in a way that won't bring harm to the trunk.

It's an important symbol: a weaving together of two societies who have always believed each other to be the enemy.

'Do you think this is gonna work?' I ask Lear. I've been reassuring Etain for months that it *will*, but still, I can't help but wonder. It's been a hard year, and it feels like there have been enough arguments, fights and skirmishes to make up for all the years that Athenas and Metis have remained separate. Sometimes it feels so hopeless: Athenas and

21

Metis were never at war – but somehow just the *idea* of rivalry seems to have been enough to make them hate each other.

It makes these steps feel like such a pointless gesture toward peace.

Lear looks at the steps for a long time. 'It's going to work, Taurus.'

'Why?' I ask.

'Because it was your idea,' he says, smiling. 'And you're the compass.'

I roll my eyes but it's nicely done: my ego starts purring like a contented animal. I kiss him. 'Come on,' I say. 'Before someone misses us.'

Etain

I'm a little disappointed when the song finishes, but it is time.

I feel something brush gently against my cheek and lift my hand to swipe away another cobweb. Wise One, where do they keep coming from? I step off the platform and walk slowly towards High Tree. Behind me, the step-holders emerge from the forest to form a sober line. There are two carriers to each one, and even then they set the steps down gently every couple of paces so they don't strain any important muscles. The Metisian magi are at their heels, preparing the magic that will bind the steps to the tree.

A few creaking strings and some errant drums introduce Eros and his little band, who strike up a tune. And it begins.

Astor – a middle-aged Metisian magi – has been the main coordinator of the steps and he's calling orders to those who asked to carry them. They've been practising bringing the steps forward all day, and they must be tired, but despite that, they're smiling at each other, holding the steps up straight-backed and unwavering.

I roll out my stiff shoulder and put my hand on the bark of the High Tree. A spider scuttles out of a crevice in the bark and darts over my hand. I'm used to spiders – they were all over the prophet house when I was growing up. Ma used to say they were the animal equivalent of prophets: spinning webs the way prophets spin prophecies. But something about this one's sudden appearance feels like an omen.

I can feel something . . . some kind of strange static under my hand. For a moment, the scene before me seems to slow. Something is wrong. There's an odd sound.

I turn my head to see the step-carriers coming forward—

It's getting louder: like hundreds of people rubbing sticks together to make a fire. There's a cry from someone in the crowd, and then – screaming.

'Etain!' Taurus yells from some way back.

And spiders burst out of the cracks between the roots of the vishaal trees. They come like water from a split pipe. Millions of them swarm up the trunks, like a storm wave surging up a beach.

My pulse explodes in my ears.

But it isn't over.

There's a hissing, drawn-out crack; a sound of branches whipping in high wind—

Something hits me hard. I'm knocked backwards, down the roots of High Tree. When I land, the impact punches the breath from my lungs. Sound disappears.

I struggle to right myself, gasping, and look up in time to see *vines* following the path of the spiders upwards; wrapping themselves tightly around each of the nine vishaal trees' trunks. They grow and swell with unbelievable speed; putting out thorns as large and sharp as fishing hooks.

My brain fumbles to make sense of it. This wasn't part of the plan. Like me, the step-holders have stumbled back, and are staring at the vines as they plait and twist over one another, tangling themselves in the branches high above us.

In a matter of moments, there's a wall of thorns with tendrils as thick as my arm. I can't see the vishaal trees at all.

Taurus

The longer we watch, the higher and thicker they grow.

I reach Etain and help her to her feet. She winces when I take the wrong arm.

'You OK, sis?'

She doesn't speak, but her face tells me she's just as clueless about this as me. A minute or so of cold silence. Then panicked whispers become anxious chittering. Still Etain can't – or won't – look away. There's a scrape on her shoulder where she hit the ground, and dead leaves in her braids. Phythia comes forward to check on her.

An outraged yell makes us look around. The cause, it turns out, is the arrival of Ade bringing with her Sabine and the rest of the Athenasian prophets. I turn to them, feeling exasperated. Aren't they supposed to be able to see the future? Couldn't they have turned up when they were supposed to and stopped this before it started?

'We only just got here. What are we supposed to have done this time?' Sabine snarls.

'It's a sign!' a Metisian magi cries. 'A sign from the Wise One!' The other Metisians seem to latch on to this. They gasp and make mumblings of prayer. I've grown up being fairly indifferent to the Wise One, thanks to my upbringing, but even I feel the Metisian part of me wanting to kneel.

'Don't be an idiot,' someone else says. 'It's gotta be someone's magic—'

'Ade's a Chosen One! She must have done it!'

I swivel to see who said that. 'Let's not be throwing around accusations yet,' I say.

'Will someone tell me what *happened*?' Sabine shouts.

Etain hasn't even blinked. Like she's in a trance.

'We were about to put the first step into place,' I say, 'and then . . . the vines. They came out of nowhere.'

'Not. Ready,' Ade snaps. Her teeth click shut after each word. 'Still. Not. Ready.'

'It *was* her!' someone yells.

Ade just smiles like a kid who won an argument. She's your warning sign if you have prophet blood and were wondering about whether to get the training to go with it: it's always hard to know how lucid she's going to be. Sometimes she's reasonably with it, other times – especially if it's inconvenient – she'll be screechy and unreachable.

25

'That's ridiculous,' says Ingrid, another prophet, from further back. 'No magic can make spiders behave like this.'

'Maybe Ade's can't,' says Einar, a member of Etain's council. He's a shit, and if I know him at all (I do) he's probably about to say something shitty. 'But someone else could have . . . Doesn't this look like the work of our old Chosen One? Where is Nine?'

Sometimes I hate being right. My stomach twists at the name: *Nine*.

Sabine shrugs. 'We haven't seen her in weeks.'

'Not ready!' Ade caws. 'Not ready!'

'Shh, Ade,' I say, reaching for her, but she grabs my ear and shrieks like a ghoul. I back off, and she throws back her head and cackles. I clear my throat. 'Einar, there's no need to blame—'

'Stop! STOP!'

Oh shit. Astor has turned from the argument to run at a small group of Athenasians. Clearly, some of them have taken advantage of the confusion to run back to camp and have hurried back wielding axes and shears. They've started to hack at the vines with their axes, but Astor's quick to get in their faces, bellowing with rage. He's swiftly backed up by another dozen Metisians – some of them his fellow magi, some of them just true-blue tree-dwellers. Us Metisians are sensitive to any intentional harm of nature. Even – it seems – the thorny stuff of nightmares before us.

It doesn't look like the axes are doing much damage anyway – the blades are somehow turned aside by the thorns, but . . . damn. Astor's one of the older Metisian magi, with his Metisian ethics deep in his bones. He's about as likely to let someone swing an axe at a plant or animal – never mind what *kind* – as at himself.

'Absolutely despicable!' he's spitting at them. 'How dare you desecrate this place? How dare you revive the wasteful habits of the ancestors? Do you want the Wise One to throw us all from the island?'

'Woah,' I say, trying to get in between them, but Enethea – clearly the ringleader of this pack of axe-wielders – is already snarling back.

'I en't waiting for someone to figure out how to get them down. I know *exactly* how this is going to go,' she growls. 'All you lot are gonna fret for ever about *harm to nature* and we're going to be out of the trees for another year or longer. Our families *need* homes, Astor. They need their lives back. They need out of that *effing* camp site, living like your lot—'

'What do you mean by that?' Astor whispers dangerously.

'Living like some prehistoricals. Get out of my way. I en't doing it any more. I en't just gonna sit around and wait for this bitch to decide my fate for me.'

Etain

Enethea thrusts the butt of her axe at me. I jerk myself out of my stupor and meet her eyes.

There's a collective intake of breath. And silence. They wait to see what I'll do with the insult. Enethea's lip curls, unintimidated by me, by anyone. Her fury makes me tired.

Something ripples along my arms; a kind of painful nostalgia for my forge, the way I felt when I stepped into the fierce heat and picked up my hammer. My hands pine for the soft leather of the handle. My heart wants the rhythm of beating the metal flat. My shoulder twinges.

'The Wise One will—' Astor begins, but I cut across him.

'The Wise One is not in control,' I say, biting my lip over the rest: *There is no Wise One. There never was.* 'We are in control. Us. *People*. It is up to us to do the wise thing. *That*,' I say, pointing at Enethea's axe, 'is insensitive towards the Metisian way. You might not agree with it, but you are obligated to be respectful. I don't know what's going on. I must convene with my council.'

'You betray your people, prophet's-daughter,' someone utters, but I don't see who. Enethea smirks.

'I expect the *Metisians*,' I continue loudly, 'to behave with a similar respect to the prophets. I have invited them here because they are part of our *communi*—'

'Prophets confuse the natural order!'

'This is a sign from the Wise One!'

There are mutters of agreement, which build into more shouts and insults, and the situation comes undone in front of me like the first picked threads in a seam.

An older Athenasian draws himself up beside Enethea. 'Why are we waiting? Let's just cut the vines down and carry on!'

'I'll be dead before your axe swings again!' Astor snarls, pulling a scythe from his belt. I try to step in as Enethea squares up to him, but they're already circling each other, just inches apart. It takes everything I have to repress the sneer of disgust edging on to my face.

'Try me,' Enethea says to him. She raises her axe threateningly, and it *is* threatening. She's greasy with sweat and the tendons in her arms are thick as rope. Her eyes are wide with challenge.

In response, the air charges with the scent of Metisian magic – a smell like moss in the crook of a branch and rain on sun-warmed leaves. Out of the corner of my eye, I can see faint green licking along the tips of the magi apprentices' fingers.

'Enough,' I say as calmly as I can.

But Enethea's not listening. *No one* is listening. She throws her weapon, the axe spinning in the air before thudding into the tree nearest to her, its blade buried in the bark. She stretches out her arms and juts her chin, daring Astor to repeat his oath.

There's a whistling sound.

An arrow shaft appears in the ground next to Enethea's foot, shot from I don't know where.

And just like that, I've lost them.

The crowd erupts. Fists are thrown, knees jerked, hair ripped brutally from scalps. Because they are revolting, egotistical *idiots*, Astor and Enethea continue to circle each other.

Holding my bad arm tight against my side, I pick up a stone from the forest floor and throw it at Enethea's head. She grunts in surprise, and as she raises her hand to her brow I hook out her foot with my ankle. She doesn't fall – not quite – but it gives me time to leap on Astor's back. He collapses under me with a scream of outrage, but my sympathy has about gone. I drive down my good arm's elbow into his shoulder blade and use my bad arm to wrest the scythe out of his hand. I bring it up just quick enough to block Enethea's attempt to retrieve her axe from the tree.

We stare at each other. I'm sweating, my arm's shaking.

'Not like this, Enethea,' I say. '*Not like this.*'

But she's angry. She's too angry to listen. She dodges around the scythe and lunges for the axe. I'm not *worried*, exactly. I've been making weapons since I was a child and I've trained with the strongest person on Erthe. Enethea's just a smith; I can take her. But I don't want to *take her*. And even if I do, how do I stop the rest of them brawling around me?

'Taurus!' I yell, still on the back of Astor.

But it's not Taurus who ducks through the flailing limbs towards me. It's . . . it's her.

I haven't seen Nine for so long that the sight of her in this moment is a shock – so familiar, and so new. She goes straight for Enethea, plucking the axe from her hand as if she's just a toddler with a toy. Enethea blinks, raises her fist, and punches Nine in the face.

I hear the crack of her finger-bones fracturing moments before *Enethea* screams in pain. She might as well have hit the trunk of a tree.

Nine swivels toward me as if nothing's happened. For a moment our eyes lock. 'I can stop them,' she says in Aula's voice, holding out her hand for the scythe.

'If you wouldn't mind,' I say, glaring at Astor as he struggles beneath me.

So Nine stands and closes her eyes and I hear a sound that's like the creak of roots deep in the earth.

And everything stops.

Taurus

What happens is that everyone becomes planted in the earth we stand on. Wood grain grows up our calves and thighs, toes become roots and heels turn to whorls.

I guess that means Nine's here. That's what we call the girl that Aula and Joomia became when they emerged from the trees – one, no longer two. I crane to look for her and there she is – two different people in one tidy package. Her skin is paler than Joomia's; darker than Aula's. Her hair isn't red or brown, it's between both. The body shape and the freckles look the same, but she is different. She's holding herself in a way I don't recognise. Not Joomia or Aula. Her eyes, when they finally catch on me, look distant – not-really-here. I salute her with a grim smile but she only gives a slight blink of recognition.

The crowd begin shouting again – still angry, even if they can no longer move to scrap with each other. *Yep, good job, Lore*, I think. *Look how united everyone is.*

'IT WAS HER!' Astor's yelling, pointing at Nine, still under the grip of Etain. 'IT WAS HER!'

The crowd start to echo his words, '*It was her. It was her!*' And not just Metisians.

Etain stands up.

'*Quiet.*'

31

The word is low but carrying, and it has the desired effect.

Etain's face is thunderous, her back is straight, her chin upright and strong. Anger radiates off her.

'Ask her!' Astor goes on from the ground. 'Ask her if it wasn't!'

Etain glances at Nine, who shakes her head. 'It wasn't me,' she says. She's frowning, squinting into the crowd. Like she's got wind of something bad. Astor scoffs, and her eyes flick to him.

He says, by way of explanation, 'You're the only one with those powers.'

Nine's face changes to pure Aula. 'If I didn't want to get us back to the vishaal trees I would've let Nadrik take the Book of Knowledge, and left you all to bump around without any memories. Would've been a lot less trouble and I wouldn't be left dealing with shits like you.'

That seems to make a few people relax.

Etain glances at Nine and gestures at Enethea and Astor.

Nine flicks her wrists, and the two of them are released from the ground's hold in a succession of cracks.

'You are going to talk your way to an agreement,' Etain says. 'And while that happens, the rest of the people will wait for you.'

What. So we're stuck here until these idiots make their peace?

Everyone rumbles in frustration, the rumbles rising to shouts and snarls. I'm almost tempted to join in, but I see Etain whisper something to Nine, and there is another volley of cracks. There's something to be said for being

Etain's brother. I scrunch my toes, and hop from foot to foot as the feeling comes back to them.

'*Of course* she freed her brother,' someone whispers. But it isn't just me. Several people I recognise as Etain's council are shaking out their feet too and filing towards her.

'I will take the council to decide what to do about *this*,' she says, indicating the thick ropes of web strangling the nine trees, the thorny vines that have brought today's plans to a halt. Etain turns her iciest stare on Astor and Enethea and points to them as she addresses the remaining crowd. 'They now hold your freedom in their hands. Their agreement will release you. Until that happens, you will all stay where you are.'

They burst into protest, but she walks away without a backward glance, Nine and the other council members trailing after. I flick off a bright red ant trying to crawl up my ankle and run to catch them up.

Astor and Enethea are still turned away from each other when I pass them, staring after Etain, fury in their eyes. Maybe they can just bond over being pissed off with her instead of with each other.

Etain

Nine and the others follow me. There are ten permanent council members, five from Metis, five from Athenas plus four rotational positions for two Athenasians and two Metisians – picked at random – to fill each month. Nine hasn't been around often enough for me to count her as a true member – though as the combined Chosen One for Athenas and Metis no one is likely to contest her presence. Taurus doesn't usually come . . . I guess I don't want anyone thinking I favour him just cos he's my brother, but in this case, I think he's going to be able to help.

The council members start talking the second we're out of earshot, and automatically step into the circular shape we arrange ourselves in for council meetings.

'Where have you been, Nine?' I whisper while they talk.

She looks at me blankly. 'With the prophets, in the Cave of Ancestors.'

'I didn't ask the prophets to leave the camp site,' I say quickly. 'I didn't *want* them to leave. But the Metisians were nervous. Athenasians are still free to visit their prophets if they want to – I still ask to hear their weather reports and any seriously grave-sounding prophecies. I want to come in person, but I've been so . . .'

I trail off. Nine doesn't say anything, and the guilt stays in my stomach, sloshing like stones in a watermill. Ever since she became one person, Nine feels . . . fragmented, almost like she's fighting to be Aula or Joomia again, but can't choose, and can't find a way to blend the two people she was together.

'Etain?' Taurus says.

I realise then that everyone's looking at me, and hastily I clear my throat.

'Order, everyone.'

'Well, what do you have to say for yourself?' Einar asks, glaring at Nine. He's polite, I guess, but his politeness only lends his criticisms a kind of legitimacy. I think he voted for me because he didn't have any better ideas and he was impressed with how I stopped the mindless, but it hasn't taken much time for him to change his mind.

Nine fixes him with a stare. 'What would you like me to say, Einar?'

'If that trick back there with spiders and then the thorns wasn't your work, who else is responsible?'

'Yeah, fine. The vines could have been me, but the spiders? Are you serious? When have you *ever* seen someone – Chosen One, Metisian magi or Athenasian – *ever* take control over an *animal*?'

'Well . . . Nadrik did,' Thetea, one of the Athenasians, points out.

I chew my cheek. She has a point. We all remember the owls.

'Perhaps they *were* the Wise One's,' says Chu. At his words, the Metisians among us trace a circle on their own forehead – a symbol of the Wise One's supposed infinite wisdom – and close their eyes like they're about to pray. Their reaction is annoyingly predictable.

I glance at Nine. It's a relief to have her here, witnessing one of my biggest problems: how can I stop them reaching for the Wise One – a god that doesn't exist? Then I have to ask myself, is that even a good idea? It might be a deceit, but it's also one of their largest touchstones from our old way of life. How can I just take it from them when it keeps so many of them holding on to sanity, to an idea of a 'bigger plan'?

'Taurus, if it *was* a person who summoned the thorns, could you find them?' I ask loudly. He actually puffs out his chest a bit. It's not as obvious as when we were kids but he still *loves* having a job to do.

Taurus closes his eyes for a moment, and then he turns and walks straight back towards the trees. 'Einar,' I say. 'If you wouldn't mind going with him.'

Einar gives me a look that tells me he knows he's being manipulated, but giving him something important to do will stop him breathing down my neck.

They come back a few minutes later with identical expressions of shock.

'Ade did it,' Taurus says blankly.

The council mutters.

'How?' I ask, incredulously, though I don't expect him to answer.

Nine considers, frowning. Then I hear her say, like Joomia, **That doesn't make any sense. No Chosen One has ever had control over animals. I've studied all eight of the Chosen Ones who came before me. Including Ade. And anyway, even if she did at one time have that ability, who says she'd be capable now? She's never used her powers as long as I've known her.**

I bite my tongue hard enough to hurt and try to keep all the frustration off my face. Being in council – well, any time I'm in public, being their leader – is like holding my breath for as long as I can. As long as I'm here, I don't show them emotions. Nothing but calm.

'What did she say?' Einar says impatiently.

Oh, right. Because that was Joomia's voice, only Taurus and I could hear it.

Nine shakes herself and repeats her thoughts from before, aloud this time.

'That . . . changes things,' Thetea says. 'If she is a danger to our people . . .'

Nine's face goes cold. 'What do you mean *danger*? She said we are not ready to go back to the trees. Maybe she thought she was doing us a favour?'

'But what does that mean — *not ready*?' the Metisian magi Merryn asks. 'How are we not ready?'

I want to answer that, but I know I shouldn't. Since Ma deemed me old enough, I've been studying hundreds of Old World theories on how to integrate different cultures. There is a particular quote I keep coming back to:

Two or more cultures hoping to integrate should keep in mind these four basic steps: ACKNOWLEDGE there is a problem, and agree to work together to solve it; IDENTIFY the causes of conflict and lay the roots of them bare — attempt then to reconcile them. They must then envision a shared goal of reconciliation and STRATEGISE how they might get to it. Finally, both (or all) cultures must determine how they might SUSTAIN this attempt at integration and continue to weed out dividers.

For the last year, I've had both Athenasians and Metisians work together in groups on a model like this, but it's been hard to get them to commit to reconciliation without a real home to put any of their plans in. I was hoping that the steps would at least help them get to the envisioning stage for a united future, but it only took Ade to put those vines in the way for everyone to drop all thoughts of unity like a sack of wet dung.

'Nine, can you get Ade to take them down?' I ask, over the council's mutinous mumblings. 'The vines?'

'I will try, of course,' Nine says. 'But we already saw that axes and blades aren't going to do it. Perhaps there really is an imbalance on the island that must be put right.'

I swallow down a spasm of anger. 'You think . . . Ade *decided* the people weren't ready?' I ask, as calmly as I can. 'She put the vines there because she . . .'

'Cos she knew you would honour the Metisians' request that no plants feel our blades so long as we live together,' Chu says bitterly. I glance around at the Athenasians in the council; all show the same tested patience on their faces.

Thetea chews her lip, as if searching for an answer. 'Very well,' she says. 'I do not think we will resolve this now, but Anassa, stop punishing our people for something they had no hand in.'

'You'd prefer them to argue?'

'No, but I'd prefer them to come to an agreement rather than being forced into one.'

'I suppose you noticed the way they were ready to spill blood back there?' Merryn says, giving Thetea a dirty look.

I lay a placating hand on Merryn's arm. 'I'm making an example,' I say.

'Without consulting your council,' points out Chu.

'There wasn't time,' I say.

'Well, if you hadn't been just *staring* at the vines for so long—'

'Am I your leader or not?' I snap.

Thetea raises her eyebrows. Taurus swallows. Einar's eyes flick around the circle, watching everyone's reactions.

'Am I your leader or not?' I say again, more hesitantly.

Einar opens his mouth.

Nine grabs my arm and cuts across him. 'It seems like Ade's right,' she says firmly. 'We en't . . . *aren't* ready to go back. If we can't find a way to get on at the sight of the first obstacle, then what hope is there of making it all the way back into the trees?' Nine doesn't wait for an answer. 'I will talk to Ade and ask her to take down the vines, but I think we need to look closer. Maybe there was something wrong with the magic that was supposed to bind us together. I can feel it in the trees, but you can *see* it for yourselves in the mess that happened back—' She stops abruptly, her eyes flashing from their usual grey to a bright, pale green and—

And a strange light flashes through the gaps in the trees, like light from the evening sun – fiery and low. It en't that, though – it can't be. The sun's already set.

'Astor!' Nine says. 'Etain, quickly! Astor!'

My people are screaming. 'Nine, give them back their feet,' I say before we've even reached the clearing, the council hot behind me.

I can smell wet, green fauna as Nine turns everyone's feet back from wood and root to flesh and toes. As we stumble back into the clearing, people are turning and running in a blind panic.

I swing around wildly, looking for the source of the light. Astor. He's engulfed in a blazing column of flame that's almost too bright to look at.

I run towards him, not knowing what I'm going to do. But Nine gets there first.

She shoves him out the way, and the light – the flame – whatever it is – goes out instantly. I see Astor get to his feet, somehow unharmed – see him turn and run – but

39

before I can follow him Nine lets out a groan of pain and I'm distracted.

Her hands are bright red and blistered.

But not for long. She channels some of Joomia's self-healing powers into them, and the blisters fade back, replaced by stiff calluses.

'Are you all right?'

He was *burning***,** she says, more Joomia now. **There's no magic that makes your body do that . . . I don't understand.**

I look up to find him, but Astor is long gone. Near to where he was standing, Taurus has paused. There's something about his pose that makes me feel sick. He's looking at something on the ground, and his shoulders are stiff. The line of his jaw is hardening like a statue. I sort of know what I'm going to see before I see it.

I reach Taurus in a few steps. I look down. There's nothing to identify the thing on the ground as Enethea any more. Her hair is gone, her limbs are shrivelled, her skin is blackened, like a log from the campfire.

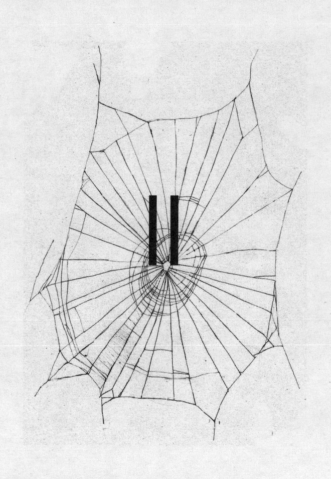

The Chosen

Now the ninth and final Chosen One has finished her task, we should, by rights, have entered the long sleep, but something has kept us hanging on.

We are bodiless, we have no agency, and indeed, we should not trouble ourselves with things our mortal selves would have wanted. We are truly part of the vishaal trees now, a seamless entity of bark and memory; root and knowledge. We should not find the actions of the ones who have come after us very interesting, for the Chosen Ones bound us, and their sacrifice was good and pure and needed.

But some ineffable thing is wrong. The people are not united. The trees that were Athenas and Metis are restless, like nervous beasts or choppy water. We are awake, still, stuck in an uncertain limbo. We have but one power, and that is to watch.

Our vision reaches far, down to the very hairs on our roots. Since the binding, we have also been able to cast our vision into the two Chosen minds who have yet to join us: poor old Ade, who did not pay Ariadnis with her life, but with her sanity. And weary young Nine – or Aula, or Joomia, depending on the direction of the wind.

What is left to be done? we wonder.

Why has the long sleep we crave evaded us?

'Not ready, not ready,' says Ade, as she is led back to the ancestors' cave with her prophet sisters. She has, as Nine predicted, refused to remove the vines that surround the vishaal trees.

Head Prophet Sabine mutters angrily about Ade's instability, her clouded mind – of which many other mouths will complain tonight.

But it is not as simple as Ade's own whim. She, like Nine, can detect the moods and changes in the trees. She cannot help but act, the way a mother bear will roar defensively over her cubs.

But of course, it is not just the trees behaving strangely. Something further is amiss – through the night and well into the dawn, the people snarl in fear and weep in rage about Enethea, Astor and the fire.

Meanwhile, Etain's council runs itself into tighter circles – wondering over and over how it was done. If Astor were Athenasian, it would be explainable – but what Metisian magi has ever caused such a combustion? Is it a sign from the Wise One? And what to do about the vines, when the Metisians will not budge on using weapons against nature? Some of Enethea's friends, mourning her, go back to the vishaal trees and hack at the vines in anger, over and over again. But Ade has cast her magic well, and the chopping serves nothing more than to make the thorns' vines grow thicker and tighter against the trunks, healing the wounds of the axes in moments.

Nine watches sadly from the shadows as Enethea's friends retire to their beds. She casts her tree-senses back to camp, where she sees Etain and her council disbanding, frustrated.

In the barracks, Taurus slides shut the screens around

his bed and finds Lear waiting for him. He smiles as they twine themselves around each other, Taurus willing himself to forget the day, forget everything about it, forget every eye twitching toward him in the council just now. Forget about Nine and his sister and the trees. Forget the steps.

Etain trails slowly back to her tent: thoughts filled with spiders and steps and webs and her unanswered question. She thinks of the simple desire she saw in the council between Taurus and Lear and wishes she could let go in the same way. She thinks of Nine. She misses Aula. She wishes she had known Joomia better.

She has piled every thought and distraction she can over the hollow space left by her mother, but it yawns then. It's just as painful hidden as it is in plain sight, and for this unguarded moment, loneliness bruises her heart. She stares at the canvas of her tent for hours, but she does not sleep.

Taurus

She comes into my tent at night. She smells good. Like a branch that's been split along the middle. Sap. Wood. Water. She doesn't say anything. When I try to speak she shushes me. She slides the covers away and kisses me right on the sternum, and then the hollow between my collarbones. I gasp. My body is a living thing.

We kiss for a while. Just kissing. It doesn't feel like *just*.

Her hands trail down me, and I trace her back with one hand. I slide my lips down her throat. My other hand stretches the waistband of her breech cloth—

'Aula,' I whisper.

She comes back from wherever she goes inside her head. 'Yes.'

It sounds like the answer to a question, not a response to her name. I hesitate. There are a million things I could say and I want to say all of them.

Then I wake up.

For a moment, I think it's still her next to me, but of course, it's Lear.

Lear. Good. Safe. Familiar. His hair is all stuck up at the back and he smells of sleep. I move slightly to the edge of the bed. He lifts half an eyelid, fumbles for my shoulder and pulls me on to his chest. I stay there for a second. I can hear his heart.

I'm thirsty. I stare at a hole in the sheets hung around the bed in an attempt at privacy. I should've sent him away, I think. Even if it meant waking up alone this morning.

'You're thinking about something,' he says. 'What is it?'

I'm lost.

'Taurus?'

'I was thinking I'll get us some breakfast,' I say, turning my head to grin at him. He kisses me, eyes narrowed in suspicion. I get out of bed and knot my sarong around my waist. It's not really light yet, but there are small, rune-spelled stones for illumination along the walkways between the beds and at the doors. I follow them out of the barracks and walk to the mess tent through the dawn-wet grass.

I push away thoughts of yesterday. I don't need to think about that, I decide.

But I'm lost.

I sigh, roll up the canvas sides of the kitchen, light a few lamps and start prep. It shouldn't bother me, to be lost. Some people are just lost people. That's OK. We try. The Etains and the Nines and the Lears of this world make up for us.

But Joomia was lost, I think. *And Aula was lost*. But they're one person now. Maybe that's what I need. Maybe I'm half a person, like they were, but no, that's not right either. Sometimes I wish I could scrape out my head like a squash and put something different inside.

I stoke the coals in the clay oven. Add more kindling. I start on the bread. I like bread. It's rhythm and muscle memory and no thought necessary. I make my own starter from potato starch, flour and honey. It's running low so I top it up before I start rolling out dough. I make thick brown rye, spotted with grain and seeds.

You were always my little cook, says Ma's voice.

I smile to myself, and catch sight of the empty water bucket. Someone's forgotten to bring the water in last night. I *told* them we were gonna need it for the stew. I pick up the bucket and head to the water butt on the other side of the camp.

I wouldn't normally notice spider webs in the grass but I do today: pitched taut between long, dewy grass stems, devoid of owners. 'What are you all playing at?' I wonder out loud, but I haven't seen any spiders yet.

The tap of the water butt is dripping silk, as if a hundred years have passed since I last came here and a thousand spiders have laid down their work and left. For a moment,

I fantasise that I'm a great hero who has woken one morning to find a century passed, and everyone he knew gone. Then I stop, partly cos I'm freaking myself out and partly because I realise there's something moving in the webs. A spider. The silk has gotten twisted around it, so its legs have swaddled against its abdomen.

I pull it gently away from the tangled criss-cross of threads. It stays so absolutely still as I pick each leg free that I wonder if it's dead after all, but when I'm finished it stretches out each limb, as if to check it still has them. Then it quivers on my palm, as if I am its web and it's testing my strength.

It strikes fast: there's a pinch of pain in the muscle between my thumb and my wrist as its fangs sink deep. I flinch, a second too slow, and it drops to the ground and scuttles away.

'It bit me!'

'Ouch,' says a voice.

I clutch my chest and spin round, but it's only Nine. 'You scared the shit out of me,' I hiss, because I'm embarrassed and because she did. There's an awkward pause. Between the trees behind her head, the sky is deep pink and raw orange. The light picks out the stray hairs that have escaped her long plait. It seems strange that someone with so much power can look so normal.

'That'll teach me to try and be a nice guy,' I say at last.

I'm sure it will appreciate the gesture later when it's caught a nice big fly.

Does she know she's doing that? Switching between her two selves? Is it confusing for her? It sure is for me.

48

'I'll try to remember that whenever I look at this scar it gave me,' I say, brushing off the silk strands from the tap. The water splashes me before I kick the bucket underneath. 'I dunno where all these webs came from. Spider version of partying hard?'

There's a strange energy about. It started yesterday, but it's still here. It's affecting everything. I don't know where it's coming from.

I'm too distracted by her not looking at me properly to react to what she's saying. That annoys me. She hasn't seen me for weeks. Not that she was exactly sociable before. Now there's no trace of my best friend in her face. No trace of Aula either. Maybe one day all of these selves will integrate and I can stop guessing who I'm really talking to.

Then it dawns on me, too late – there's a reason we're meeting like this. She doesn't bump into anyone at all unless she can help it. I say gruffly, 'What is it?'

'There's smoke coming from the forest near the base of the cliffs,' she says, looking relieved that I asked. 'Etain thinks it might be Astor.'

I do a quick calculation. Obviously, if they see smoke, Etain will need to send a search party in that direction, and if she's smart (and she always is), a second one to scan the surrounding area for signs of Astor if he's already left.

'She wants me to go compass on him before any other search parties can find him,' I reason, turning off the tap.

'Especially Metisian search parties,' Nine says, nodding. 'See if you have better luck finding him than I have . . .' Then she gives me a strange, kind of shy look. 'I can go with you . . . if you want.'

'We're gonna have to be fast,' I say in mock warning. 'Are you sure you're gonna be able to keep up?'

I can't stop my eyes wandering back to her as we run together. I know it's weird, but I'm kind of wrestling with my feelings. Like: she's Aula. And Aula and me . . . But she's also *Joomia*. And they kind of look the same. So . . . so have I been – er – *dreaming* . . . about my best friend? I keep glancing at her, kind of messing up my compassing. No. No, I never thought of Joomia like that. Only Aula. So how do I feel about Nine?

Oh, man. Not the time, Taurus. Concentrate.

We're both barefoot. Together we make hardly any sound. It's difficult though – every bird call flattens my concentration. Or maybe it's her. I stop every ten yards or so to reorientate myself. It's like trying to stand on one leg when you just woke up. My balancing point is . . . off.

I realise at one point that I've just led us in a circle, but I don't get a chance to be embarrassed cos a few minutes later I trip and just about lose my sense of Astor all together.

I stop, about to let out a curse.

Nine says, 'Taurus. What's that?'

We're framed by pine trees now. I follow Nine's finger and see black marks scuffing the trunks at hip height. On the tree closest to us there's a soot-black handprint pressed deep into the bark. Resin seeps from it like blood. I stare . . . and there's something else.

Nine approaches, hand outstretched. Then she sees it too.

An ant. It's the length of my finger and the colour of a

deep wound. Its pincers are narrow and corrugated, dark as scars. As we watch, it scuttles over the handprint with its abdomen raised, as if in defence.

Ignoring my wordless protest, Nine reaches out and carefully places her hand just below the insect on the trunk, presumably so she can ask the tree what it makes of this passenger. For a moment longer, nothing happens.

Then the ant quivers, its abdomen extends, its pincers clench and unclench. I get the unpleasant idea that it smells us. It confirms this a millisecond later as it swivels and bolts downwards, right at Nine's hand.

I shout a warning, but Nine simply twitches her finger to make the bark peel back. It opens like a hungry mouth and snaps down over the insect with a yawning sound. For a moment there's silence. A shimmering lichen creeps up from Nine's fingers to cover the handprint. She lets out a long breath.

'What was that?' I ask.

Something that shouldn't be here. It . . . it didn't feel the way a normal ant would feel. The tree couldn't sense it.

I say, 'I think I saw an ant like that just before Astor . . . well. I just thought we might not have seen anything like that before because of the altitude of the cities or—'

There's a cracking noise. We both jump. The bark Nine buried the ant under blackens and splits. I'm expecting to see pincers emerging, antennae waving furiously—

But there's only a puff of smoke. We watch it rise and dissipate. Then a there's a flash and the place where the handprint was is licking with flame.

Nine gasps, drops her hand to a nearby root. With a

violent stutter, the flame goes out. Pine sap splatters out of the wound in the bark and almost immediately hardens in reddish-black blobs.

And all around us, the forest floor begins to move.

More ants?

But no, it's spiders. Normally I wouldn't call them preferable, but at least they've not mutated to ten times the size I'm used to and started setting things on fire.

They're emerging from under every single rock, fallen log and pile of rotting leaves. Hundreds of them. They give the tree a really wide berth, clambering over each other and around each other, a few crawling over my feet, but they don't make any detours up my leg like you'd expect. The place where the spider bit me on my hand starts throbbing. The only direction they're going is away. It makes me think maybe we should too. I'm just about to suggest that when someone steps out from behind a nearby tree.

I'm so jumpy I roar and pull Nine to my side.

No – OK, OK – I let out a shriek and duck behind Nine, who doesn't even blink.

It's just Ade. She comes over to us in her bizarre, collapsible gait, like some young animal. She always looks like she's waiting to lean on something. 'Boy,' she says. 'Don't be afraid.'

I don't bother trying to tell her that I'm not afraid. I'm obviously *terrified*. The spiders' sudden emergence. The unified direction of them. The thought of that ant's pincers.

'What are they doing?' I whisper.

Ade's under-eye prophet scars give a seashell-gleam as she says, 'Leaving. The spiders are leaving.'

'Leaving?'

She smiles, like she knows what I'm about to ask.

'Where are they going?'

Etain

Late morning, I'm trying to stretch out my shoulder when Astor's whole damn family pay me a visit. His sons – Mur, Chiva and Ineb – and his mother, Medea, all pile into my tent.

'I'm trying to find him,' I say. If they're here, I'm guessing they didn't see the smoke. I decide not to mention it.

'We know,' Medea says coldly.

Wise One, spare me from matriarchs. About the only thing Athenas and Metis *can* agree on is having an abundance of cranky old family leaders who always know they're more right than you are and how you should be doing it better. And who don't mind saying those things to my face. Every. Damn. Day.

'Our concern,' Medea continues, 'is what you intend to do with him once you've found him, and how you plan on stopping all the Athenasians from murdering him when you do.'

'Why don't you let me deal with that?' I ask.

'I would, if I trusted you to lead these people, but I don't.'

Astor's sons take in a breath. I finish the stretch I'm in the middle of and laugh. 'That's refreshing. Why don't you tell me what you really think?'

Medea's mouth crooks reluctantly.

'I sent Taurus and Nine to stop anyone from hurting him,' I say.

Her mouth puckers. 'I do not want that abomination anywhere near my family,' she hisses.

I sigh, and glance at her grandson, particularly Ineb. Taurus told me he used to be cheerful and helpful and smart, but that was before Nadrik stole everyone's memories. Ineb was one of the mindless who came after us as we headed to the Cave of the Ancestors. He was one of the mindless who was unlucky enough to attack Joomia, and was turned to wood because of it.

There were twenty or so mindless Joomia turned to wood. When she came out of the tree as Nine, one of the first things she did was to try and turn them back. It didn't exactly go well. In fact, it was lucky that any of them survived at all.

In the months she'd been in the tree, their bodies had started to forget how it was to be quick, to be flesh and blood and burning energy. When Nine brought them back to themselves it was all Phythia and her healers could do just to keep them breathing. Their memories were returned, but their bodies weren't.

I was there when it happened, biting my nails to their beds as I watched them all slowly asphyxiate – until at last Phythia managed to work a spell that would force their lungs to inflate and deflate for them. Once that rhythm came back, it got a little easier – but none of them have yet managed more than a few words of speech. Ineb is one of the lucky few now able to walk.

'I can never work out,' I say, 'if you all hate Nine cos half of her is Athenasian, or cos you're too stone-headed to see that that half of her also helped to save your lives.'

Mur bristles. 'Do you call this a saved life, Etain? Ineb robbed of all his senses and Pa turned into a walking flamethrower?'

I give him a very steely look. 'Would you rather you were dead, or without your memories? Would you prefer for Ineb to still be a tree?'

Medea snarls and gestures for her grandsons to exit ahead of her. 'I'll find him myself then,' she says, and I find I don't have the energy to try and persuade her otherwise.

'Fine,' I say, and turn back to my exercises, but I feel her lurking in the entrance.

'Something else?' I say.

'What about Ade?' Medea says.

'What about her?'

'Has *anyone* tried to convince her to take down the vines yet?'

I grit my teeth. I wonder if she's been talking to the council. They've been at me since sun-up.

'Well, you can ask Nine – the only one who Ade actually ever listens to – but wait, I forgot, you think *she's* an abomination, right?' I turn to enjoy how that comment goes down.

It's not what I expect. The look Medea's giving me is dangerous. 'Unless you want her blood on your hands, Anassa, you'll want her to dismantle those thorns.'

'Is that a threat?' I say as calmly as I can.

'No, girl,' she says. 'It's a fact.'

At noon, the search parties I sent out return, but they're missing two people. Hours later, Nine and Taurus return with Ade, all three of them talking about ants and spiders. I know Medea and Astor's sons are watching me shrewdly from a way off. Ugh.

I decide to give Taurus a break and order a group of ten to continue the search for Astor and now the missing people too. But when I open my mouth to tell him and Nine that I don't know what to do about ants and spiders, Nine cuts me off. **It's all right, Etain**, she says. **I'll investigate it. You should try to sleep.** Surreptitiously, I try to study her – to see if her mind-voice coincides with a more Joomia-esque expression, but I can't see anything that stands out. Maybe I just didn't know Joomia well enough.

Taurus gives me a look that tells me I'm being rude cos I'm ignoring Ade, and I give him one back to tell him I don't have *time* for Ade, for anyone really, but especially not for her. I think about what Medea said. 'Can you take Ade back to the prophets on your way, Nine?' I ask.

'Of course,' she says, putting her arm around her.

Ade hisses and grabs my arm. For a second, the scars around her eyes turn iridescent. 'I find you on an island. I find you in a boat,' she snarls.

'Yeah, OK,' I mutter. She's all over the place. She loses interest in me in a millisecond and turns to the camp at large. 'NOT READY!' she yells.

'And please, please get her to shut up,' I add loudly.

'If you can't get her to take down the vines, at least get her to do that.'

Nine nods, and everyone goes back to their business. Taurus hangs his head, like he's disappointed in me.

'Give me a break, Taurus,' I say, rubbing my temples.

'Ade hasn't done anything wrong,' he points out quietly. 'Ma would want us to take care of her.'

Taurus, you don't know what Ma would have wanted cos you only saw her about twice a year when she'd accumulated enough guilt about leaving you and Ade in Metis to send her down that staircase in the owlery.

I hold the words prisoner against the back of my teeth with my tongue, trying to scare myself into imagining what would happen if I said them so there's no danger of me actually doing it.

He rubs my shoulder. 'Sorry. I know you've got a lot to think about.'

'I'm fine,' I say reflexively.

'OK,' he says. 'But I'm always here if you need me.'

'I don't,' I say, then I shake my head. 'I mean . . . I didn't mean that. It came out wrong.'

His smile is quick, covering the flash of hurt. 'All I meant was, you don't have to do all this alone,' he says.

Wise One, I *can't deal* with him looking at me like that. He's sensitive. I get that. Maybe I would be too, if I was ever able to take my guard down. As it is, I'm in this *endless* battle not to hurt him with an accidental harsh word or gesture.

I feel worse when we get into the mess tent and it's all, *Taurus! Over here, brother! Thanks for helping out earlier, Taurus. Sorry about my boys earlier, Taurus. I like what you did with your dreads, Taurus.* Like I said before, maybe Lore got us the wrong way round.

I sit down next to Merryn, Head Magi of Metis, who's smiling knowingly at me.

'Always been a bit of bright star, that boy,' she says.

'You have *no idea* how much I wish he was an arsehole,' I say to her, glaring as Taurus claps hands with Eros and sits down with some of the older citizens. 'Wise One, he's so . . . *sincere.*'

'An affectation, perhaps?' Merryn offers, although she doesn't look convinced. I think we both know his affability is genuine.

'How am I supposed to compete with that?' I say hopelessly.

Merryn pats my shoulder, looks mortified when she gets the wrong one and, for lack of a better option pats my head instead, which makes me feel about two years old. 'He doesn't have your responsibilities, dear. Leaders are not the ideal candidates for the well-liked.'

I snort into my broth. 'You can say that again.'

Taurus

Lear is shitty with me because I left early with Nine. I guess I forgot about breakfast.

We try to get back to our usual chores. Everyone's tempers are frayed and fraying faster. Stupid snipes feed stupider arguments. Fights break out. No side's better than the other. Metisians bitch about the Athenasians.

Athenasians gripe about the Metisians.

Lear's fuming. 'What is it they're afraid of?' he snarls. 'Liking each other? *Changing* one tiny bit of their stupid narrow minds?'

The thing about people getting angry is it makes me refuse to be. 'I don't think it's change they're scared of,' I say.

Lear rolls his eyes. He's such a nice guy most of the time. Some people wear anger like a cape. Etain wears it like that. When Lear wears it, it's ugly. Like maggots under dead skin.

The day goes on and there's more than insults. We find one middle-aged Metisian weaver, Sorrell, calling out an old Athenasian magi on shoddy spellwork and next thing you know we have another brawl on our hands.

'You're acting like children!' Lear roars, shoving both of them away from each other. 'Grow up! Learn some diplomacy!' He stalks off, and I follow him, leaving a handful of shocked people behind us. Lear isn't known for his temper.

We walk beside each other in silence, and then he says, reluctantly, 'I shouldn't have lost my temper.'

'Do you think maybe you need to let off some steam too?' I ask. 'You've been like a wildcat with a thorn in your foot all day.'

'You mean because I shouted at them? But that was just to get my point across. I'm not actually angry.'

'Right.'

'They're just being so *childish*.'

'Yeah, well. It's hot, the work is hard, the days are long, and holy hell – *the midges today*.'

It's only then that I realise he's stopped walking with me for a few paces. I turn round.

'Why do you always have to be so *neutral*?' he says. 'Our people are falling apart!'

I rub my face. 'OK. What do you want me to do about that?'

'I want you to act like it matters!' he says. 'Shout, get angry . . . *anything*.'

'Shouting, yeah. That's the only way to show you care about something.'

He draws his bottom lip through his teeth and scuffs his heel through the earth.

'I don't know if you've noticed,' I say. 'But there are more important things happening here than me not saying goodbye to you this morning. Etain asked Nine and me to go and look for a missing man before some other, angrier people from *our city* did it first, OK?'

He fish-mouths at me. 'You honestly think I'm that petty?'

'Oh, come on. You were ridiculous about Joomia, before.'

Lear spreads his hands, fingers wide. 'How about *asking* me what's wrong, Taurus? How about you don't presume to know what I'm thinking?'

I retie my loosening dreads. 'Fine, what's wrong?' I ask.

'Etain,' he says, pointing back toward camp. His finger is shivering, like saying her name is a malediction. 'That's what's wrong. She's refusing to make real decisions. Like with these vines. If she hadn't delayed us setting up the steps for so long, maybe there wouldn't have been a chance for old Ade to summon the spiders. If she hadn't *invited* all

60

the damn prophets to the ceremony, or if she had just let Athenasians at the vines when the spiders first arrived, it might have worked, OK!'

I stare at him. 'You're full of something today.'

'You don't see it? They're sniping at each other now, but pretty soon they're going to need someone to blame. That's how it works. They're angry. They have a right to be angry!'

'So Etain should have seen Enethea being burned to a crisp coming?'

'That's not my point.'

'What is your point?'

'You follow her like a *dog*,' he says. 'You're fucking *blind*. You followed Joomia and now you're following your sister. Maybe it's time you grew a spine and thought for yourself.'

It's like he's slapped me and left me reeling in the dirt.

Ow.

I'm lost.

When I wear anger, you can't see the maggots. They're deep inside, chewing at my tissues. I say, 'If you and all the frustrated ones want to go and start your own camp, no one's stopping you, Lear.'

'Maybe we will,' he says. And he gets up and walks away.

Etain

Another day goes by and *still* no one finds Astor.

Three fights get brought to me and halfway through my dressing-down of the last culprits I start feeling the telltale signs of my period coming – a clammy heat in the small of my back and a hot, heavy feeling rolling up my legs to my kidneys. There have been signs all day, I realise: a whining, intermittent headache this morning and the feeling that all my clothes have changed shape: clinging and coarse against my skin.

I'm standing at the time and manage to knock over a pile of papers before I turn to the fighters and attempt to issue a reprimand, but I've kind of lost my thread by that point. I have to give in and send them back to work.

I go back to my tent as soon as it gets dark enough to justify it, and just lie there on my stomach, missing Ma, and thinking of all the herbal teas she would have brought me.

I do my best not to move for a while, but it's hard not to and every position is uncomfortable and sweaty. Every time I close my eyes, Astor is leaning over me with a flame flickering in his bare hand, or ants are crawling over me or spiders are coming out of my mouth.

When some of the discomfort eases off, I take a stone spelled with illumination from my tent. I walk to the river, dunk myself in and crawl out, panting. I want to be in my forge. I want a piece of metal to smooth under my blows. I want to sweat until all my frustration is leeched out of me. I want a fierce heat to burn out my thoughts.

What are you doing? I wonder. *What on Erthe are you doing, Etain?*

I walk into the forest. It's probably a stupid thing to do. Wild dogs, snakes and other things share the shelter of the trees with us, but right now I don't care. I just want movement.

I don't know where the webs come from.

One minute, the path is clear. The next I'm spitting spider silk. It's strange how the sensation of walking into a spider's web can't be mistaken for anything else – the snag of the silk against your forehead, the pull of elastic threads along your chin. When I look up I'm expecting to see one or two of them – maybe catch a glimpse of the spinner scuttling back under somewhere dark.

But there en't one or two.

They're *everywhere*. Dripping off the overhanging branches, criss-crossing across the path ahead, frosting the leaves of every fern and bush, far as I can see.

'How are you here as well?' I say aloud. 'The vishaal trees aren't enough? What do you want?'

But, of course, there's no answer.

You'd think with that many of them there'd be *some* kind of noise, a hissing or clicking or something, but they're eerily silent, almost as if their mass is swallowing any sound in the surrounding area. After a moment or two of watching, I notice they're actually moving away – winding further into the trees in an ambiguous direction.

I wonder, if I follow them, if I'll find their nest or their queen or . . . *something* I can put a stop to.

And not much further along, I find it.

Ade.

I feel my mouth getting pinched.

She's sitting cross-legged in a clearing, back straight, eyes open and unfocused, the thick bands of scar tissue under her eyes glowing slightly. The spiders are crawling all over her, sitting in her wild, reddish-brown hair, swinging from the collar of her embroidered tunic. Their shapes blur into one roiling pattern. I get the same sensation from watching them as I do from watching prophets scry into a mirror or a deep bowl of water. A blurring of *here* and *now*; a distortion of *when*s.

Ade's mouth moves, and low, scuffing words come from the back of her throat. My skin prickles. Something en't right about the twitch of her jaw, her unseeing eyes, her rigid posture. I've seen prophets mid-vision plenty of times, but nothing like this. I want to turn and walk right past her, pretend I never saw her. Who would know?

You would, I think. Cos the golden rule of the prophet house that rooted me to any room I walked into where a prophet was having a vision unsupervised roots me where I stand now:

Never leave a prophet having a vision alone. She could fit and swallow her tongue. She could lash out at herself or others. She could be drawn out of her body by the strength of the vision, or be driven mad by something she sees there.

'She's already mad,' I mutter to myself. 'It's not like any more visions are gonna hurt. Ade en't my problem.'

If only. My toes curl. Frustrated. Cos here's the truth:

She's my problem, cos she's Nine's mother.

She's my problem, cos she's this island's most powerful prophet, even if she can't make enough sense most of the time to string a sentence together.

She's my problem, cos my mother was in love with her. And she was in love with my mother. Something about those words, even just thinking them inside my head makes me want to hit something.

'She's already mad,' I say firmly to myself. I turn to leave.

Ade's head snaps up sharply and every single spider in the clearing freezes. It's incredible how still the scene is after being occupied with so much movement. A sick feeling clutches me between the shoulders.

'Someone there,' Ade says. She's not looking at me. Her head cranes and swings on her neck, questing like a pack animal that caught a scent. I back up a few paces. I suddenly wish I was wearing my tool belt.

'I know you're there,' Ade says. 'Who are you?'

'The daughter of Ashir,' I say carefully. Ade doesn't always get names but she always gets Ma's.

'Ah,' she says. 'Anassa.'

I can't remember Ade calling me anything but *girl* the whole time I've known her. It sets off warning sparks in my head.

'Who are you?'

Ade's face splits in a wide smile, showing all her teeth. A puppet-like grimace. 'Watch your horizons, Anassa.'

There's a few seconds' pause before she coughs, sighs and stretches. She stops when she catches sight of me, still rooted to the spot.

'Ade?'

Her shoulders hunch, like she's expecting a telling-off. 'Had to,' she says. 'Had to do it! Spiders kept talking.'

'Spiders – what do you mean, Ade? You were *talking* to them?' I feel my voice rising – I'm still remembering the strange, guttural movement of her throat as the spiders crawled over her. My heart's still trying to escape my body through my mouth.

'Talking to me. No one else listening. Just Ade. Poor Ade.'

'Ade, that wasn't you speaking just then, was it? Who was using your mouth?'

But she's not looking at me. She's gazing sleepily at the spiders.

'*Ade*.'

She looks up. 'Spiders are leaving,' she says. 'Follow spiders?'

When I can't think of a way to leave her here that won't make me feel cripplingly guilty later, I say, 'Yes.'

So we do. It en't difficult to track them – the forest ahead of us is so thick with arachnids that the ground looks less like earth and more like water. I worry Ade will tread on them, but actually I'm much more of a liability. My feet are heavy and purposeful even when I don't mean them to be. Ma used to say she could hear me coming cos of how much my tread sounded like a stamp. In comparison, Ade glides on, light-footed as a goat.

She – and the spiders – stop a few hundred yards short of the beach.

'What's here?' I ask.

'Spiders. Spiders are leaving.'

'They're not,' I say irritably. 'Look, they're staying around here.' She turns to look at me, head cocked. *She can't help what she is*, I scold myself.

'You angry, girl,' she says.

I feel my face heat. 'No.'

'Yes,' she says, rubbing her nose like a little kid. 'I'm sorry. Sorry about the vines.'

'Can you take them away then?' Hope rises inside me. Maybe I can fix this after all.

But she shakes her head.

'Then *I'm* sorry, but you being sorry doesn't mean much to me, Ade.'

'Trying, girl,' she says. 'Trying to get better.'

I sigh, because that's nonsense. If they're untrained, prophets don't *get better*. Their minds are ruined for good.

For no apparent reason, she flinches and shrieks, 'No. No, no, not – not! NOT READY. NOT READY.'

I let out a snarl of frustration. 'Why, Ade? Why not?'

She puts her face in her hands and moans. 'She's gone. She's gone.'

My pulse trips. I have an idea I know who *she* is. I'm at the edge of a void I've been skirting for months. Ade looks up at me, as lucid as I've ever seen her and I'm so frightened I can barely get the words out. '*Don't*,' I whisper. 'Don't say it!'

But she takes a long breath and says, '*I'm* . . . not ready, girl. Not ready to go up there. To the new trees. Not without her.'

Not without my mother. That's who she means. Every part of me fills with her words and turns to bright, flaring anger.

'*You're* not ready? *YOU* aren't ready?! You – you *selfish* – you—'

But I can see her losing her grip again, and a second later she's mumbling the words to a song under her breath, as if nothing's happened.

I'm back at the vishaal trees, watching spiders swarm out

67

of the ground; I'm staring down at Enethea's ruined body. I'm watching the line of funeral marchers carrying my mother's body wrapped in blue cloth for the sky funeral.

I'm too furious for anything more considered than the most hurtful, bladed words I can think of.

'I wish it was you,' I choke out. '*I wish it was you who'd died.*'

As soon as the words are out of my mouth, the clearing goes silent. *Ade* goes quiet.

There's a heavy stillness, like dry ground waiting for rain.

And then, as if a bird has dived into their midst, the spiders scatter in every direction. They move so quickly, it's like they dissolve into the dead leaves.

'Oh,' Ade says.

Something explodes out of the trees to my left. I swivel, and see a tall, dark, man-shaped blur heading straight for me. I don't have time to do more than step back from his path. He blazes past, catching my arm as he goes, hitting me with heat, like standing in front of open flames, though there's no light, just warmth. Next comes pain: my skin shrieks, as if a brand has been pressed against it. I can smell the flesh on my arm cauterising.

'Girl!' Ade yells. 'Girl, you all right?'

'Astor?' I call as the man comes to a stop. He whirls round, though the moonlight doesn't touch his face, and comes at me again.

I pick up the first branch I can find and hold it up, but he keeps coming, dead set on me like a hammer on a nail.

Ade screams. I swing the branch down like a sword. It

swerves him away from me but the branch breaks into pieces as it touches him and bursts into gouty yellow flames.

I swear. He turns again. I stumble back. He makes for me.

'Astor, stop! It's me! It's Etain!'

But maybe that's why he's attacking.

Something catches under my hasty feet. I fall back heavily, hitting my head.

He's nearly on me.

Ade calls out a note. It's like she's run a lance through my skull, and the magic swells — cold as stones in a river and smelling of old caves. I clap my hands over my ears and shut my eyes—

I feel a brief flare of heat, and then it's gone, and there's silence. When my hearing comes back, I can hear running footsteps. I scrabble on the ground for something to defend myself with. I'm panting, throwing out my feet and arms wildly in panic. My foot catches something hot and I freeze, terrified.

But nothing comes for me. I stay there, eyes still closed, listening for the sound of ragged breath, the light tread on leaves. I wait, and then, steeling myself, scramble to my feet.

Still nothing. I blink, take a deep breath and wait for my eyes to clear. The forest and the beach beyond it comes slowly back into focus. I pitch around, but the trees are quiet, and there's no one there. 'Ade?' I whisper. 'Ade?'

I lean against the nearest trunk and pat myself over. The edge of my left hand is agony from the branch that turned to flames, and there's a blister the size of a lemon coming up on my arm from where he first ran at me. There's a wetness between my legs too, and the sharp pinch of urine, but that's the least of my worries.

'Ade?' I say again.

'Here, girl.' I can see her outline now: several feet away and bowed over like she's been hit in the stomach.

'What did you do? Where did he go?'

But Ade slumps on to the ground, whimpering.

'Ade? Are you hurt?'

No spiders now, not one. Just the thick white webs, heavy with dew in the branches overhead and among the tree roots. I'm not looking where I'm going as I tread towards Ade. I trip over something and sprawl flat on my face.

I get up, shivering, wanting to cry.

Instead a silent scream clutches my jaw and holds it open.

Because I've tripped over a body. Still smoking. Skin blackened, eye sockets hollow, teeth showing through the now lip-less mouth. Just like Enethea, but of course it en't Enethea.

It's Medea. Astor's mother.

Taurus

When Ma and I met up, she asked some weird questions, you know? I mean, when I was fifteen she was still asking cute stuff like: 'What's the tallest thing you've climbed this week, Taurus?'

I was all, 'I live in a tree, Ma. And the highest point of the tree is the passage that I have to climb to meet you here,

70

at Ariadnis, which is higher than any tree in Metis. So, here. This is the highest point I've had to climb this week.'

She flushed. 'Can't a mother ask her son a light-hearted question?'

I thought, *Sure you could if I was still five. What am I still doing here?* I said, 'Only telling you the truth, Ma.'

She pulled me to her. 'Hang in there, kid.'

She'd say stuff like that. *Hang in there, kid. One day, when this is over.*

Those things hadn't sounded like a distant thing when I was younger. They sounded like *soon*. When she said stuff like that, I thought she was saying that eventually my mission would be done. That one day I'd go up to Athenas to live with her and Etain. Or they'd come down here to live with me and Ade.

There was other stuff going on the year I was fifteen too.

Joomia still wasn't showing any signs of power. I didn't know then about Ramon, the first person she turned to wood. She'd kept it a secret. Nine only recently figured out how to reverse that process – but back then it was the same as if she'd killed him. It was an accident, of course, but it scared Joomia out of using her powers again for a long time. You could say I wasn't the most sympathetic person in the world about that. Not to her face or anything. I just didn't get why she was so reluctant to be important.

There were times when I wasn't sure what I wanted more: to be important so everyone would think, *That Taurus guy – he's important*, or because if I was important . . . maybe Ma wouldn't have left me there in Metis, by myself.

Hang in there, kid.

71

This time she didn't follow it with any reassurances. And I got it. There wasn't even anything special or meaningful about the way she said it. I just . . . got it.

Oh.

It's not going to happen.

And then I knew:

I'm going to stay in Metis for ever.

That night, I brought someone back to my hut for the first time. It was Kaseem that night, but it could have been anyone. I hadn't realised how exquisite it would feel. To hold someone, naked, against you, limbs tacky with sweat, warm stomach to warm stomach, hands running down your back, swelling, gasping sometimes: teeth, your head on their chest after, listening to their heartbeat.

It was addictive.

I was going to stay in Metis.

I guess I thought I'd try to find someone who thought that was worth something.

Etain

I slap my leg and peer at my hand. Five ruined mosquito bodies, and five tiny smears of blood on the bandages across my palm. I wipe it on the waistband of my tunic and try to concentrate on what Einar is saying. Flying insects everywhere, zipping around my ears. Everyone is scratching and slapping themselves and glaring at each other.

I couldn't bring Medea's body back by myself. When Nine and a few others went to recover it, they found another, further away, that turned out to be Ineb, Astor's youngest son. Taurus said I vomited when they told me that, but I don't remember.

We stand in the clearing beneath the enormous trunk of what used to be Knot Tree. Many people have come to bow their heads over the bodies; to murmur a song. Nine stands and waits for the Athenasian and the Metisian magi to finish murmuring their funeral rites, and then she slowly crouches and puts her hand on each blackened corpse: Enethea, Medea, Ineb. The change is subtle: the charred skin seems to darken and then loosen. It's a strange magic: I blink, once or twice, and then the bodies are just piles of earth. It's like my mind can't follow the change, so it rearranges: weren't they *always* just earth?

Some people spread the earth around the base of the tree, just as we did with the remains of the people we lost battling the mindless under Nadrik's spell. Another song is sung, another long speech. I give a quiet blessing, hardening my expression against their stares, which are boring holes in me, and the sting of insect bites.

Mur, Astor's eldest son, comes up to me after it all. His face is empty, like a shucked skin. He doesn't say anything; he doesn't do anything. He just stares into my eyes, his hand gripping the shoulder of his younger brother, and shows me everything my decisions have cost him.

The gathering trails back to camp in groups. Taurus and Lear must have argued or something: Taurus is swapping intense looks with a girl called Rhcan.

Nine comes to stand beside me. She watches Taurus too, her face blank as always, but her eyes are dancing. **He never**

did know what to do with uncomfortable feelings, she says.

I laugh, and say, 'Name me someone that does.'

I keep hearing Medea saying, *I'll find him by myself then*. I want to go back and say something to stop her, want it so desperately I'm struggling to swallow enough air. I just keep thinking about what will happen if we *do* catch Astor, and manage to restore him somehow. What will he do when he realises what he's done?

'How's Ade?' I ask.

Nine bites her lip. **Phythia's doing what she can for the burn.**

I saw it. A great, red, angry strip of skin, larger than the two brushes I'd sustained. She's still lying in Phythia's tent, sleeping it off. *I wish it was you. I wish it was you who'd died*.

Wise One, imagine if those were the last words I'd said to her. I still haven't told anyone the real reason she interfered with the setup of the steps. Why? Cos secretly, it's something I was thinking too? Cos I'm afraid to go on without my mother?

'What was it like when you knew you'd killed someone?' I ask.

Nine looks at me sharply. 'What do you *think* it was like, Etain?' she says.

I press on. 'Like, did you start feeling guilt right away or . . . did it eat you slowly?'

I'm still half thinking about Astor, about the idea of waking and discovering you'd unknowingly murdered the people you loved the most, when her face hardens. So I guess she knows that I'm also thinking of my mother, thinking of the fact that Aula was the one to kill her – however accidentally. Thinking of what Taurus has told me about Joomia and Ramon. That Joomia was the one who turned so many people to wood. That she only managed to turn some of them back.

'I owned it. I ate it whole. I put it inside me,' she says, suddenly savage. **I embodied every bit of remorse and self-hate I could muster.**

I blink, and every bitter thought towards her changes from icicles to water. 'Sorry,' I say.

Don't try to push your guilt off on me just because you can't stomach the consequences of your decisions.

It genuinely would have hurt less if she'd hit me. I deserve every word.

'You think Aula and Joomia en't here,' she says, 'but they are. I am them, even if I don't always look or sound the same.'

'I'm sorry,' I say. 'I know they're there. I can hear them – I mean, *you*. It's just . . . difficult to process.'

It's not an excuse, but I don't know what to say that will make her feel better.

There's a silence, and then Nine speaks, breathlessly. 'It's like you and Taurus both think that because I'm neither of them, I en't going through the emotions they would either. It's like you don't even want me around any more, and it en't fair, OK? I know I've messed up this joining somehow and I know I killed Ashir and Ramon and I let Lear fall and I know I can't be either of your best friends any more, but can you stop treating me like everyone else did when I was just their Chosen One?'

The tears sliding down her face like a kid who's been punched catch me off-guard. 'Oh Wise One, Nine,' I say, pulling her to me. She seems to sag a little, as if in relief; she puts her arms around my waist and cries hard into my shoulder. Shame burrows its way into my throat, deep into my stomach, and leaves a hot weight in my limbs.

'You en't the only one with a prophecy over your head.'

'I know,' I say. 'I'm sorry. None of that stuff's your f—'

It *is* my fault, she says. I'm the Chosen One. I'm supposed to unite everyone.

'Like I'm supposed to be leading everyone,' I say.

She squeezes me gently, and I'm glad she can't see my face.

She lets go after a little while, and we stand there, thinking, and it's a little restful, even if I can hear midges rather than the comforting clank of engines and the smell of fried food. Instead, the air fills my nose with the damp of the earth, and the sharp wood of the trees, and I'm reminded of why we have to make all this work: because it's the only home we have. I love this place, these trees, this island. I love them. I can't ruin it, or let anyone else ruin it with the same mistakes our ancestors made.

'You don't think you could make everyone forget again?' I ask her. 'Forget who they were, forget Athenas and Metis, and just remember being one, and loving the island?'

She smiles sadly. 'Yeah, I've been thinking that too. But it wouldn't be wise, Etain. I reckon they have to learn. We all do.'

'Yeah,' I say, half-hearted. We lapse into silence again for a few minutes, just looking at the scattered earth around the base of Knot Tree.

'Spiders,' she says eventually. 'Spiders. They ran from Astor?'

She doesn't seem to expect me to answer though, cos she's looking in the direction of the ocean, as if she's willing herself to see any remaining arachnid scuttling towards an answer.

'You tried to warn me something was wrong,' I say. 'You said . . . the joining didn't completely work?'

No, she says carefully, but with conviction.

'Do you know why yet?'

She shifts, as if she's weighing up how to tell me. **No. Not yet. It's like . . . like magnets that should meet, but can't. Or a loose stitch or** — she smiles a little — 'a casting defect in a forge. Something that's loose in the trees . . . in me.'

'Can you fix it?' I ask, knowing the answer.

'I dunno. It might not be just mine to fix. We're missing something. A missing ingredient or . . . factor. I don't know. Maybe I messed it up somehow.'

I shake my head. 'That doesn't make sense. If you had, how could the trees have given you back to us? This . . . defect . . . it's got to be something else.' I pause, thinking of the disparity among everyone, worse now than it was before. 'Is it us? Is it that we're still not united?'

She rubs her forehead.

'Or,' I say, nervously, 'could it be something to do with the spiders? Or whatever's happened to Astor? Or that ant you were talking about?'

'Yeah,' she says. 'Yeah, I think it's all related – the spiders and the ants and Astor too . . . Etain?'

'Yes?'

I think we need to go and see the prophets. I think we need to see them *now*.

I pause. 'I can't, Nine. I promised the council . . .'

'Out of respect for the Metisians, you promised the council you wouldn't make any *decisions* based on prophecy. Not that you wouldn't visit them.'

But I carry on chewing my lip, uncertain.

I'm half-Metisian, she goes on. I'm not sure even *they* know why they mistrust prophecies so much. It's like an untraceable prejudice they stick to until it grinds them into the dirt. You're allowed to *challenge* them sometimes, Etain.

She holds out her hand.

Taurus

People are dead, so people who aren't drink.

I'm right there with them. I wasn't close to anyone who died but I got my own problems. I know that's selfish, but knowing it doesn't make it different. Actually, it makes it worse: now I have real ammo to hate myself with.

Why am I so lost? I decide it's because I miss Joomia. I miss her all the time. I miss sitting in silence with her and I miss making her laugh and I miss the stink eye she'd give me if she thought I was behaving badly. I think about hugging her and it makes me sad. Really sad. Maybe I'm just a really sad person. Maybe that's what lost is.

Why am I lost? Maybe it's because I miss my sister. She's so busy. She has to be, I get that. I just don't get why she won't talk to me about things. She won't talk about Ma.

Aula would have, I think. No one talks to me like Aula did. Like the world was a nut she wanted to crack just so it would leave her alone. I got that about her. For sure, I did.

Rhean was a friend of Enethea's. We've only been talking for an hour but I can tell she wants to jump me. She looks really sad too. I mean, she's flicking her hair and stroking my arm and lowering her eyes to my crotch, but somehow every movement is filled with sorrow. Grief does weird things to people. Is that why I'm horny too?

We're minutes away from needing to go find somewhere private when Etain taps me on the shoulder.

I can tell she's behind me, so I lean my head back until I can look her in the eyes.

'Sister sister,' I say. I waggle my eyebrows at her. It makes me dizzy.

Rhean giggles.

Etain keeps her Leader Face on.

'How much of that have you had?' she says, narrowing her eyes at the pitcher of ale in my hand. Someone brought out a few of the ale casks we'd managed to scavenge from the ruins of Athenas for the funeral. Probably not a great idea to drink so much, though.

'Some,' I say. (OK, I've lost count.)

There's the tiniest flare of Etain's nostrils to let me know just how thrilled she is with me. 'Great. I need you. Come with me and Nine.'

I wink at Rhean. I say, 'To be continued.'

She gives me a winning salute. I wobble to my feet. Etain grips my arm and leads me out of the camp site.

She starts scolding right away. 'You are being cruel,' she says, leading me through the trees as Nine skips ahead. 'Lear was *right there.*'

I'm drunk enough to know that if I wasn't this drunk, I would seriously object to this conversation. Like Etain the human shrew gets to tell *me* about being cruel? I imagine saying this for a moment. Really, I just want to tell her to loosen up. To let go a bit. Instead, I say, 'Oho. Keep your restrictive relationship parameters to yourself, little sister. Not everyone in Metis wants an exclusive relationship.'

'Sorry to state the blatantly obvious, but Lear *does.* I wouldn't care if both of you were happy venturing elsewhere, but he en't, and you're hurting him.' She has to push aside a thorny branch and waves me ahead of her so she can let it swing back after I've passed.

'How would you know anyway?' I ask her. 'Been having secret little chats?'

'I just bother to read people on a deeper level than whether they want to have sex with me right then and there.'

I put a hand to my chest. 'Ouch!'

'It's kind of beside the point, Taurus: even if you were *both* up for being non-exclusive, it's not exactly tactful to make a move on someone else when they're *watching* you do it.'

'You're grumpy,' I say, 'because you haven't got any in a while.'

'You're deflecting, because I'm right and you hate it.'

'Well—' I begin, but there's no comeback. Sometimes, with Etain, I feel like she's the only one who understands me. And sometimes I've never felt more judged. I sigh.

'Maybe there's just things we don't get about each other.'

She pounces on that one. Damn it. It must have come out in my tone. 'Like what?'

I don't say anything.

She spreads her arms. 'Like what, Taurus?'

I shrug. 'I'm wondering how you could have let Ade get in the way of Astor.'

'What is it with Ade?' she says. 'Look, she's *fine*, Taurus. She's *alive*. She was just there at the same time—'

'But she got hurt,' I say. I'm about to chicken out of saying the rest. The challenging look on her face draws the rest out of me though. 'It just sounds like she saved you and you didn't do a thing to help her.'

'You're calling me a coward.'

'No. I'm just saying. I know the spiders wouldn't have stopped me from defending someone I'm supposed to care about.'

'Well, I *don't* care about her,' she says. 'Happy?'

'Definitely not,' I say, mentally recoiling.

We keep walking, stiffly, irritably.

'Just say it, Taurus,' she says. 'Whatever it is.'

'How can you say you don't care about your people? You're supposed to be *leader*. Our Anassa. You *have* to take responsibility for what happens to them!'

She throws back her head and laughs. 'So I should be taking lessons from *you*? Anax of responsibility?'

'At least I care about them!'

'Caring about people isn't the same as liking them,' she counters.

We glare at each other. The air between us is stiff.

81

I stop abruptly, registering the direction we're headed in.

She turns back. 'What now?'

'Where are we going?'

'To see the prophets.'

'Why?'

She hesitates, and then she says testily, 'I'm trying to include you. I thought that's what you wanted.'

I rake my hand across my face. 'Include me? So this is about my feelings?'

'No, it's about not knowing what's going on and trying to shed light on it.'

'And what are they gonna shed light on, Etain? What do you think they're gonna tell you? That this was all *supposed* to happen? That Astor was *meant* to kill his family?'

She bites her lip, hard, and I can tell there are words poised on the edge of her mouth. I watch her swallow them. 'I didn't know you felt that way about prophets,' she says quietly. 'If you don't want to come . . .'

'I'm not talking about the prophets—'

'Fine,' she snaps. 'I didn't know you felt that way about *me*.'

I open my mouth and close it. Pain arcs briefly across her face.

'I didn't mean—' I begin, too late.

'It's fine, Taurus,' she cuts across me. 'Go back to Rhean. Go and get it out of your system. I just thought you were the compass. I thought you wanted to help me.'

I watch her leave. Why did I even let that conversation start? It's not what I wanted to say. What was it I wanted to say? *Help me. I'm lost.* A mosquito lands on my neck. I slap it away.

I'm being an idiot. She's going to the prophets. Which means she's looking for answers in a familiar place. She's just as lost as I am.

Etain

I haven't been to the Cave of the Ancestors in months, and it looks very different from the last time I was here.

The few miraculously unbroken mirrors, bowls and books I retrieved for them from the ruins of Athenas sit on rickety shelves standing at intervals around the room. Parchment, leather-bound journals and books on Sight are crammed alongside them – the prophets must have gone back to Athenas themselves and done their own scavenging, and those fabric hangings weren't here last time, nor was that cauldron. There's a vast metal bowl too – at least as wide as I am tall, and high enough to bump my hip. I remember it vaguely from one of the scrying rooms in the prophet house, used when prophets needed to throw their vision wide and concentrate their powers into one reflective surface.

Nine is already here, standing at the side of the bowl with the other prophets. Ade's notable only by her absence. Normally one of them would be holding her hand, keeping her under control.

I wish it was you.

I shake my head and look back at the bowl. It's full of

still, clear water, and reflects almost perfectly the ceiling above. I'm so distracted by it that I don't immediately see Sabine, standing to my left with an unreadable expression on her face.

'Sister,' I say hopefully, but her face is cool and remote; her eyes narrow, taking me in.

We're supposed to kiss – four times, once on each cheek, the other two in the air above the eyelids, as if in blessing of the Sight. Obviously, I en't a prophet, but they're my family – they heard all my teenage tantrums, wiped my butt when I was a baby, made my birthday presents. Doesn't seem to mean much to them any more, though.

'Good evening, Etain,' Sabine says. 'What can we do for you?'

'I was hoping for some help,' I say. The word *help* echoes thinly against the cave walls.

'I see,' she says.

'Sabine,' Nine says warningly. Sabine rewards her with a single, cutting glance that asks if her authority is being questioned. Nine says nothing more, but one eyebrow quirks.

Sabine looks back at me, inscrutable.

I put a hand to my sternum as if I can support the heaviness gathering there. 'I don't know what I'm doing, Sabine,' I say. 'I never had to work without visions before, and I've never needed them more than now.'

'What do you need to know, Etain?' Sabine says. There's something dangerous in her voice, but I'm too tired to tell what it is.

On the other side of the scrying bowl, Ingrid shifts irritably. She was better friends with Ma than Sabine, but wasn't up for leading when Ma died. With Sabine's eyes boring into me, I wish she had been.

'I just thought you might have been on the lookout for Astor, for what might have caused his . . . um . . . madness.'

'And?'

'And . . . and I wondered if you might have found a way to take down the vines that won't offend the—'

There's a general hiss from the prophets around the bowl.

'The Metisians,' I finish determinedly.

Sabine considers me. 'I'm guessing you want this information without making any attempt to integrate us back into the camp?'

I bite my lip, trying to find an answer, but she continues before I can.

'And I'm guessing you want this information in spite of the fact that the blame for the spiders is being directed at us and circulated *around* the camp without a peep of intervention from you?'

Ingrid opens her mouth, perhaps to defend me. Sabine silences her with a look.

'You want this information, despite the fact that one of our own risked her life for you and your brother in a multitude of instances – none of which you've seen fit to pay back?'

'Ade only did any of that cos Ma asked her to.'

It's out of my mouth before I can stop it. This stupid, child's response to provocation. *Take it back*, the better half of me says. *Take it back!*

But I don't.

'Sabine,' Nine says angrily. 'Ashir would have wanted—'

'Ashir only ever cared about prophecy as long as it helped out her children,' Sabine snarls. 'Which would have been fine if her children gave a shit about us.'

I shut my eyes against her words, but they rip right through me anyway. In the silence left around them, no one but Nine will look at me.

'I understand,' I say, at last. 'I'm sorry.'

Ingrid looks up, but she can't do anything. The prophets need a leader, and they have one.

Taurus

'Did you hear that?'

Rhean rolls off me, panting. 'It's the sound I would have made if you could keep your focus.'

I sit up on my bed and listen again. Screaming, sobbing. Not just one or two but several voices. Rhean sits up too now.

'Anassa!' someone calls into the night. 'Anassa!'

I get out of bed without a word and fumble for my sarong.

Rhean looks like she's tempted to stay, but she sighs heavily and swings herself out on the other side of the bed.

'It's probably nothing,' I say, brushing the privacy curtain aside. I haven't got the sarong knotted properly and Rhean's tunic's coming off her shoulder.

Of course we run into Lear at the entrance to the sleeping tents. He sees me first. Something complicated crosses his face, like he's glad to see me and he knows he shouldn't be because we argued. He wants to keep his stance, he's about to forgive me. I can see it all. Then he spots Rhean.

I close my eyes and curse myself, and then I'm past him, walking back through camp, others emerging at the screams. I make for the Cave of the Ancestors, where I guess Etain will still be, where I know—

I nearly trip on something lying on the ground. Something smoking, something hot. Someone – Phythia – lets out a yell before I do, though, and I come up short.

Another body, blackened and burned like the others.

'Astor,' Phythia says in a low rasp. 'I caught sight of him, running through. He didn't look any different, Taurus. But everyone he brushed past . . .' Her voice wavers. 'He didn't even seem to *see* them. Has he gone mad?'

I follow the screaming that's echoing across the camp now – and as I look along the pathway that sits above the main encampment, I see more bodies, strewn at intervals. There are at least eight of them—

'*Where* is the Anassa?' someone yells.

'Taurus—' Phythia says warningly, but I'm already running. My head swims with drink and the smell of Rhean's hair and the *look* on Lear's face, but I run through it, trying to compass.

She's not at the Cave after all, but at one of the smaller beaches, about a mile from camp. She's standing a little into the surf, looking out to the horizon as if she wanted to go further but couldn't make herself.

'Etain!'

She jumps when she hears me and it's almost as if I can

87

see the reverberation of our argument jump back and forth between us.

'What?' she says. It takes a second, but then the mask comes down, and she's all Wise and Powerful Leader, cloaking the other version of her. Then she sees my expression.

'Oh Wise One. Taurus, what is it?'

The camp is a wreck. Canvas is ripped and scorched around the main barracks. Pots and pans from the mess tent are scattered and upturned in the grass. 'Where is everyone?' Etain asks.

But the council tent, lit by floating Athenasian lights, draws her. Her answer is laid out there in front of it.

Ten.

Ten bodies on the grass, blackened and curled in on themselves like dead beetles. I choke, hand over my mouth. Etain just stares – blank, despairing – as we draw closer.

Beyond the bodies are her council; Einar stands out in front, looking grim.

'Where did he go?' a voice calls, and Nine runs forward from I don't know where.

Chu points and Nine sprints off in the direction of his finger.

'Where are the people?' Etain asks Einar as soon as she's near enough.

'The magi have taken everyone down to the beach for now,' Einar says. 'It seemed the most easily defensible against fire attack.'

Etain nods, looking relieved. 'I must go to them.'

'No,' Janaelle says. She glances at me, and I try to read her face, but she looks away quickly.

Etain frowns. 'What do you mean, no?'

'Into the tent, Lady Etain,' Thetea says. 'Your council needs to talk to you.' She hesitates as her eyes land on me. An unexplainable dread expands in my stomach the longer she looks at me.

'You should come too, Taurus,' she says.

Etain

They stand around me in an austere circle. The council tent is unscathed, but I can still smell char and burning as the wind flaps the canvas.

'What does the council wish of me?' I ask, thinking desperately of those bodies while schooling my face, resisting the urge to smooth my braids.

Einar takes a deep breath. 'We have arrived at something of an impasse.'

'Because Astor ran through and got you all scared?' Taurus snarls.

'Ran through and killed *ten people*, Taurus,' Ior says. 'One of them was a *child*.'

'Whose child?' I ask.

'Alma's,' says Merryn.

'Chima,' I say. Sweet kid. All fuzzy twisted hair and big brown eyes. I blink furiously.

'My lady,' Chu says, 'where were you?'

'I was . . .' I know the smartest thing would be to lie.

To tell them I was out walking, or something. But I'm so tired. 'I was with the prophets,' I say.

There's a collective intake of breath.

Hastily, I say, 'I was just making sure they were . . . all right.'

'Not to ask for guidance?' Janaelle asks, her eyebrow raised.

'What's the harm in her asking?' Taurus says loudly, like he's forgotten what he said to me. But I can see the guilt written all over his face, as easy to read as a toddler's frown. They can see it too.

Janaelle's mouth gets small. 'It was my understanding that when we elected you, you promised never to use the prophets to aid your decisions about the rest of the people.'

'You don't understand—' Taurus starts, but I cut him off with a shake of my head.

'Well, you can rest easy,' I say, 'because they wouldn't share any visions they might have had with me anyway.'

Einar's jaw works as if he's chewing on a hard heel of bread. 'So tell us, *Anassa*,' he says. 'What's next? Now that thirteen people are dead and vines with thorns the size of sickle blades blocking us from our true home cannot be taken down. Now that there is a murderer on the loose risking the lives of everyone?'

'I am hoping we can work together,' I say evenly, looking around. It should sound like a putdown but instead I feel as if they're looking down at me. 'Ade had her reasons for doing what she did,' I say. 'Perhaps, as Nine said—'

'Are you really trying to justify the word of a madwoman

90

and her barely-vocal daughter?' Kaseem says, cutting me off.

I stare at him, wounded. Apart from Sander, he's usually the first to take my side in a debate.

'My lady,' says Chu gently, 'you know as well as anyone that prophecies en't always accurate. Ade en't like your ma or Igra and anyway, the prophets who are left barely have any of their usual tools, right? Maybe the chances of them making an accurate prophecy about our fate in the new trees en't that great, let alone Ade by herself . . .' He looks at the rest of the Athenasians, as if for confirmation, and each is nodding with a *fair point* kind of expression.

I grit my teeth. 'Did you ever work in the prophet house, Chu?'

'No, but—'

'Do you know how prophet magic works?'

'No, but—'

'Where did you work again? The Episteme plateau?'

'Er . . . yes, Lady Etain. In the library.'

'And you're set on identifying as male, right?'

He blinks at me. 'Y-yes.'

I nod. 'Unlikely you know much about prophecy and how it works then.'

I take a breath and realise I'm bristling and furious. It's all over me, in my hands and gestures and eyes and posture.

'Perhaps . . .' Sander says, looking nervously at me. 'Perhaps we all ought to calm down, give it a day, ask the Wise One for His . . . or Her . . . blessing.' he adds, looking askance at the Metisians. Perhaps organise some prayers.'

I purse my lips. 'That's thoughtful, Sander, but I don't

think the Wise One is going to—'

'Perhaps we should ask for His blessings now,' Einar says, looking at me. He's testing me, I know it. 'Maybe He—'

'*She*,' Merryn objects.

'Einar—' I say.

'Or *She*,' Einar amends, 'can tell us the answer to the question our leader is so keen to avoid—'

'*Einar*,' I say again.

'O Wise One!' Einar casts his head back and stares at the ceiling. 'What do we do now? What do we do with our brother Astor, whom you have seen fit to writhe in flame—'

'That's *enough*,' I shout. 'Einar, that's enough. You *know* what happened to people in the Old World when they started to believe in a place that consumed people by fire.'

'Are you saying the Wise One has no place like that for us?' Einar counters.

I clench my fists. I can see the smile wanting to inch on to his face.

'Perhaps . . . perhaps we *have* offended Her,' Merryn says.

'Perhaps we weren't meant to join the trees at all,' Kaseem mutters.

'Is it a test?' Janaelle wonders. 'A test to determine the faithful?'

Taurus explodes. 'It's *not real*,' he snarls. 'The Wise One isn't real! It's a device Lore implanted in our memories when she took out Allah and Jehovah and Buddha and Jesus!'

They draw back from him like he's mad.

'He didn't mean that,' I say. 'He's just—'

'Or perhaps . . . the Wise One is testing our leader,' Einar says.

'Etain doesn't speak for the Athenasians,' Kaseem says to the Metisians.

'You elected her!' Taurus snaps.

'Enough!' Einar says, echoing me. 'Lady Etain, what is your answer? What will you have us do now?'

I spread my hands. I'm on the edge of some emotion, but I'm not sure what, like they're forcing me to bare parts of myself that should be hidden. 'I don't know what you want me to say.'

'Can I take it that you are not planning to take us back to the trees?' Einar says, his anger cool and distant over his folded arms.

'I'm not saying we can't go back *ever*. I'm only saying that there's a fairly large obstacle to overcome here. Perhaps it's not time. Would it be too much to ask for a little patience?'

There's silence – the usual mix of coldness and scepticism when it comes to this question, but there's something different about a few of their gazes. I know about reading people. I've been developing *that* skill since I apprenticed to Nadrik all those years ago.

I take a sharp breath in, and realise I know what's coming. That's why we're in the tent. So they could force the answer out of me they already knew I would give.

'Oh, I see,' I whisper. 'It's come to that, has it?'

Chu, Sander, Thetea and Janaelle at least have the guts to look me in the eye.

'What?' Taurus says, blinking around.

'They're voting me out,' I say. I feel winded. 'They don't want me to be leader.'

A few fleeting glances tell me how right I am.

From the other side of the tent Einar says, 'Little to no progress has been made since the Chosen Ones were . . . er . . . *retrieved* all those months ago. Something has to change.'

'You cowards,' Taurus spits. 'You said nothing before.'

'We have come to cross swords with Etain *several* times since we trusted the prophecy of your late mother that she would be leader,' Einar says calmly. 'Etain's rigidity has meant no progress for us. This must change.'

'Prophecy!' Taurus laughs. 'Yeah, I see, Einar. All you idiots from Metis are still holding on to your old prejudices!'

'Actually, it was a collective decision,' says Thetea. She bows her head to me. 'My lady, with all due respect, you have been voted leader and yet you refuse to lead. I have attested that I knew you to be a quick and deft negotiator, a keen observer, a skilful handler of social customs . . . all these things I saw in you when you were Scribe of the Anax.' She hesitates, then adds, 'Recent events, I believe, have shaken those skills loose.'

I close my eyes. It's like I've been holding a set of scales with hundreds of arms. I've been trying to balance each arm, shift the centre so that each one will align. It's taken all I have to balance them. And it's not enough.

Recent events . . . shaken those skills loose. Does she mean my mother dying? My city being destroyed? Ade? Or just Astor? Just Astor and all these deaths? The scales tip. Drop from my hands.

When I open my eyes, the tears slide out. As if they needed any more evidence that I'm unfit for this.

'You helped us keep hold of as many citizens as we could, Etain,' says Janaelle. 'You led us out of Metis. You saved us. But maybe that was all you were meant to do.'

'Ma was so sure,' I say, my voice thick. 'She was so sure.'

She nods, as if she understands.

'I accept the council's decision,' I say. 'I ask its permission to leave.'

'What?' Taurus snaps. 'Etain – no!'

'Permission,' I say, looking at Einar. I know it will be him they vote for next. He's sure of everything. He says things and he believes in them. Janaelle's right – that used to be me. It's not any more.

'Granted,' Einar says. 'Of course.'

I turn heel and get the hell out of there.

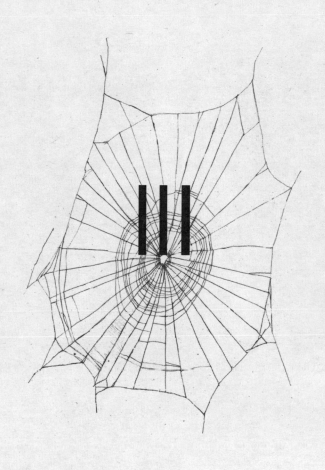

Taurus

When we met up – Ma, me and Etain – we alternated the location. Sometimes it would be at the bottom of the footpath of Ariadnis. Other times, right at the top of the tower of Athenas, in the owlery. When I was fourteen, Ma suggested it would be easier to meet right in the middle: the entrance to Ariadnis with its strange arch of phosphorescent mineral bulbs. Those bulbs followed me into my sleep, I swear. I dunno why. They made me feel like I had skin mites.

I could tell Etain didn't like it there either. She had a look on her face the first couple of times that I figured meant she usually walked past Ariadnis quickly without looking at it. I saw it as my job to stay calm for both of us. I'd act as if this place, with its powerful tug of magic, didn't make me want to run screaming in the opposite direction.

I knew Etain found me impressive. I totally got a kick out of that, especially because she didn't seem impressed with anything much. I wanted to keep it that way for as long as possible.

I never expected for the dynamic between us to change so dramatically. I always remember the beginning of that change as the time she dared me to touch the mineral bulbs in the entrance arch.

I was rattling off the usual things about an issue that Mathilde had had to solve.

Out of nowhere she came out with it: 'I dare you to touch the bulbs in the entrance.'

'What?' I said.

'What do you think will happen if we do?' she asked, a little breathlessly.

This was weird behaviour. My sister was a quiet, stoic little kid. Mostly she just listened, stony-face-attentive, to all the leadership crap Ma had commanded me to pay attention to. Etain heard it all, week after week. I tried to nudge a smile from her when I could, tweak her hair, get her to talk about her day. Sometimes I managed it, sometimes not.

This time though, there'd been something different from the off. Her eyes glinted when she'd mentioned Athenas in her steady little voice. Her fingers plucked restlessly at her tunic and the small metal bracelets which she'd claimed to have made herself. (I couldn't quite believe that. I know that sounds like mean older brother stuff, but she wasn't the Amazon Warrior she is now. She was a little squit.)

'What do you think will happen if we do?' she said again.

'Nothing good.'

'How do you know if you don't try it?' Her small tongue snaked out and licked her lips nervously.

'Because there are legends about it, saying nothing good,' I replied, watching her sideways.

'You're afraid,' she said, testing the waters of an ego challenge.

I laughed. I was the *master* of the ego challenge. 'Yeah, I am, sis. But fear keeps us alive, right?'

'Sounds like something a coward would say,' she said.

I knew from her tone it was an insult. I raised my eyebrows. 'Well then, I guess I'm a coward.'

She stamped her foot. 'I'm gonna be leader! I order you to do it!'

'Order me?' I asked.

She was panting suddenly, her fists clenched. Her eyes were wild and angry and scared all at once.

I looked toward the arch. Then back at her. Finally, I shrugged. What was I thinking? I don't remember. I said, 'All right. If that's what makes you happy, sis. I hope you can cope with what happens if I get hurt.'

I sauntered casually toward the arch, swaying my hips. Still trying to make her laugh. She didn't. I smiled and reached, real slow, for one of the bulbs.

Her face. I never forgot it. Tensed and agonised. Breathless. I didn't know *what* kind of dangerous game I was playing, but I suddenly knew it was going to break one of us. Up until then, I'd been sure it was going to be her. Now I wasn't so sure.

My fingers inched closer—

I was going to touch it—

There was nothing for it now—

I let my arm flop to my side. I was sweating. 'If you're so desperate to do something you're not allowed to do, you do it yourself, Etain,' I said. My voice was shaking – I guess from feeling danger's sword swishing past me.

She burst into tears. I wonder, even now, if she would have stopped me.

I stared at her, this furious little thirteen-year-old girl, in

101

utter disbelief. 'What the hell is *wrong* with you?'

'I'm *never* allowed to do anything,' she sobbed. 'I have to study the old kings. I have to be Nadrik's pupil. I have to be the leader cos what if someone else does it and fails?! What if they lead us to disaster? What if Nadrik finds out what I'm supposed to do? Aula does whatever she wants! And you – *you* get to do whatever you want! It's not fair! It's not *fair!*'

Etain put her head in her arms and howled. I'd never seen anything like it. I put my arms around her and let her cry against me until her sobs faded to snot and breathlessness. I knew there were pieces of this story that she hadn't told me, bits that I didn't understand.

But I began to get something about her then. Yes, Etain was quiet and restrained, but that wasn't shyness. That was expectation. Her burden was so heavy that it was sinking into the building blocks of who she was.

Maybe it had already sunk into me.

The Chosen

At dusk, he climbs into the crow's nest and peers at the island through a battered telescope. His name is Vulcan. He is tall and beautiful, with a long coil of braided hair wound around his head.

'How far?' the captain calls from the deck.

'Close,' Vulcan says, his voice raw with anticipation.

He waits for the island to draw closer in the telescope, till he can see the silhouetted tree tops clearly in the glass.

Then he descends on the rigging and walks back to his cabin.

There is a plated copper box in the corner, aged with verdigris. The lid is decorated with spirals of silver wire: a sunburst shape set into the top. The lock is cold against his fingers. He fumbles for the key hung around his neck and the lock springs open under his other hand with a quiet click.

The ant queen sits inside, her swollen abdomen throbbing with pale light. She is about as large as his forearm. He gazes at her for a moment, so delicately, seamlessly made – each piece of her fitting together with precise symmetry. Her mandibles open and close slowly, as if she were asleep, or in a trance. Perhaps she is, but there is no way to tell for sure. Her eyes are always open.

Carefully, he touches a finger to her thorax, and immediately her antennae twitch, her body stills.

'It's time,' he says. 'Wake them up.'

Etain

I walk without purpose or direction. I don't want anyone. I don't want anything. The tears that were so potent in the tent won't come now, when I need them. It would be a relief to break down here, by this tree or the next, and let out these stones under my breastbone. But nothing comes. Not sadness, not even relief.

I hear Igra's words to me, not long before she died: *Thing about prophecy. It sort of makes you who it says you're gonna be, most of the time.*

The worst thing en't that they're right about me not being fit to be the Anassa. The worst thing is that Ma was wrong.

'STOP, MA! JUST STOP!'

I turned and put my hands over my head. The day was hot, and there was shade in the palace gardens under the olive trees.

It was just some stupid thing.

We'd been going over a hypothetical situation where Ma would pretend to be a pissed-off citizen and I'd have to be me, diplomatic leader. If she didn't like the answers I was giving, she'd push harder. My limbs were aching from metalwork earlier in the day, and I hadn't had much sleep, but it was just a normal day. It must have come out of nowhere for her – I didn't usually let her see me feeling the strain – but I couldn't help it that day. It was coming up to a year until Aula would go into Ariadnis, and I could feel that everything was about to change.

Ma had never mentioned when I'd become this fated leader; I'm not sure she actually knew herself.

I sat down on the grass. Ma sighed and sat opposite me.

She considered me. I always kind of resented how little of her physicality I'd inherited. Taurus was always much more like Ma: lithe and elastic, practically bird-like. Our father had been an engine worker. I might have made something good with him, Ma used to say fondly, but the engines work against us. When I was older I figured out that she meant that he'd died working in the engines, not long after I was conceived. That happened sometimes, when there was a fault or the magi's safety runes hadn't been replaced soon enough. Anyway, I'd inherited my build from him. On good days I knew I was strong and tall, but on others I just felt bulky and clumsy. I just didn't see myself in her at all.

'I know this is hard on you, sweetheart,' she said.

'No, I don't think you do,' I snapped.

She thought for a while. 'I know you might resent me for it one day. Maybe you already do. I knew that from the moment you stirred in my belly.'

'But you did it anyway.' I look up from my hands. 'You did it anyway cos that's what prophets do.'

In the space between us was every hug she'd kept from me, every moment she'd barred me from going to bed before doing one final task, every friendship or romance she'd curtailed. She made that space. She carved every inch of it, and I hated her.

And maybe she saw that, because she crawled over to me and took my face in her hands. 'Yes, I did,' she said fiercely. 'Because I have Seen the woman you will become and the man Taurus will be. And I have Seen the hardships you will face. And I have Seen you conquer every one.'

I threw her off. 'What, that makes it better? Cos you love the people we will become rather than the people we are now?'

She stared at me, and I stared back, shocked at myself. Because I'd done what I thought was impossible. I'd made her cry.

'Is that what you think?' she whispered.

I was shaking. I didn't have the strength to push her away.

'Etain. Look at me. I am so proud of you. You are the strongest person I've ever met. You bear this burden that fate has given you, and you do not break. But I do not love you for that. I love you because you are my daughter. I love you because you make me laugh and cry and you teach me about myself. You are a true leader.'

I was crying too now. 'But it's so hard.'

She wrapped her arms around me. 'You will find a way.'

'But what if I need you?'

She held me tighter. 'I'll be there.'

'But what if you're not?'

She held me tighter, but she didn't answer. There wasn't an answer to that, I guess.

I start to run, propelled by echoes of the council's words, each one a hard splinter in my head, threatening to crack me open like a nut. I run until the sun is swallowed by the trees and I have to slow and pick my way through the trunks, reaching out for each one in the darkness.

It takes me a while to register that it's strangely quiet – usually, the further into the trees, the louder all the non-human sounds become. At night, it's owls of course, and other night birds. Sometimes you'll hear wild dogs yapping at each other from somewhere across the island. But here, deep in the woods – wherever I am – the loudest thing is me. I try to breathe quieter. Maybe I've wandered into dog territory without realising. If they're watching me . . .

If they are, they only get dangerous if you go near the pups, I tell myself. *Just head for the shore. Which way?*

I stop, my palm on the nearest trunk, and listen.

Something scuttles over my hand. I snatch my arm back against my chest. Something snags under my feet.

I trip—

Almost find my feet—

Overbalance.

The sound of my fall is impossibly loud. A black shape bursts out of a tree nearby. My heart thunders against my ribs, hard enough to bruise. Wing beats, and then the shape lifts away into the sky.

Just an owl.

Quiet again.

Shaking, cursing myself, I get to my feet. I master my breathing.

Leaves crunch quietly behind me. A twig snaps.

I turn and look, but the darkness is so thick it makes it easy to imagine the floor is no longer leaves but an oil spill or a pool of quicksand that will swallow me whole. *It's something minding its own business*, I tell myself. *Come on, Etain. Where's the sea?*

I listen for the quiet *shhh* of the waves. *Left*, I think, turning in that direction. There's a skittering noise from somewhere nearby. I try not to pause.

Walk, I think. *Put your hand out for the next tree.*

It's no big deal. I've been reaching for every tree since it got dark and I didn't think about it until now. I force my hand out and take a step forward.

See? Wood. Now get moving.

I take another step. And another. The trees are cool. A slight breeze weaves through them. I start to relax. I can even hear water again – a little stream.

I reach out for the next tree and my hand meets something that en't bark at all. It takes me a fraction of a second to register that it's skin against my palm, hot and tacky with sweat and coarse with hair.

My lungs stop working. Every single muscle in my body freezes, tightens in on itself, stops. There's only one person it could be.

'Hello, Etain,' Astor says.

Taurus

I need to find Etain, but I'm too sad or angry or maybe even too desperate for the compass thing to work. If I was only panicked, at least I'd get an idea.

Einar gives the order for the people to return to the camp and posts magi around the edges to look out for Astor. I watch as he welcomes everyone back.

He glances at me. 'You'll be wanting to find your sister, Taurus. Don't want her wandering about with a murderer on the loose.' He's been playing not being smug well until now, but when he turns away I can see it lurking in the corners of his mouth.

A vivid fantasy fills me: grabbing him by the jewels and squeezing until he collapses. *Feeling smug now?* I'd say. *Still think you played that well?* I savour every second of his imagined apology.

Then Lear grabs my shoulder. 'Taurus.'

The thing is, anger at Einar is easy. Anger at Einar is just anger. But anger at Lear—

'I tried to tell you,' he says. I say nothing.

'I didn't want it like this,' he says. I say nothing.

'I'm sorry it worked out that way, OK? I didn't want—' I keep my mouth shut and stare at him.

'No?' he says. 'Nothing?'

I just glare at him.

He makes this big show of shrugging. He stops, turns back. 'You know what's funny? I feel guilty, but I haven't even done anything wrong.'

I say nothing.

'Can't you at least apologise? We argued once and suddenly you're sleeping with Rhean?'

I say nothing.

'You can't even see yourself, can you?' he says.

'What do you want from me, Lear?' I ask.

He shakes his head. 'How about some honesty, Taurus? You're acting like this is the first time you've done this. You pick up people, try them on and chuck them aside. Of course I was jealous of Joomia! She was the only one who got close to you who you didn't immediately replace with someone better. And you still can't see why I get jealous when you go off with Nine now?'

He takes a breath, rakes his hand across his face.

'You know what I think? You're just waiting for someone to actualise you. This compass thing isn't working for you the way you thought it would, is it? You can guide other people, but you don't even know where to begin directing yourself.' He makes to leave, comes back again. 'Etain lost her leadership because she wasn't leading. She knows that, even if you don't. Go and find her and bring her back here. She shouldn't be out by herself.'

I stare after him as he leaves and I'm shaking with I don't know what.

I think about going straight over to Sabine to ask for Lore's journal. That would show them all they need to see about who should be leading.

Only it wouldn't. Would it? *It's gonna take more than an old prophecy to get them to see what you need them to see.* I watch Chu and Thetea moving the last body into Phythia's tent. I should have helped.

I stride off towards the river, thinking Etain might have come this way. I swat off midges every other step. The heat doesn't help my mood, even as the sun moves into its downward slope and paints every dark branch gold. The river bank is empty when I come to it, so I decide to follow it towards the beach. Maybe Etain retraced her steps from where she left Ade.

Every hundred yards or so, I try to compass but it's still stuck like a shit that won't come. *This compass thing isn't working for you the way you thought it would, is it?* Lear's words are crowding everything else out. When I finally stop, the last few drops of light are being squeezed out of the twilight. I'm nearly at the beach.

'Taurus?'

I jump. 'Stop doing that,' I say.

Nine leaps, all graceful, from her side of the river bank to mine. She shouldn't be able to clear it, but at the last second, roots spring from the ground near my feet and throw themselves out for her to run down. They slither back into the earth once she's reached me and the smell of her is so reassuring I nearly put my nose in her shoulder.

I couldn't find Astor, she says. **Even the trees can't help. It's like he's found some way of masking himself from them.** She shrugs. **Could you try?**

I shake my head, unable to speak.

She peers at me. 'You all right?'

I open my mouth to tell her, *yeah, of course*, but what comes out, without warning, is a sob, and then I'm on my knees on the damp earth with my face in my hands.

Oh, Taurus. She gets right down on the ground with me, puts her arms around me. For a second it's like I've got Joomia back. That makes me cry even harder. **What happened?** she whispers. **Taurus. Tell me what's wrong.**

'Those people who died. Ade and Ma . . .' *And Lear's so mad at me. I'm lost. I'm so lost.* I take a breath and roughly swipe my arm across my eyes. 'Etain got deposed,' I say.

Nine sighs heavily. 'I thought you were going to say that. I hoped not, but . . . is she all right?'

'She's devastated. Wise One, what is she going to do?'

There's a pause. My eyes are closed. I shiver as she slowly traces her finger over my cheek. I let her do it. When I open my eyes, she's close. There's an energy humming between us.

'What is this?' I ask. 'What's going on here, between you and me?'

She snatches her hand back like I've burned her. Her eyes flick backwards and forwards, confused. 'Aula's still in here,' she says.

'Joomia too,' I say. 'And I don't think she's that into blokes. Definitely not blokes who are her best friend.'

111

There's a stiffness between us that's right between something happening and something not happening. She twitches a hand over her plait and brings the subject back. 'Anyway. Etain . . . I thought she *liked* leading. I thought she wanted to do it . . . for herself. But it didn't work.'

'You think the prophecy was wrong?' I ask.

'I dunno what to think any more,' she says. 'Two weeks ago I would've said your ma and Ade wouldn't have risked their lives on a prophecy that only had a fifty-fifty likelihood of coming true. But then Ade pulled that stunt with the spiders and the thorns. I didn't think she was lucid enough to use her powers now. She never had before. I would have said *Lore* wouldn't have trapped us in the cities, apart, unless she knew that it was the only way at the time, but the more I think about it, the more ridiculous it seems – *Taurus, get down*!'

There's this *ripping* noise as Nine yanks me to the ground and we both throw our arms up against a sudden flare of light. I have this wild thought that the sun has decided to come back up. My next thought is it's Astor, mad and blinding, setting things ablaze. Nine rushes to put herself in front of me. I tense myself, blinking against the light.

But it's not Astor. The branches of the trees above us – as far as I can see – are wreathed in golden light. They're like the tiny little magical orbs we used to hang around Metis to light the pathways in the dark.

'What the hell?' I whisper, squinting at them. There are hundreds in every canopy, casting their illuminations warmly through the leaves. Alone, each light isn't even that

112

bright. Combined, they're so bright it's like standing in daylight.

I walk to the nearest tree trunk and peer upwards. I think Nine realises what they really are at the same time I do.

'Taurus . . .'

'Yeah,' I say hoarsely. I don't want to make any sudden moves.

They're not lights. They're ants.

Etain

When the lights erupt around us I don't understand it, but I assume it's Astor's doing. I'm just grateful that I can see, even if it means something worse will follow. I only want to *see*.

We are both still frozen, my hand against his chest. I'm afraid to move.

He looks the same as he did when I last saw him, though he's lost most of his clothes, and his feet are bare. His body is scored with scratches and smeared with the stains of green lichen, earth and soot. His face is upturned, his eyes swimming with the lights above us. He's transfixed. His heart is accelerating under my palm. His skin, I realise, is heating up: a sudden, unnatural heat as if he's stood too long in front of a forge. But it doesn't stop there, it surges. Hotter. *Hotter*.

Very slowly, I take my hand back and try not to shake it. My palm en't blistered, but I think it would have been with a few more seconds' contact.

113

'Something is about to happen,' he says breathlessly. His head snaps left, then right. 'Coming.' He sniffs, glances at me as if he's forgotten I was there. 'Etain.'

'Astor.'

His blow knocks me backwards. I stagger against the nearest tree, clutching my jaw. He's howling, limbs flying everywhere, hitting trees and ferns around us in a wild, meaningless fury.

Then he stops, breathing hard but otherwise perfectly still. Blood dribbles out of his nose in a long, syrupy cord, over his lip, down his chin. I watch as a drop falls to the ground. It hisses as it hits the earth and steam slips up in its wake.

'Army of them. ARMY,' he calls. There's a flicker above us, and I get the feeling that those lights en't *just lights*. 'From the water!' he says, then yells, 'FROM THE WATER.'

I inch away, praying he keeps ranting, but a branch snaps under my foot and he whirls on me. 'YOU. THIS IS YOUR FAULT. YOU SHOULD HAVE BROUGHT US TOGETHER. YOU SHOULD HAVE BROUGHT US HOME!'

He takes a handful of my braids and there's a singeing smell as the extreme temperature of his hand dries them out like grass crisping in full sun. He brings my face close to his. I can feel the heat radiating from him.

'I'm not the leader any more, Astor,' I choke out, wincing as his fingers brush my scalp. His breath is sugary and hot as a bellows.

'You should have brought us together,' he repeats in a flat, hard voice.

And he shoves me, snapping my head back—

Taurus

Screams from the direction of camp. A giant gout of flame, shot into the air, tall as the vishaal trees. Yelling.

I move towards the sounds but Nine grabs my arm.

How can I not have seen them? she whispers, still looking upwards. **There are thousands of them. Thousands. And I—** She stops and bends to put her hand on the nearest tree root. **I can't even tell they're there when they're right above me.**

'We're gonna have to go,' I say.

More screams. I start towards them.

Wait, Nine says. **Just a moment.** Her eyes slowly turn from brown to palest green and flick backwards and forwards, like she's following something beyond sight. I keep glancing up at the illuminated ants, waiting for them all to start moving at once. If I listen closely, I can hear a kind of hum. Like they're speaking to each other.

Nine twitches. She stands up. Points far off, beyond where the cliff rears up out of the forest. **Etain. She's with Astor.**

I whirl in that direction. Then look back. 'And at camp?'

Strangers coming to shore . . . she frowns. **I think . . . I think it's a ship.**

We stare at each other. *If we're the last island on Erthe . . . how could it possibly be a ship?* We're both thinking it – we've made our own little fishing vessels, but a ship means something different. I swivel back and forth, torn in half.

Nine bites her lip, nodding to herself. 'I'll go to Etain. I'm faster. You go to camp. Listen: don't be seen if you can help it. I don't know what they're here for or how they got here or why but—'

'Fine,' I say. 'Fine, *go*.'

She takes a running leap back across the river, vines from the opposite bank snaring around her waist to haul her across. She lands heavily, rolls and jumps up again. Leaves and branches sway in her wake. I feel sick. *Astor*.

More screams from camp. *Put it out of your head, Taurus.*

I can't, but I have to. I start to run.

The Chosen

The ants have done well, spreading themselves so thoroughly. They work because they are so simple: so ignorable. They have no mission beyond climbing into the trees, tapping into the forest's own mysterious magic. They are invisible, even to Lore's Chosen One. And all they have to do is sit there and light the way for Vulcan.

From the prow of the boat, he sends a jet of flame into the sky to announce his presence to the islanders.

He has brought his best men. They are tall and armoured in bronze, their long hair swept up under helmets. They carry torches and longswords and shields that can block a galloping bull without a dent. The people of Lore's island stand no chance at all.

Vulcan signals for the gangplanks of each ship to be pushed out, and the men march down them, on to the sand. Vulcan watches some of Lore's people come out of the forest toward them, their expressions shocked and wondering. These are magi, he guesses, sent to investigate. Despite their awe, they are cautious: their fingers glow with an alien magic.

From the ship, Vulcan signals his dartsmen. They take aim, fire. The magi drop soundlessly with the hits, their spells dissolving on the tips of their fingers.

'Find the rest of Lore's people,' Vulcan orders. 'Surround them.'

Taurus

They come out of nowhere, in armour as golden as the lights. They're holding torches, throwing them at the tents the way you'd throw clothes on the floor. The canvas goes up in flames as quickly as dry tinder. People stream out of the tents, yelling in panic. When they try to run for the trees, the golden soldiers stop them, more and more of them pouring in.

They spread out quickly, moving like synchronised parts of a great whole, standing in implacable lines at the fringes of the camp. Blocked in, nowhere to go, my people huddle together.

But they don't cower.

Athenasians and Metisians alike face outward, fierce and scared but ready to fight.

I'm a coward. I'm just beyond the first perimeter of the trees, out of sight. What the hell am I gonna do? No one's been hurt, I guess, not that I've seen, but maybe that doesn't matter. The lit-up ants in the trees, the burning tents, the armour and the weapons, the way they've boxed everyone in. They're not exactly friendly. What do they want?

'What do you want?' Einar repeats my thought, loud and clear. I'll say this for him: he's front and centre with the magi, arms spread as if he's gonna protect everyone by himself. None of the golden soldiers answer. Slowly, they walk forward from all sides. Everyone in camp shuffles backwards, in on themselves. I can see them bristling, tensing.

Then Janaelle emerges from the burning council tent, brandishing one of the spelled sticks she used against Nadrik's army of mindless. I recognise it instantly. She gestures fiercely towards one of the soldiers and vines snap whip-like from the tip, curling around one soldier's ankle and throwing him on to his back. Behind her, Sander shoots an orb of fiercely spinning air he's conjured, blasting another soldier's hand.

And just like that, there's chaos.

Etain

I come to in agony.

The back of my head is one raw, unidentifiable ache. I think I'm lying on the ground. My sight is blurred and sliding, and I can hear someone moving around some distance away. Astor. I try to sit up, but my head hurts so badly I can't help letting a hiss curl out of my mouth.

The footsteps pause.

'Sleep now, little leader. Sleep.'

I clench my jaw and force every muscle in my body to move. I don't get much further than my elbows when bile rushes up my throat and I have to turn my head sideways to be sick.

His foot catches me across the jaw, and I collapse back, shaking.

'SHE LED HER PEOPLE TO DESPAIR,' Astor screams to no one, although to my ears it's like he's shouting from somewhere much further away. 'SO THEY BURNED HER AS A TRAITOR.'

And he presses his hand, burning hot as coals, into my stomach.

The Chosen

Vulcan buckles a leather strap to the ant queen's box and slips it on his shoulder delicately. He marches through the woods, glancing at the camp where his golden soldiers have contained Lore's people. He notes, with satisfaction, that Lore's people are fighting back. That's good.

He must be quick. He opens the lid of the box to check on the ant queen, murmuring a request.

Immediately, the ants in the trees halt their golden light. Vulcan blinks in the darkness and waits. Then a trail appears for him: just a few ants alight now, showing him the way through the trees.

He shuts the lid of the box and, holding it tight against his side, begins to run. The trail flashes past in a blur and when he stops, he knows he is close.

'FIRE. FIRE FIRE FIRE FIRE!' screams a voice, laughing to itself.

Vulcan peers through the trees to his right. Ah, yes. Astor. The large man that the biter ant he'd sent out had infected with fire. Unknowingly, he's been doing Vulcan's wishes – spreading fear, panic, *discord*.

He watches as Astor skips around, occasionally brushing the trees around him with a hand, sending up smoke and leaving blackened handprints. 'Where's Etain, Astor?' asks a voice. 'Where is she?'

Vulcan peers around the tree and sees her. Yes, Lore's Chosen One is just as the ants described – tall and strong-legged, with a long rope of hair the colour of red clay.

'Astor,' Nine says, 'please, what have you done with her?'

Astor claps his hands and swings his head. Blood sprays from his nose. His body is not holding the fire very well.

'Etain?' Nine yells. 'Where are you?!'

'NOT HAVE HER!' blares Astor. 'NOT HAVE.'

And he launches himself at Nine. She catches him and swings him away from herself, and as he hits the floor and rolls she stamps her foot. But Vulcan anticipates the weight behind Nine's foot – his nervous system has extended through the ants. He can sense the tiniest shock wave ripple through the root system beneath him. Through the ants, Vulcan can feel the trees around them – not move exactly, but *respond* to her magic. There's a crack like ice breaking, and carob-coloured bark travels up Astor's body like scales. He has only time to let out a single, mournful cry, like a child denied their favourite toy, before the bark obscures his mouth and face and branches grow swiftly from his head and shoulders, putting out leaves, putting down roots.

Vulcan has seen enough. He steps out from between the trees and runs full pelt at Nine. She doesn't even see him as he bowls her over, doesn't register his existence until she smashes back against the roots of an old cypress, and looks up, eyes wild, breathing hard. When her gaze finds him, it is plain that she expected to see Astor, but her eyes narrow in a kind of recognition.

'Guess you're the one with the ship,' she says, standing up and jerking her head so the joints in her neck crack.

'That was impressive,' Vulcan says, nodding at Astor's frozen form. He sets down the ant queen's box. And he runs at her again.

Taurus

There was a moment of panic when the lights went out again, but by that point the tents were pretty well up in flames and at least we know the terrain better than them. Merryn and Ior work Metisian earth magic with Athenasian battle magic to trip the golden men or hold them while others rush forward to snatch their weapons.

Further away, Sabine and the prophets sing protection over the heads of the people. Metisians – *Metisians* – are guarding prophets, fighting with whatever they have to hand: poles from the ruins of the barracks, pots and pans from the mess tent. Janaelle is unstoppable. She downs five soldiers at once with her spelled magi-stick, screaming and whirling as more come rushing at her.

But no matter how many times the golden soldiers are downed they get up again as if nothing's happened. Partly, it's their armour. It's gotta be reinforced or something because nothing – not the vines or our own improvised

121

weapons or even the swords stolen from their hands – seems to be doing any damage.

They're so fast, their bare arms and legs taut and curved with elastic muscle. How are we managing to challenge them at all?

And they're smiling. They're enjoying the fight. Like this is what they came for and we're giving them exactly what they want. They laugh with maniacal enthusiasm when one of us throws a particularly skilled shot at them. Like my people are putting on a show.

I can't just stand here watching my people battle against the ultimate enemy – whoever they are. I gotta find *some* way I can help. The only thing I can think of is joining them. It's stupid, reckless, but I'm about to do it . . . when something stops me.

A sound – some kind of explosion further back in the forest. The force of it slaps the ends of my dreads against my back.

I whirl around, hearing a yell that's gotta be Nine. I run towards the noise. Two hundred yards or so back from camp, the trees have been relit with the strange ant lights. I stop in front of a tree that has been split clean in two. The stump remains, fragments sticking jaggedly upwards. As my eyes move to the top I take a sharp breath. A bloke is picking himself up from the remains. He looks about my age, maybe a bit older, tall and elegant. He's wearing a simple chiton/chlamys combination (he's doing it in style, I'll give him that), with a long queue of black hair wrapped around his head (no doubt very fetching when it's done properly, but given he's just been thrown headlong into a tree it's looking a bit . . . saggy), and golden-brown skin. Nine's marching through the forest to my left, and all I can assume is that she just threw him into that tree hard enough for it to break. *That's my girl*, I think.

But he's dusting himself off – he *survived*.

A second later I see why.

As Nine comes – picking up speed as she goes – he braces himself, draws back a fist . . . and punches. She flies back, skidding along the ground. Then he's on her. They're wrestling, their blows splitting the air like thunder. It's like some kind of fictitious titan battle. *This guy's as strong as she is*. When Nine rolls away from a blow and his hit goes wide, wood chips and leaves fly up. He lets out a wild laugh, just as nuts for the fight as his soldiers, and tries again.

She kicks him off her, throws herself on top of him. Pins his arms with her knees. He struggles, his bucking limbs nearly throwing her off. She grabs his face with both hands and closes her eyes.

CRACK.

The ant lights go out.

I blink, trying to peer through the gloom. Above us, the moon is bright but nothing compared to the illumination we had before. My eyes – slowly – adjust.

'Nine?' I call.

She's picking herself off her opponent. As I come closer, I see he's not skin but wood – frozen, immobile, the grain of the bark making curlicues of his nose and cheek. Her magic ace-in-the-sleeve.

'Shit,' I say.

She rolls over, panting. There's blood on her cheek. I've

123

never seen Nine with so much as a cut finger.

'Who was he?' I ask, staring at him, not expecting her to answer. She shakes her head, and I help her up. 'Come on,' I say. 'We've gotta help the others – where's Etain? Is she OK?'

She shakes her head again – really out of breath – and points in the direction she came from. 'I dunno,' she says. 'I couldn't find her. But I—'

She stops. A horrible clicking noise is rising like some kind of sinister applause. As we whirl around, we see ants scuttling down the trees behind us, rippling over the grass like a tide. They reach the golden man and swarm over him, thousands and thousands of them, thick as a blanket, and as they bunch together they start to glow again. His arm twitches. Then his leg.

'Taurus, run! Run!' Nine yells. We've barely taken two steps before he's free, and behind us. She veers sharply right. I watch the ant lights illuminate a path for him as he follows her, and soon they're out of sight, although the sounds tell me that their battle's resumed. I follow, painfully slowly, running towards the noises and the lights, left then right then left again, but they're further and further away, until finally the lights come to a stop in the distance – right at the foot of High Tree.

I pick up my feet and sprint towards them. 'Nine! NIIIINNE!'

I'm too far away and I'll never be able to stop him anyway. But I don't care. I'll do whatever it takes. I run until the air in my lungs feels like fluid. My chest aches to take a breath it can't draw, my legs are ready to sink beneath me. I limp towards the tree.

Nine's collapsed against the vines, her breathing ragged as mine. The golden man holds her there by the shoulders.

'. . . that was a good try,' he's saying. 'I didn't expect that last part.'

'What,' she pants, 'do you want?'

He doesn't answer, and the ants are crawling towards him again, too many to count. They crowd over her as he grips her in place, struggling against him. They crawl across her feet and up her knees, flocking up her torso, climbing her hair. Nine doesn't make a sound, even when they reach her face and pile over her mouth, her nose, her eyes.

'NINE!' I scream, and I try to run for her, but my legs won't obey me.

The ants light up, but this time it's no gentle glow. It's the same sunlight burst that came out of Astor. It blinds me, and for a few terrifying minutes I can't hear anything either. All I can feel is something shaking the ground beneath me.

I hit the floor, cowering. Slowly a noise comes back, first a whine and then a ringing and finally a fierce sucking wind that shrieks around me, pulling at everything I'm made of.

It stops abruptly and completely. The silence it leaves is absolute.

When I open my eyes, blinking white spots out of my vision, the first thing I see is the vishaal tree. Beneath the webs, there's a gash in the bark, like a wound. A huge, vertical line right up the colossal trunk. It looks just as impossible as a cut in the sky. Sap dribbles down the trunk in gouts like blood from a wound.

I try to look for Nine, but my head won't work properly,

I'm sick from the light, dizzy and wrecked from the run here. I put my head in my hands and try – and fail – to breathe evenly. The light fades, my vision blurs.

I hear ants scuttling like they're inside my skull.

The Chosen

By the time Karragan has arrived at the camp, he is satisfied to see that Lore's people have been subdued and are now huddled in the centre of the clearing, surrounded on all sides by his men. In his full captain's armour, only the flame motif tattooed on his neck, beneath his Adam's apple, distinguishes Vulcan's deputy from his soldiers.

'Report,' Karragan says to the nearest soldier. The soldier murmurs an answer in his ear, too low for their prisoners to hear. Karragan's mouth thins in displeasure. He casts a critical eye over their captives. There is something wrong with his stomach. He *ought* to feel victorious, but looking into their faces is harder than he thought. He sees a mirror of his own family. It feels quite different from what Vulcan promised them all.

But perhaps . . . perhaps he is only too tired to appreciate it. After all, look at this place. Trees, shrubs, grass, fresh water. And *space*. So much space. Yes, Vulcan has delivered on that at least. Karragan is only tired, that is all. It was a long voyage.

He rouses himself and says, loud enough to be heard by all, 'Who is the leader here?'

One of his men hauls out a short-statured man, broad

and leathery-skinned, who glowers up at Karragan with small, squinted eyes and an amusing amount of defiance.

'Name?' Karragan asks.

'My name is Einar. What do you want with us?'

'I'm asking the questions, Einar. You are the leader of these people?'

Einar nods.

Karragan's hand is so swift that all Lore's people see is Einar's head snapping back as Karragan breaks his nose. Einar doubles over, and blood sprays down his face.

Karragan shakes his head. 'You are relieved of this duty. I will present your new leader shortly.' He pulls Einar up by the shoulder and turns to his soldiers. 'Wait here.'

The ant lights lead Karragan inland to his master, standing beneath the great trees they saw even when the island was no more than a blot in their telescope.

Vulcan nods in recognition.

'The Etheling, sire?' Karragan asks.

'I undid her. We will leave her here for now. No one will come near this spot until I say. Then we will harvest her bones.'

'Congratulations, sire,' Karragan says. 'She was obviously quite the opponent.' He looks around at the splintered trees, the deep scuffs in the earth. Then he frowns as a shape on the ground stirs. 'An escapee,' he says, bending down to touch the cheek of a young man. He wrinkles his nose. 'So decorated.' He touches the beads and coils of golden thread decorating the boy's long dreadlocks. 'All this kohl around their eyes.' He tuts. 'They're all like it. Men almost indistinguishable from the women. Long-haired and faces

127

painted. As little respect for ancestral convention as your sist—' Karragan stops himself, and swallows. 'Forgive me, sire. I forget myself.'

Vulcan purses his lips, half-amused, half-irritated. 'They are more backward than I'd guessed,' he agrees. 'I would have expected nothing less of Lore, but *Kreywar* surely would have left his influence here . . .' He shakes his head, shuddering. 'How can they let a woman stand as their champion? Their Chosen One?'

Karragan shakes his head, mirroring his master's disgust. 'There is something else, sire. We've secured the shore, but there were far more magi than we were expecting. Even the mundane among them have a lot of *skuld* blood.'

For a moment, Vulcan's eyes dilate in alarm. Then he shrugs. 'It is nothing I did not expect. If you are worried, perhaps it will help to know that I am not.'

'Thank you, sire. It does help.'

Vulcan nods once. 'Good.' He jerks his head at the boy on the ground. 'If he's alive, take him back to camp.'

'Of course, sire. You must rest before you address the people. I'll take care of everything.'

Vulcan nods again, his thoughts perhaps darting ahead to whatever speech he plans to make. He locates the ant queen's box, and shoulders the strap. 'Give me an hour,' he says, and darts off through the trees, light-footed as a deer.

Karragan looks back down at the young man and hauls him on to his shoulders in one deft movement. He looks back at the ruined vishaal tree. The unmoving bodies of thousands of ants cover the roots, their lives spent at the will of the ant queen, and through her, Vulcan. There are many more of them crawling away though, and still more lighting the scene from the trees.

Karragan nods, satisfied, and takes off back to the camp site at a run, the ants lighting the way.

An hour goes by. Two. Three.

The pile of dead ants stir.

It's just a shuffling, bleary movement at first. Then it becomes a deluge, an eruption, the husks of ants flying everywhere as two young women stagger up out of the mulch, more dry insect bodies whispering off them. In tandem, they take a shuddering gulp of air, then catch sight of each other. For a moment, they're frozen in total disbelief. In the next second, they're in each other's arms, clinging.

Aula.

'Joomia.'

What . . . what happened?

'What did he do to us?'

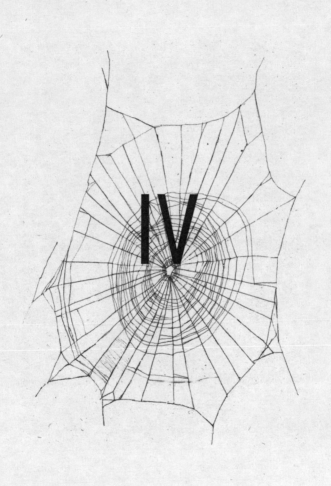

Etain

I wake, but my eyes won't open.

Is my arm trapped? I can't feel it.

Get up, Etain.

But I know without trying to move it en't gonna be that simple. This is a limb-by-limb job. A finger first – but even that takes a kind of desperate strength I'm not sure I have. Panic followed by adrenaline makes the finger move, and then my hand. My eyes don't exactly open, more like peel apart. The air stings. There's smoke billowing past my face. That explains the smell. There are white fragments in the air – like slow rain.

I'm on my side. I roll on to my back.

I black out.

I come to.

I try to sit up and pain from some unknown place makes me swoon.

I black out.

I come to.

The arm that was trapped under me – the arrow arm – twangs in agony. I lie there and breathe tightly through my teeth.

I black out.

I open my eyes slowly.

I can smell singed hair – now I think about it – and when

133

I persuade my other arm to move up high enough to reach, the braids on the right side of my head crumble like sugar between my fingers.

I wonder if I should sit up.

I try it. Black again.

Fire.

My tongue is like a piece of stale flat bread between my teeth. I take a deep breath. There are more twinges and shoots of pain. My legs are aching. My stomach is roiling, hissing with acid. My throat feels scraped and scarred. Is it snowing? How could that be?

Fire.

I try to move again, but everything is screaming in protest. Another deep breath, followed by a series of raucous coughs.

You can't just lie here.

One movement then. Quick.

I clamp my lower lip under my teeth and do it. Blackened splinters of wood tumble off me. Whimpering, I rest on my hands, my vision swinging dangerously close to nothing.

No.

I look around. *There is a tree trunk – just there. Get to it. I don't care how you do it.*

I manage all fours, but I have to stop, have to allow for the world to spin madly out in every direction.

When I come to, I'm face down this time, but I know I can only have passed out for a few seconds. *Get up. All fours again. All right. Good. Get to the trunk.*

I move. One hand. One knee forward. Stop.

Again. One hand. One knee. I look up.

Not there yet.

Snow . . . still falling.

One hand. One knee. One hand. One knee. Hand. Knee. Forward.

I reach the trunk, shaking, wanting to cry, but even as I drag in the first dry sob, I realise my body just en't up to it. I don't have enough water for tears. I don't have enough breath for crying.

Waste of time anyway. Now get on your feet. Use the trunk. Do it.

My fingers find ridges in the bark and I heave. It takes three attempts.

For a moment, I'm up: bent over, leaning heavily, but up. My vision is still swinging, but as I look around in front of me – not back, I must not look back – my brain rewards me with a word: the stuff falling from the sky.

Ash.

I try to take a step, but something is wrong. I can't stand up. I glance down at myself.

I wake up on the ground again.

OK. That was bad. Ow. OW. No, don't cry. Just . . . just don't stand up. And . . . and don't look down at yourself. And . . . don't look back. If you stay here you'll suffocate from the smoke.

My skin feels tight against my skull. It reminds me of—

Anvil. Hammer. Forge.

My mind thinks slowly. When I was in the forge, I drank, because that's what you do when you get hot.

OK, you need to drink. I sway at the thought. *Yeah, water. Get to a stream.*

How, if I can't stand up? I try to think. *A branch*, I decide. *A long, straight branch.* I manage to find one a short crawl away and, from there, I lever myself into a bent-over shuffle, like an old woman. I manage to move without passing out again, shifting with the branch, painfully slow. When I stumble into the stream it is probably blind luck or ingrained direction. I bend to put my face in the water and my tongue snakes out, lapping it like an animal. It tastes bitter, but I drink until my belly feels swollen. Then I kneel on the bank and pant . . .

Taurus

I wake up with sand under my head and Sabine over it. Well, I say *wake up*, but I'm so sluggish I feel like I've been coated in glue. A moan burbles out of my lips. The prophets are around me and Phythia is taking my pulse.

'Kid, you all right?' Sabine hisses.

I don't manage to answer.

I don't exactly pass out again, but there's a moment I become more aware of what's going on around me and it's because a voice has cut right into my head. It pushes my weariness to the edges of my mind and pokes my brain awake:

'People of Chloris. People of Metis and Athenas.'

There's whispering around me. Phythia's pulled my head into her lap. The ant-man – it has to be him, even

136

if I can't raise my head to see him.

'My name is Vulcan. I come from Govinda, an island pulled up from the water just as yours was. I understand that you were not aware of other islands until now, so perhaps this is a rude awakening. For that I apologise. Our people are descended from the people Kreywar Brenwar and Lore Sumati and saved after the comet, just as yours are.'

His voice is surprisingly gentle, as if we are animals he's wary of frightening. *Animals*, as opposed to *people*.

'A long time ago, Lore betrayed our people and blocked us from this land. While you have been coddled in your cities our island's resources have withered as yours flourished; our population has quadrupled while yours was controlled.

'I will not pretend that we are not desperate. I will not pretend that we come to *ask* for resources. You have them, we do not, and we *will* have them. I know of your traditions with the trees, but our need is greater. It will be less painful to simply give us what we need.

'Do not think you will be rescued or that there is a way out: I have destroyed your Chosen One.'

Was this the way the Erthe felt as the comet hit it? A hole blown deep in its side, throwing up water, changing the surface of it for ever.

'The person meant to hold you together is gone. If you do not wish to be harmed, do not cross us.'

'Nine,' I whisper. 'Nine.'

Etain

I wake up next to the stream, throw up, drink again, creak to my feet, still bent over.

The smoke's lessened, but it's still there.

I hobble on.

I come to a familiar-looking cave and remember that from here the sea is that way, and that way, and that way. I try out one direction, but I hear voices not far off, and I only think, *I can't be seen like this* because my clothes en't covering me any more and Ma would say it en't decent. I turn the other way. Yeah. No one goes to that other beach.

I know I should eat; but I can't find my appetite and I don't want to risk eating anything I en't sure won't poison me.

Keep going.

When I reach the beach, I crawl into the surf. The waves sweep up my hands and wrists, cold. I let out a gasp and manage two shaky sob-like heaves from my chest before it hurts too much. I don't know what to do after that. The air looks clean, but I can still smell smoke. I see movement in the trees a way off and stumble to hide behind some rocks cos I still en't decent . . . and . . . and another reason, but I can't remember.

I'm not sure I sleep exactly, but when I move again, it's night, and it's raining, and I'm freezing.

The thought bubbles into my head: *You can go back to the cave*.

The journey back is the hardest bit. I'm even more

disorientated, even more hungry, even more thirsty. In the dark I end up losing my stick. I have to give up searching for it and go on all fours. I feel and guess and creep. But I do get to it. The miracle is that there is – unmistakably – light coming from inside the cave. Flickering orange light.

Fire.

I back up, remembering but not remembering. Something inside me stamps like a nervous goat. But where else am I gonna go? I crawl inside. A narrow passage. Paintings daubed on the walls in ochre paint. Comet. Wave.

I remember a song—

The word: *prophet.*

And then I'm inside the cave, and I was right – there is a fire. And a person next to it. A tall figure with strong limbs and wide hips and eyes that widen in shock at me.

I use the wall and pull myself slowly on to my feet, though still bent, still gritting my teeth against the pain.

Etain? the figure asks in a voice that en't a voice.

I close my eyes, and remember.

'Yeah,' I say. 'I'm alive.'

The Chosen

Aula comes back late in the afternoon.

'They're preparing for something,' she says. 'The soldiers. But I can't tell what. I don't understand it. They've separated everyone into groups. I lost sight of where they took Taurus, but he was with Ade and Phythia, at least. Those ants are *everywhere*. I squashed every one of them I saw – *eurgh*, they were disgusting – but I keep worrying about what you said, Joomia. What if the ant man can use them to see, the way you can see through the trees?'

I might have an idea about that, Joomia says. **Only, first you need to see—** She gestures towards the corner of the cave and Aula sees Etain, curled up under blankets.

'You found her,' she whispers, her knees trembling.

Joomia manages to catch Aula before she topples over. **Please, no more than one invalid at a time,** she says. **She found *me*, actually. Just as I was about to go out and look for her again. She's woken enough for me to make her drink and eat, but nothing more than that. I think she thought I – we – were still Nine, if she recognised me at all.**

'Is she hurt?'

Astor got his hands on her, Joomia says. **Her stomach. I bandaged it.**

Aula swears. 'What on Erthe did you find to put on it?' she asks. 'The prophets don't have herbalist stuff in the cave, do they?'

No. That's what I was going to tell you. I know mint is good for pain, honey for infection and . . . and sometimes in Metis we used sap from the vishaal trees.

Aula eyes Joomia's hands, puckered with quite a few bee stings, and blinks in surprise. 'Sap?' she wonders aloud.

Vishaal trees are inflammable, so I thought the sap might be good for the burn. It won't do her any *harm* anyway. I blocked off the entrance to the cave as well as I could before going out. Mint and sap were easy enough – I made sure I wasn't seen – but the only bees' nest I knew about was in an old gum tree Ade found a while back. Do you remember?

Aula groans. 'Yes, I do bloody remember. All the stings we picked out of ourself.' She exchanges a look with Joomia at the strange pronoun. 'But that's wild-dog territory, Joomia.'

Yes, Joomia says, pushing back the sleeve of her left arm to show Aula several red, rapidly healing toothmarks.

Aula swears again.

As soon as they got my scent they were on me. It was so strange, Aula – they never usually attack unless we provoke them, do they? I turned most of them to wood while I got the honey, but since I have to be in sight of something to reverse the change, I had to get away fast afterwards, and one of them caught up to me and got hold of my arm.

'Ouch,' Aula says, touching the wound gently with her fingertips. 'So why *did* they attack you? Did you find out?'

Joomia nods. **When it bit me, I saw why.** And out of a pocket she produces the long, inert body of a red ant, exactly like the one she and Aula – as Nine – managed to smother under the bark of a tree. **It was buried in the dog's ruff**, she says. **All the way up to its head. Like a tick.**

'You think . . . you think *that's* how he knew so much about us? His ants were kind of . . . spying on us – through other animals?'

Other animals, Joomia says. **And maybe Astor too. Maybe *that's* where his weird fire powers came from.**

Aula rubs her forehead, looking dazed. 'Why him and not the dogs?'

Joomia shrugs. **Maybe it's different in humans? Maybe the ant in Astor's a different kind?**

'So where did you learn healer stuff?'

141

From healers in Metis, Joomia says. **Merryn was Head Healer before she became Head of the Magi and then Elder of Wise Tree, and actually Einar—**

'Ugh. Einar,' Aula says automatically and Joomia gives a reluctant grin.

Anyway. Etain bashed her head pretty bad and she was seriously dehydrated, but she'll be all right now, I think.

Aula sighs. 'Then we only have to worry about the fact that she got deposed and her people are enslaved.'

Etain

Flames searing against my stomach. Smoke curdling in my lungs.

SHE LED HER PEOPLE TO DESPAIR, SO THEY BURNED HER AS A TRAITOR.

I choke.

Etain!

I jerk against the hands holding me. 'I can't breathe!'

Shh. It's all right. You're safe.

I turn and see the fire burning beside me. I shriek, kicking away from the hands, stumble to my feet, try to run. I hit a wall and fall back.

Etain!

'Get me out. *Get me out of here.*'

I'm going to, just let me help you. The hands reach out of the dark and help me to my feet. **This way.**

There's a shoulder supporting me. My vision blurs. I allow the hands to help me walk, and we pass a narrow place. Then I feel cooler air on my face and reach toward it. I'm not fast and I half expect the hands to pull me back, but they don't. They let me feel my own way along the tunnel and stumble out into open air.

It's driving rain, and there's a forest and it's dark green and earth-brown. I hobble out into the downpour and collapse, trembling as the water floods down my face and hair and skin. I imagine that steam is coming off my skin.

Someone comes to sit next to me.

I peer up at them, through the rain. 'Joomia?'

She smiles. **Yeah. It's me.**

'How . . . *how* . . .'

She smiles grimly. *Nine* **had a run-in with . . . with someone very powerful.**

I stare at her. She's just the same. Even with her hair soaked, black with the rain. Her skin is darker than Nine's and significantly more so than Aula's; her freckles are almost invisible. She's wearing pale-green prophet robes and staring out toward the forest. I shake my head.

'What happened?' I croak. 'Where is everyone? Where's Taurus?'

At the northern beach, she says. **They can't escape. They're being held there.**

'What? By who?'

She chews her lip. **Men. From another island.**

Another island. Those words echo around my head for a long time, waiting for me to make sense of them. But I can't. The world is spinning. 'What . . . what do you mean? How . . . why . . . ?'

I don't know, Etain. I don't know. They came out of nowhere.

Their leader . . . he's strong, like Aula. And he has these . . . these *ants* **. . . It was him. He split us in two again. Etain . . . he hurt High Tree. It's wounded. It won't stop bleeding.**

Although this makes little sense, something about it rings a bell. Vaguely I remember a strange voice . . . and lights . . . I remember thinking that they weren't just lights.

'How?' I ask. 'How could he do that?'

She bites her lip. **Well . . . you know mine and Aula's magic is different—?**

I latch on to the name before she can get any further. 'Aula! Is she—'

She's alive, Joomia says soothingly. **She's keeping watch on the beaches. Looking for Taurus, mainly. And Ade.**

I try to keep my head above my own rising panic. 'Are they . . . are they alive? Are they hurt?

I don't know, she says after a horrible pause. **But I don't think so. Now they are in charge, the men the leader brought with him don't seem to be massively violent unless someone tries to escape.**

I try to take deep breaths, but my mind keeps painting images of my people trapped there. Ade. And Taurus. Oh Wise One. I imagine a hundred men with ants' heads instead of human ones, brandishing whips and screaming in a language we can't understand.

Stop it. They're people, I say to myself. *People* can *be reasoned with*.

I mentally shake myself. 'Sorry. You were explaining. About how that . . . that man . . .'

Joomia shakes her head. **It can wait, Etain. You're still healing. You could use some more sleep.**

Sleep. As soon as she says the word I feel it wanting to creep back over me, but I shake my head. She gives me a quizzical look.

'I don't want to dream,' I say.

Don't worry about Astor, she says. **He won't be coming for you out here. I took care of it. Or, Nine did.** She pauses and looks at me. *Really* looks at me. It's funny, I've been so used to people just seeing what I was putting on my face. Seeing a leader. Why would they need to look any closer? She says, **It's not Astor you're worried about, is it?**

I can't make myself answer her. When she takes my hand, my pulse jumps.

The rain gets worse, growing into a storm that rages beyond the mouth of the cave, so bad that Joomia asks me tentatively if I mind going back inside now. She doesn't bring me far in – just to the other end of the tunnel, so I can still see daylight through it. Sleep wants to cling to every crack of me, but I wake every few hours. Memories of the burned bodies, of Astor screaming, of my deposition – they chase me back toward the boundary between true sleep and dozing.

I don't know how much time passes. A night. Maybe two. Dreams come, fuelled by what Joomia told me: faceless invaders; a man with ants. They crawl over me, into my mouth, down my throat. I wake up yelling.

Joomia brings me outside when she can, forcing water down my throat, and then a few spoonfuls of lumpy stew. I can't manage more than that without being sick. One time, when I wake up screaming in a kind of battle rage, she pulls me up and makes me walk around the cave.

145

Another time I wake, I watch her moving about the cave. She does some stretches and tends the herbs around the entrance, occasionally looking out at the rain. She takes a clay jar of olive oil and rubs it in circles over her skin. I sleep quieter after that, dreaming of her long brown fingers pushing knots out of my shoulders.

I have a feeling it's morning the next time I wake, as Joomia pushes something into my hand. I feel her take a seat near my feet and I can hear that the rain's stopped and birds are chirruping from the trees outside. I peer out between my eyelashes. There's light pooling at the end of the cave's tunnel and a peach, warm from the sun, is cupped in my palm.

I stretch tentatively, but nothing twinges, and so I take a deep breath and sit up. Aula, not Joomia, turns to look at me with sad, weary eyes.

It doesn't feel like any time's passed. It could be a morning in Athenas, maybe after we'd dragged ourselves back from a party at Sander's on the Water plateau. She'd stay in my bed, and whoever woke up first would be the one to bring juice up from the kitchens. Plus flatbread, tomatoes, anything to neutralise a hangover.

I smile. 'It's you.'

She gives me a crooked smile. 'It's me.'

I reach for her hand. She squeezes my fingers gently. 'I'm here.'

'Where's Joomia?'

'Washing in the stream.' Her eyes search me. 'You feeling all right?'

I'm about to give her a gruff answer, but to my horror my eyes fill and my mouth wobbles as the memory hits me.

'Oh, I see,' I whisper. 'It's come to that, has it?'

Chu, Sander, Thetea and Janaelle at least have the guts to look me in the eye.

'What?' Taurus says, blinking around.

'They're voting me out,' I say. I feel winded. 'They don't want me to be leader.'

I haven't replied with words, but still Aula says, 'Yeah,' looking at me. *Knowing* me. 'It's been rough, hasn't it?'

I half laugh, even as the tears fall. 'Stupid,' I mutter. 'It doesn't even *matter*. Not with everyone captured. What the hell am I crying for?'

'Oh Wise One, Etain. Give yourself a *break*,' Aula says. 'Listen, I know what prophecy feels like when it's hanging round your neck like a medal you didn't ask for. And I grew up with you. I know I had it easier – I guess cos your ma didn't *know* what the prophecy about me looked like. She didn't know what to do with me. Yours was straightforward: you *lead*. So she made you into a leader with everything she had.'

I shrug. 'It doesn't matter,' I say, determinedly wiping my eyes, fumbling to remember where Joomia said Aula's been. 'Did you find . . . is everyone . . . ?'

'Some people got hurt in the fight when they got here,' she says, and I can hear the effort in her voice to keep it steady. 'But it doesn't look like they're here to murder. Then again, they en't exactly here to mingle either. I found Taurus. He's being kept separately from the others. I'm not sure why. Some bloke called Karragan made the order. I'm worried someone's told them about Taurus's compass thing. Or maybe they're trying to find you?'

'What for?' I say. 'I'm nothing any more.'

Aula rolls her eyes. 'OK, let's shake off some of the self-pity. That's not you.'

'Self-pity?' I say, stung.

'Look: the prophecy said you were going to lead. It didn't say when or how. The way I see it, you're alive. And as long as you're alive, it en't too late to be the leader you were prophesied to be, OK?'

I wait for her words to stop stinging so I can consider them properly. She's right. I've got to *do* something.

'OK,' I say at last. 'So we're going to get Taurus out.'

She raises an eyebrow. '*I'm* going to get Taurus out.'

'I feel better.'

'Like hell you do.'

I get to my feet, shakily. 'He's my brother.'

She considers me with her head cocked. Then she grins. 'That's more like it.'

Taurus

On the third day, they split us up. I'm wrenched from Ade's stubborn fingers and taken to another tent, alone, guards all around. I'm left to sit there and stew. I don't understand it. I pace, trying to figure out a plan, trying to catch some words which will help me figure out what these people *want*. But they hold even the smallest conversations out of earshot, and as it gets dark, I start to despair.

148

There's a pallet in the corner, taken from one of our camps. I lie on it, and trace the strange canvas wall – woven wider and thicker than the canvas we make. It smells musty and bitter. There are sounds from outside the tent – the usual sounds of the night but also voices with strange, unfamiliar accents, and I still can't make out what they say.

I drift off. When I come to, I'm not alone.

There's a man in the doorway, and two golden soldiers either side of him. He carries a candle in one hand and a tray filled with food. I recognise the grains, the clay jar of honey, the dried fruit. It's from our stores.

He comes forward. The golden soldiers station themselves at either side of the entrance. He sets down the tray and candle in front of me. Then he sits cross-legged on the floor, a few paces back. A multitude of necklaces and bracelets click as he settles himself. There is something dangerously sleek about him, even in the movement of his hand rearranging his jewellery.

He touches his chest. 'I am the captain of these soldiers and our leader Vulcan's deputy. My name is Karragan. You should eat,' he says, gesturing at the food.

I don't move. He leans back on his hands. The gesture pulls the tunic taut against his shoulders. He looks at me with his chin up like we're sparring.

'Eat!' he snaps, shoving the food tray at me, making me jump.

It's not bravery that stops me, but my mind still floundering.

He picks up a dried apricot from the floor and strikes

like a snake – in a split second his fingers are wedged against the back of my neck, his other hand pushing the fruit roughly against my mouth. I struggle against him, but he's strong. The apricot hasn't dried properly, and the syrupy juices run down my chin. I can't move him, so I reach with my fingertips for the tray and slam it down on his head. Food goes flying everywhere but he lets go.

I stare, breathing hard.

He's back in his cross-legged position. Poised. As if nothing has happened. He picks up the fallen apricot and puts it in his mouth whole, grinning at me as I watch, his mouth full of pulp. He takes the dented tray and flattens it back into shape, the muscles in his forearms flexing. Something in the back of my mind grunts its appreciation. Climber's muscles, like mine, and I spot his hands are scarred from old scrapes.

He's looking at me with renewed approval too.

'You people have some fight in you.'

'Who *are* you?' I ask.

'I am your destiny,' he says, and lets out a crowing laugh at his own joke. His soldiers join in, as if they were waiting for the cue.

I shrink. OK, yeah, I'm afraid.

'No!' Karragan barks. 'You were doing so well! Fighting spirit – that's what we like! Do not come over all cowed now, boy. Keep up the fire!'

I stare at him. I don't understand how he can be like this. I try to say something else, but my face breaks. I cry. Messily. Nine is dead. Nine is dead. *Nine is dead*.

Karragan watches me with distaste. Slowly, he retrieves

the meal he brought for me piece by piece and eats it, lazily. Waiting.

I wipe my eyes as something dawns on me. 'You're speaking Babel. You're speaking my language.'

'*Our* language,' Karragan says. 'Didn't you hear Vulcan? We have much in common, you and me. My people, your people.'

'What do you want from us?'

'Resources. Food. Really, you should have been listening.'

'After you attacked us? Stole from us? *Murdered* us?'

'He's not asking. At least *you're* alive, Son of Ashir.'

I can tell from his face he knows what that name will do to me, and he's right. It's like an electric current shooting through my foot.

'How do you know my mother's name?'

'I told you. You, me; my people, your people. Much in common. Or maybe I just asked around.'

'Get out!'

'You can't make me.'

And I lose it. I scream and launch myself at him.

He lets me. He sits there, taking the blows I'm raining on him as my yelling strips my throat. He doesn't move an inch. When I stagger away, panting, he fumbles at his neck and draws out a row of beads with glyphs that look similar to the ones the Athenasian magi use.

'Protection runes,' he says, just as I work it out. 'Good effort, though.'

I have to lie on my back. The world is spinning. I can feel the tears drying on my hot face, like a kid after a tantrum.

'What is your name?' he asks.

151

'Taurus,' I croak. I don't have the energy to withhold it. He likes that a lot. 'Ha! Not a cow – a bull! Very good!'

'Where are the rest of my people?'

'All safe, tucked away in the other tents on different beaches. Three meals a day and walks around, provided they do the labour that Vulcan asks and there are no miscreant actions.'

I will not pretend that we come to ask for resources. We demand them. You have them, we do not. Our need is greater, and there is nowhere else for us to go.

'You mean like slaves.'

Beyond the tent, I hear a loud, harsh cry that's halfway between a bird call and a dog's bark.

Karragan's expression falters. He glances back to the opening of the tent. The guards have not moved during our entire interaction. Well, they haven't had to, have they? He doesn't *need* them.

'Marchib, Vasilé,' he says. 'If that was the Etheling calling, I sincerely hope you are only still here out of politeness to me.'

They blink, bow to him, and leave. Something changes when the tent flap falls shut, but I can't put my finger on what.

My skin prickles. 'Now what?'

'Now the soldiers are going to find out that that call was a diversion,' he says. 'Your friend Lear gave you away.'

'What do you mean?'

'I mean, he told me you have a special skill. That you can . . . find things.'

'No,' I say. This is dangerous. *Damn you, Lear.*

Karragan narrows his eyes at me. 'Yes.'

'*No*. He doesn't know what he's talking about.'

He picks apricot pulp from between his teeth. 'I think he does. From the way he was going on he knows you *very* intimately. Oh, don't look like that. I think he only told me so you'd be kept safe.' He rolls his eyes. 'My brother might not have killed you, but if he had found you before me he may not have kept you *safe*.'

I don't know what to do with all that. What comes out is, 'Your brother?'

His hands go to his necklaces, fumbling for a moment and pulling one back over his head. Something strange happens to his face, as if it's being spelled. The *bones* in his face change, and a fold develops in each corner of his eyes, making them appear thin and angled – like Lear's. His lips are suddenly plumper than before, and his head is round and hairless but for a faint prickle of black stubble over his scalp and where his eyebrows ought to be. He looks like—

'Vulcan. He's my brother,' he says. Yeah. I see it now. It wasn't that the necklace had caused a spell to trigger, but the removal of it has removed the spell. What I'm looking at is his *real* face.

He had disguised himself – not from *my* people, of course, but his own.

He puts the necklace back on. His face changes back – and it looks bulkier, rougher by comparison.

'You're not supposed to be here,' I realise.

He smiles. Or at least, he stretches out his lips. 'As far as my brother knows, I am still at home on our island. He would certainly be . . . unhappy to see me here.'

153

'Overprotective?' I ask.

'Something like that.'

'Surely your people would have noticed two Karragans running around.'

He rolls his eyes. 'I have more than one disguise.'

'So where's the real one – the real Karragan?' I ask.

'Probably asserting his second-in-command status over the other soldiers. Or, equally likely, mooning over my brother,' he mutters. 'Who knows? Who cares? But I want your help, young Bull. And unlike my brother, I'm not going to ask for something if I can't give you something.' He stands up. 'Get on your feet. I am going to help you escape.'

He yanks me up by the arm. My legs are shaking.

'What's wrong?' he asks. 'You want to stay here?'

'What do you want me to find?' I ask. What is it that he wants so desperately that he has to disguise himself to fool his brother?

'A journal,' he says.

My chest hitches. 'What journal?' I try.

He rolls his eyes again. I've never seen someone make that gesture so elaborate. 'You know which journal I mean,' he says.

Yeah, I do. There's only one journal he could possibly be interested in. I'm kind of disappointed. I already know exactly where that is. No tricks required.

'Lore lived on my island before she came to yours. You know where her journal is, Bull?'

'No,' I say.

'Yeah,' he says. 'You do. Or you can find it.'

He picks up his candle and goes to peer through the flap

of the tent, smiling smugly. 'We should go – the guards will be back when they realise the alarm's false. When I say run, we run. You're going to take me to that journal.' He grips my arm and pulls me into him. 'Don't try anything sneaky on me. You will not like the outcome if you do.'

'I wasn't—' I begin, but he knows the truth, and he smiles again. I think about testing that claim, but if he's got powers anything like his brother . . . I hear the hissing of those ants again. I think we both know I'm going with him.

'I want your name,' I say.

'I bet you do,' he says, and he looks me up and down and blows me a mocking kiss. I squirm and he grins. 'My name's Sol,' he says. 'Now let's go.'

I follow him blindly out of the tent, plunging through undergrowth, brushing aside ivy, dodging around tree trunks.

'We're running until they can't hear us and then you're gonna tell me the rest of it,' I pant.

'Rest of it?'

'The truth,' I say. 'What you're really here for.'

I can tell he's rolling his eyes at me again. Then there's a shout not far off and a flare of brighter light. Sol swears. 'They're back. Move, Bull! Faster!'

I sprint as hard as I can, and he keeps pace with me easily, always close enough to grab me if he wanted. When we're much further down, just north of the vishaal trees, I slow down to a fast walk.

'Go on then,' I say, panting. 'Tell me.'

He waits for his breathing to even out before he begins. 'Ever heard of manifest destiny?'

'No.'

'You know how there used to be a lot more white people. In the Old World?'

Old World. That's what we call the world before the comet too. Who *is* this guy?

I say, 'Yeah, I heard that. I've seen pictures of them.'

'They used to have this crazy idea called manifest destiny – that it's inevitable that they would conquer a piece of land eventually.' He shakes his head. 'My people think that's a great idea.'

I frown. The ants' clicking noise keeps rattling around my head.

'And you don't?'

He says, 'I think there might be another . . . there might be another way. But I need that journal. Which way do we—?'

But he goes silent as we draw level with the vishaal trees. He looks up and up and up, his eyes going round. I like that my home does that for him. It does that for me too sometimes, and I've lived here all my life.

He clears his throat and whispers, 'Which way now?'

There it is again. Clicking. I guess I'm exhausted or mad. Something. I'm opening my mouth to answer him when something – someone – slams into us, knocking us both down.

I hit the ground hard, and cough as I try to drag air back into my lungs. When I look up, I see a girl holding Sol against a nearby tree by his throat.

'Nine,' I gasp. The relief shudders through me so powerfully it makes it hard to get up. But then she turns her head, just slightly. It isn't Nine.

'What do you reckon?' Aula says casually. 'Feed him to

Etain, let Joomia go all magic vines on him, or shall I save them the trouble and rearrange his face now?'

Aula Aula Aula Aula, my mind says dumbly, dancing in little giddy circles.

I open my mouth to answer—

But there's the clicking noise again. It's not in my head. It's here.

'What is that?'

I get my answer before Aula can reply. A writhing, moving shape nears the vishaal trees, like a spill of sugar syrup. A leakage of brown fizzing liquid spreading itself along the forest floor—

Coming toward us—

Ants.

Thousands and thousands of ants.

Sol claws at Aula's hand as his eyes go round in desperation.

'He was helping me escape, Aula,' I say.

'No. That's what *we* were doing,' she says, but after a moment, she lets him go.

'We?' I ask, but Sol cuts in before Aula can respond.

'They're coming,' he mutters, massaging his throat. 'My brother is near.'

The ants close in on the vishaal trees and sure enough there's Vulcan striding out with them, only a matter of yards away.

'Joomia's here too,' Aula whispers to me.

'And Etain?' I ask.

But she doesn't answer because there's a crack so loud I can feel it in my molars.

The Chosen

The ants chew as they go, loosening the fibres of the trees in their path.

Slowly, slowly.

And then, all at once, fifty trees fall, neat as a stack of cards being fanned on a table. Vulcan's ants are so precise the trunks always avoid smashing into the trees around them.

Etain chokes down a cry at the collapsing trees and staggers to her feet. Joomia sinks to her knees. Aula lets out a long, animal howl.

Taurus

I clamp my hand over Aula's mouth, but the damage is done, and Vulcan swings round.

'Who's there?'

Sol glares angrily at Aula, but her face is blank, still horrified at the trees. I'm just glad she's not in rage mode.

The Chosen

Aula, Joomia says, **make the bird noise we talked about.**

Taurus

Aula moves my hand and holds me away from her. She trills softly. *What is she doing?* An answering trill echoes from across the clearing.

Vulcan turns in that direction instead.

Aula trills again. The answering chirrup is closer this time. I relax a little. She knows what she's doing.

It takes a few more goes, but Vulcan seems to relax. I guess he thinks he's disturbed a bird. Something like that. Sol looks like he sat on one. He's rigid, eyes darting everywhere. I wait for him to look at me. Then I mouth, hard and angry: 'What. Is. He. Doing. To. Our. Trees??!'

'Harvesting,' he whispers. 'He's harvesting.'

'What do you mean?'

'We need resources, Bull. I told you.'

My mouth feels dry, like I'm going to be sick. The stumps of each tree are lumpy and exposed, like skinned kneecaps.

Taurus. I can see you.

I turn my head.

Joomia.

My vision blurs with tears. She's coming toward us, slipping silently between the trees, pulling Etain by the hand. I don't make a sound. It's unbearable. My best friend, my sister—

I peer around the tree, but Vulcan's still looking in the other direction.

Etain grips my fingers. She looks weary and unsteady on her feet – but alive.

'Who's this?' she mouths, eyeing up Sol and his robes:

very obviously not Athenasian or Metisian.

Sol's jaw goes hard. He doesn't say it, but it's all over him, for sure: *Take me to the journal, Bull. Take me to the journal or I'll yell for him.*

Sometimes my instincts are OK. Sometimes they lead me down into the centre of the shit pile. But sometimes, like when I accidentally spilled wine on Aula, they put you in a place you want to be.

I don't *think* Sol's going to rat on us, but he's desperate enough for the journal to pretend like he's going to. I whisper, 'This is Sol. He's coming with us.'

Etain

With Vulcan still distracted, we pile back into the Cave of the Ancestors.

Taurus looks the way I feel. He kisses my forehead in a weary *I'm glad we're alive* way and I decide not to tell him about the burn yet. I've definitely healed, from the glance I gave myself as I put on the clothes Joomia found for me, though I don't want to see it in full light yet. I catch Joomia's eye. We hold each other's gaze. One. Two. Three.

She starts a fire and Taurus prepares roots for a pot. It's absurd how quick and everyday that feels, but no one's denying we're hungry. I'd nearly forgotten about the newcomer (Sol, I think that's what Taurus called him) until he stands up. He's tall enough that it makes us all focus on him.

'Is it here, Bull? Will you at least let me look?'

Aula's right eyebrow is ready to arch off her face. '*Bull?*' she says.

The familiarity of her tone knocks a laugh out of my chest. The novelty of her being here hasn't worn off. She gives me half a wink in return and I feel, for a moment, like perhaps things aren't going to be as bad as we thought.

Taurus gives us the fish eye. 'He's calling me Bull because I'm manly and imposing,' he says, deadpan.

'Who is he?' Aula asks.

In answer, Sol removes a necklace from the multitude around his neck. I can hear the faint crackle of magic as it comes away, taking one face with it, and leaving behind another that's very similar to the man we saw near the vishaal trees.

'He's Vulcan's brother,' Taurus says, I think because Sol's pose suggests his appearance answers everything. 'From what I can gather he's disguised himself to get to the island and try to find Lore's journal before his brother does. I dunno if that's true, but he did help me escape, and he didn't seem to want to be seen by his own people, so there's that.'

I eye Sol up, trying to see what he thinks of Taurus's description, but his face is blank.

'How do *you* know about Lore's journal?' Aula asks.

'My island has prophets too, *Chosen One*,' Sol says.

'Then why have ours never Seen you?' Aula asks. It's a good point. And what's he talking about with *another island*?

'Because your prophets have never *heard* of my island, so how would they even begin to cast their Sight toward us?' Sol replies.

161

Aula looks unconvinced, and ready to voice just how implausible she finds that idea, but Taurus cuts across her.

'Am I right then, about your brother?' he asks. 'Is he looking for a compass and a journal, same as you?'

Sol considers. 'My brother is here to take your island, to use it for its resources and its potential workforce. He'd certainly like Lore's journal thrown in, but it was my luck that your . . . er . . . *friend* Lear told me about your finding-things gift before him. Though my brother is far from stupid, and he's brought prophets with him, so it won't be long before he sets up a line of interrogation to find the journal. If you want to save your island from him you're going to need to let me see it quickly.'

'What for?' Aula asks.

Sol sighs dramatically. 'I don't have time to explain *everything*. Be a good little Chosen One and get it for me?'

Aula shows him a fork-fingered Athenasian gesture that he won't misread as polite.

He smiles appreciatively.

Taurus looks like he's hoping I'll intervene. I dredge up the tatters of Leader Etain and steel myself.

'You want us to give you a highly prized magical artefact after your brother and – for all we know, *you* – invaded our island, cut down our trees, captured our people, split our Chosen One in two . . . did I miss anything?'

Sol bridles. 'What was so awful about them being split in two? You *seem* happy they're here.'

I falter. 'I . . . I *am* happy,' I say. I turn to Aula. 'I *am*. It's just . . .'

It's more complicated than that, Joomia says. She pauses,

162

and we all look at Sol, waiting for a comeback. I think it dawns on us all at the same time that he can't hear her. Apparently those rules still apply.

Damn, she says. **Aula, will you—**

'We joined our cities by joining ourselves,' Aula says reluctantly. 'If we're not joined, then the question is: *can our people ever unite*? See the problem?'

'Not really.'

'Well, your brother turned one of our people into a walking flame-thrower, so I guess unity might be beyond you.'

'This is ridiculous. How do I prove myself then?' he says, shaking his head in exasperation.

Start by telling us why you want the journal, Joomia says. Aula translates.

Sol sighs, but I get the feeling he knew it would come down to this. 'Fine. Fine. You know about Lore and Kreywar?' he says.

I'm almost not surprised to hear those names. 'What do they have to do with it?'

'Everything,' he says. 'I told Bull here: we – my people – are descended from their people, just like you.' He chews his lip, I suppose thinking of where to begin. Then he says, 'I don't have a lot of time, so I'll try to tell you this quickly.' He pauses for a second. 'I suppose it starts with magic. Do you know how we came to have magic, Bull?'

The other three glance around at each other. In the stories we were told as children, the Wise One gave our people magic in the same breath as condemning them to be trapped in Athenas and Metis. I guess this was supposed to

163

be an 'opportunity' to show how wise they were but it seems pretty ghoulish to me.

I say, 'There was a meteorite shower, before the Comet and the Wave That Covered the World.'

Sol nods.

Taurus says, 'What? Where did you hear that?'

'Yeah, where did you hear that?' Aula demands.

'Ma told me about Lore and Kreywar the same year you went to Ariadnis for the first time.' I glance at Taurus and wince as I see him sorting this into another thing that me and Ma had tucked between us, but I don't know how to make that better.

Sol continues. 'There was no magic on Erthe until then, but when the meteorites came, the communities they landed in began to develop . . . certain abilities. They could harness the energy of their own bodies – in the living things around them, even in the latent energy of the air. Several brands of magic began to develop.

'The most mysterious of them was *skuld* magic, what we now know as prophet magic. It could be said to be the purest kind of magic, and also the most unwieldy – seriously damaging the mental faculties of those who have not had the training to use it properly. *Skuld* magic is connected to the invisible fabric of what will be, what won't, what is, and what could be, and is best cast with the voice – that is, against a melody. It cannot be woven into spells, but it can be used in a more general sense – for healing, or beckoning, or lifting spirits.'

It's strange – I never thought of prophecy as being a magic in its own right—

'The second type – *serpil* magic – took its cues from botanical life: the power of growth. It is a slow-moving, time-allowing magic. It can make bridges out of fig roots, speed the healing of wounds, bring down buildings with a fungus . . .'

'Metisian magic,' Taurus says.

'That is what I have gathered you call it, yes,' Sol says. 'Then there's the more precise kind, *oluwaseyi* magic – enforced through runes and glyphs and letters; sketched on to surfaces to hold the magic in place. I think your . . . Athenasians use this sort.

'But there was also a rarer kind of magic: one that bound people and places together. Depending on the place the person was born, *etheling* magic could bond them to mountains, or to rivers or seas or trees or plains. In one or two cases, it might bind people to other people, or even animals. It worked differently from the other kinds, because it was innate to the user's body – impossible to teach, and impossible to remove. Many years later this came to be known as—'

'Chosen One magic,' Aula says.

Sol nods in acknowledgment. 'For you, yes. In Govinda – the island I'm from – it is known as *etheling* magic.'

'So, your brother has – er – *etheling* magic too?' I ask, putting the pieces together.

'Ten points, Anassa,' he says. I frown when I hear the title, but he either doesn't notice or doesn't care. 'You can help me with the next part: Lore and Kreywar.'

I could tell this part in my sleep. 'They predicted the coming of water and the erasure of the land. Like other new magi, they managed to save a great number of people by building a fleet of sub-aquatic ships that would stick to the ocean floor when the comet hit and float above the water when the storms of the initial impact had died and the oxygen levels had equalised. Lore and Kreywar were supposed to be among the first magi, or among the first prophets, depending on who you ask.'

'They were all four,' Sol says. He's enjoying this, I can tell. 'They saw the future, they could cast *serpil* and *oluwaseyi* magic, and they were also blessed with *etheling* powers. Perhaps they were particularly close to the meteorites that fell before the comet. In any case: we know that Lore was born in rain forest, and so her *etheling* powers were of trees and plant life. Kreywar, however, had an altogether different kind of power – he could call up magma from Erthe's core. It must have taken him a long time to come to terms with this power, or there wouldn't have been any need for a voyage at all. But voyage they did, looking for the island they had prophesied, so they'd be able to settle on land once more. Only when they were at the edge of desperation did it occur to them that the islands they sought might be ones they would make themselves.'

Sol leans forward, eager.

'So Kreywar reached into Erthe's core, poured in his power, and called up a volcano now known as Izanami, like the Old World goddess. The volcano's creation was so powerful that it tore apart the tectonic plates of Erthe's crust and from below the surface came great spouts of magma. An island formed before Lore's and Kreywar's eyes. This was Govinda.'

He rummages through his necklaces then and pulls one pendant out to show us.

'What does that one do?' Taurus asks.

Sol frowns. 'No, no, this is just a necklace. My mother gave it to me,' he adds proudly. 'Kreywar's mark.'

We peer at it. A round, onyx disc, etched with a volcano's peak rearing above spiralling waves.

He sighs, and puts it back. 'For a while, it appeared they were saved. From seeds they'd carried aboard one ship, Lore grew new life upon the land. From the genetic ark collected by great scientists aboard another, they recreated enough animals to make a new ecosystem. But patterns re-emerged. Human conflict re-established itself.'

The next pause is heavier, and Sol's voice goes quieter. 'Kreywar was killed in one of these conflicts. Lore and Kreywar had foreseen such an event, and had woven, with their considerable power, a spell that would allow humanity to begin again. For many years, Lore, under the pretence of scouting the ocean, had been planting new life on another island, Chloris – this island we're standing on – born from the crack that Izanami had made, larger than the first island, and perfectly formed.

'She lured half of Govinda's people to the island under the illusion of gathering more resources, pretending that the island she and Kreywar had created had only just been discovered. As soon as the people set foot there, the trap she and Kreywar had spun with their various magics snapped shut.

'And so, the people forgot their origins,' Sol says. 'And remembered only what Lore chose for them to remember, living out the myth that she and Kreywar had made for them – Wise Gods and wisdom.' The words are dismissive, but I can hear some curiosity in them too, and more than a little longing. 'And there they have been ever since. No Govindan ship could reach them. They could sail directly at the island, but no one could come within a hundred feet of the shore.'

'Part of Lore's magic,' Taurus says thoughtfully.

'Yeah, OK, nice story,' Aula says. 'How is this supposed to help us?'

'I am not quite finished, Chosen One,' Sol says, clearing his throat. 'When Lore's task was done and her people were safely trapped on Chloris, building the cities they would later not remember building, she travelled to Izanami to lay Kreywar's bones to rest. It is said that they are still there, in the deepest passages beneath the volcano and that, one day, should her people have need, they should venture there to retrieve them.'

Taurus

My feet are cold. I move them closer to the fire under the pot and the stone around it warms them.

Sol stretches. 'See where I am going with this?'

'Not really,' I say. 'Why would anyone want to retrieve his bones?'

Chosen One magic, that's why, Joomia says. **Or *etheling* magic, if that's what he wants to call it.**

Aula squints at her. 'What do you mean?'

168

Well, it's like he said, isn't it? *Etheling* **magic is innate to the body it inhabits.**

'So if you died and I dug up your bones I could talk to trees and make vines grow?' I ask, wrinkling my nose.

I guess you'd need prophet blood – what did he call it? *Skuld* **blood. You'd probably need to have the Ritual of Acquisition as well, but yeah, in theory, my bones would still hold the magic, like yours would, Aula. If that story is right and Kreywar really could open tectonic plates and control magma, if someone had Kreywar's bones, they could make more land . . .**

More land. Wow. Well that's something to think about. Now I get it.

'His island *is* massively overpopulated,' I say.

'That en't our problem,' Aula says.

It is if his people are going to invade us and take our resources, Joomia says darkly.

Sol's head has been questing back and forth between us and Joomia. 'She's just explaining what you mean,' I say.

He eyes her. 'She mute?'

She's right here, Joomia mutters.

'It's a weird magic,' I say. 'Only people who were there when she was born can hear her voice.'

'Why doesn't she get an *oluwaseyi* tattoo put in near her voice box?' he asks.

I frown, and Joomia echoes me. Etain and Aula look at each other in surprise.

'We'd . . . never thought of that,' I say finally.

He snorts. 'Yeah, I probably wouldn't either if I'd been brought up to believe some bullshit about a Wise God and made to fear one type of magic or another.'

'No, instead you were brought up to believe that your island should dominate all others,' Aula sneers. 'What's wrong with Izanami if you're so desperate for land? Can't your brother sail your people over there?'

'To an active volcano?' Sol asks, skewing his mouth incredulously, obviously doubting her sanity.

'If it's like the volcanic islands I've read about in Old World books, it probably has land *around it*,' Aula says defensively.

'Well, maybe it does,' Sol says, 'and maybe my brother *could* sail our excess population over there. But it's never been found. Not by anyone.'

'What, no one's thought to take one of those boats you came here in and have a good, old fashioned scout—?'

'Of course they have. *Hundreds* since I was born. Every one of the trips has failed.'

'So what makes you think *you're* going to succeed?' Aula snaps.

He shakes his head at her. 'That is between me and my own god, little Etheling.'

Aula rolls her eyes, but I get a hunch and follow it. 'A prophet told you that you would,' I say. 'I'm assuming you have prophets on Govinda?'

Sol's face sobers. 'It was the first and last prophecy she made.'

'Who?' Aula asks, but I reckon, from the inflection in his voice, that I know.

'Your mother?' I ask.

He flinches. It's not much, but I still see it. He presses his lips together, and I can tell he's annoyed to have given himself away.

170

'Prophecies aren't always accurate,' I say. I don't look at Etain.

'No, but the map my mother Saw in Lore's journal ought to be,' he says. 'Come on, where is it?'

Joomia puts the lid on the pot and goes over to a shelf, pulling down a bark-bound book. Sol didn't need my compass skills to find it after all. It's been in the care of the prophets ever since Joomia and I found it. **Let him look,** she says. **It's written in Hindi. He'll need me to translate it unless his people study Old World languages as thoroughly as they studied Old World domination habits.** She holds it out to Sol. **Tell him if he's not careful with it I'll make bamboo shoots grow through his toenails.**

Aula relays that one pretty gleefully. But he's as careful with the pages as if each were sharp as a blade. He turns slowly, all the way to the back. And then: all the way to the front again.

His expression, eager until now, falters.

'Not what you were looking for?' Aula asks.

He turns the pages a little faster. I feel Joomia tense up next to me.

'What *are* you looking for?' Etain asks.

He's gone all the way to the back again. Something seems to catch his eye.

'This last page is thicker,' he says, almost to himself. 'Yes, look, there's a fold where it's not stuck together properly. How about a knife?'

What is he going to do? Joomia asks nervously.

'A knife?' he asks again, looking up. 'Oh, don't be ridiculous. I'll be *careful*.'

171

As if it's her own beating heart, Joomia picks up the knife we used to cut vegetables and cleans it on a corner of her tunic before she hands it over.

Carefully, Sol thumbs the thicker page and runs the knife along its edges. He puts the knife between his teeth and slowly peels the page apart.

His eyes light up. He hands the knife back.

'Here,' he breathes. I feel my pulse thump in sudden, unexpected excitement. We crane in to look over his shoulder.

It's a map, drawn carefully in browned ink.

I recognise our island immediately, vaguely rhombus-shaped, with the cliffs and Athenas plotted on to it. There's a small squared-off section next to it, showing the trees of Metis located underneath the cliff, otherwise invisible from a bird's-eye view. A small, simple illustration of an owl flaring its wings is above it, and scored beneath its tail feathers, a name: Χλωρις.

Joomia taps it. **That's Greek**, she says. *Chloris*.

'Chloris,' Taurus echoes. 'That's what your people call our island – this island, right?' he asks Sol.

'Of course,' Sol says. 'How did you *not* know? Haven't you read the journal?'

'We thought we were the only island left on Erthe,' Aula says defensively. 'And technically we've only been living *on* the island for just over a year.'

I watch Joomia trace her finger across the page. To another island. It's more circular than ours, with some flecked lines that I think are meant to be trees, and hunched black shapes which must be rocks. Above it is another animal symbol. An ant.

Govinda, Joomia says.

Sol turns the page. The map continues with the ocean drawn in small curved waves. Far off, on the other side of the paper, there's another shape, another island. And at its centre, immediately recognisable, a volcano. More labels — and another animal symbol . . .

'A spider,' I say hoarsely.

Izanami, Joomia says.

Etain suddenly takes Sol's shoulder.

'What?' he asks.

'Take us with you,' she says.

Etain

Sol shakes his head. 'I don't need tag-alongs.'

I stand up, ignoring the other's mystified looks. 'What will *you* do with Kreywar's bones?'

'Make more land,' Sol says.

I shake my head. 'So you don't have a plan.'

'Plans are not a luxury I can afford, little Anassa,' he says. 'Govinda has been overpopulated, overcrowded, underfed and underdeveloped for longer than I've been alive. Our people have been taking to the seas, looking for more land for the last *twenty years*. Some come back in despair. Others don't come back at all. We have known about your island for ever, but Lore's spells that kept you from us were too strong for our magi. We could have sailed towards you for years and never have touched you. We presumed the spell would break eventually, but we did not

173

expect it to happen in our lifetime. You must see that you – your island – represents hope for us.'

Taurus snorts. 'Yeah, I totally understand. Turning us into slaves is the only way forward here.'

'I already told you,' Sol says. 'Manifest destiny. Your ancestors got given a reset. *My* ancestors still have that unfortunate thing that Old World white people had. When they see land or people that are different, they go, *Hey! That looks like something we can dominate and turn against itself!* You know about that, right?'

'You're defending what your brother is going to do to us?'

'No!' Sol snaps, losing his temper. 'I'm trying to find an alternative!'

I say, 'All the more reason to take us with you.'

Everyone turns to me. I can tell what they're thinking. I know I must look exhausted and shrunken – not surprising after the last few days. But Sol doesn't look at me like I'm mad. He looks like he knows *exactly* what I'm thinking.

'What's the *real* reason you want to come?' he asks.

'The same reason as you,' I say. 'Your people need land. I need your brother off mine.'

Sol shakes his head. 'I said no.'

'You can navigate one of those boats yourself?' I ask.

He hesitates. 'I'll be fine. I'm gonna steal one of the trimarans they brought for storage.'

'But even that would be better if you had more people?'

'What do you even know about sailing? I saw your little fishing boats,' he laughs.

'You could teach us.'

174

'Not enough time. And too much energy.'

'Fine. So let's say we find you paper, and you copy the map, and you're out at sea and it falls overboard, or rain gets it or you run out of food and end up eating it cos you're so hungry? What then?' I'm not giving up on this. I hope he can see it.

'I said, I'm going alone.'

I glance very briefly in Taurus's direction. 'Seems to me that what you need is a compass.'

Taurus sits up, surprised, and Sol's eyes narrow. Aula looks at me nervously. She can sense the resolution that's stolen over me, but it's not the type she's used to – that I'm used to – carefully honed, iron-forged. It's something new – a little raw, a little desperate, a little reckless. But it has to be worth it.

If I can get those bones, I can trade them for our people. I can save us – free us from Vulcan.

Sol looks at Taurus. I bite my lip, anticipating his reply.

'I'll take you, then,' Sol says to Taurus at last. '*You* could come.'

Taurus

I think about that. Yeah, I think about it.

Has there been anything, ever, that's rested on my decision? And this would be purpose. *Real* purpose.

I look at Etain, and it's obvious why she wants this so bad – if she trades those bones for her people's freedom, she can look like a hero to everyone who deposed her. And Aula will go with her because they're tighter than rope twine, and Joomia will . . .

Actually, I don't know what Joomia will do. She's looking at me. Her smile is sad, but it's always been a little sad. **Don't even think about it,** she says to me. **I'll follow if I have to.**

I smile back. 'Sorry, Sol. But if I go, they go with me.'

Sol makes a snarling noise in the back of his throat.

Aula grins maliciously. 'Is that a yes?'

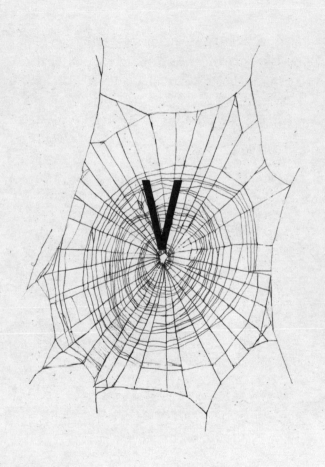

The Chosen

Vulcan surveys the line of resigned islanders as they walk toward the western side of the island, the area he has decided to harvest first.

'You look tired, sire,' Karragan says. 'Why don't I find you somewhere out of the sun?'

Vulcan has a pounding headache. It's not unusual – it's from all the information the ants send back to him, so much that he often cannot process it very well. Occasionally, he fits from it, but Karragan usually plies him with knotgrass tea before that eventuality.

'I want to commence the interrogations this evening,' Vulcan murmurs under his breath, ignoring Karragan's question and the sun baking his back. Ignoring his tunic clinging uncomfortably to his hips and the unclean slickness of sweat under his arms and between his legs. 'Have you found anyone who might know where the journal is?'

'No, sire,' Karragan says. He has not told Vulcan about the missing boy. He has certainly punished the soldiers responsible, though. 'But I'm sure we'll find the ones you need. Even if they are not among the captives, they will not go far.'

Vulcan runs a hand over his head, tucking the stray hairs that have escaped from his long braid behind his ears.

'Do you like it here, sire?' Karragan asks.

In truth, Vulcan cannot believe that such a place exists.

He has sailed to look at it before, when his father was alive, though of course they couldn't get close. But they are here now. Whatever protective magic was keeping them away has gone. It is so beautiful – so cool and green and alive – that it fills him with a shivery emotion he doesn't know how to name.

Vulcan remembers Karragan and offers a shrug in reply to the question. He has a strange feeling. The fight with the Chosen One of Chloris has weakened him, but it is not just that. When he thinks of her – the Chosen One – he sees the fierce look on her face, the wild, sinewy elegance of her fighting, the fear in her eyes as his ants swarmed her. He cannot stop seeing that last thing particularly. Is this feeling . . . guilt?

You had to do it, he reminds himself, thinking of what his father said: *So long as she stands, the island will be protected from you. You must undo her*.

But wasn't she his own kind? Wasn't she Chosen, like him? Soon he must retrieve her body from his ants and clean it back to the bones so her power can be his. He fingers the long scar on his forearm from the operation that replaced his own radius bone with his grandfather's and his ulna with his great-grandmother's. His left hand now does not grip properly, the result of the difficult surgery, but the magic of the hive mind and strength of ten men are his. He just wishes the headaches would ease up. Five years. Surely that's long enough to adjust? He is a little nervous of what will happen when he has one of the girl's bones – will the headaches become full-blown migraines? Will he be able to cope with that much power?

He heads back towards his camp, rubbing his temples.

'Shall I ask them to prepare a meal for you, sire?' Karragan asks.

Vulcan nods, and Karragan scuttles on ahead.

On the north-western shore, Vulcan checks in on the medici's tent first. 'Better?' he asks, looking in at Astor. His ants recovered the man a few days ago. There's no need for the medici to answer, though: Astor's eyes are bloodshot, his chest is heaving, and his body has lost a frightening amount of weight, as if it were consuming itself.

Vulcan wrinkles his nose in annoyance. Well, at least it did the trick of scattering them, scaring them, whilst allowing him to see the goings-on around the island before he arrived himself. Yes, he can see through the ants on their own, but it is better when the parasites make a bond with something – or someone – whose vision works in a similar way to his own.

'How long does he have?' Vulcan asks the medici.

'Not long, sire,' she says. 'His temperature won't stay down.'

Vulcan swears, but he's used to how quickly the victims deteriorate if their body rejects the venom. He hopes Astor is not an indication of how his ant-impregnated soldiers will fare. 'There must not be enough *skuld* blood in him to keep him going. That happens sometimes. Hold him for me,' he says.

The medici sighs, pulls on some heavy-hide gloves and grasps Astor's arms. Vulcan presses his fingertip to the back of the man's neck, where the abdomen of one of his parasite-type ants still protrudes. Astor screams, bloody flecks of saliva frothing out of his mouth. The medici winces at being splattered and Vulcan grits his teeth as he feels the man's skin heating up. He holds on, trying to clear his mind, to keep the clamour of the ants in his head down to a singular command.

Not as much. Slow the toxin.

Astor slumps, his hand catching the medici's tunic. She jumps back as it starts to smoulder.

Vulcan sways, clutching his head. The headache pounds, like knuckles against hard wood, and fades slightly. The medici rushes to hand him a water skin, and Vulcan wrings it dry.

'Well,' he says, ignoring the tight pain still gnawing at the back of his skull. 'That ought to—'

'Sire!' Karragan explodes into the tent, face grey, eyes round. 'Quickly! Quick!'

Vulcan's senses jangle, panic making him stumble as he follows Karragan out of the tent, toward a soldier watching their fleet – or rather, what is *left* of their fleet of ships.

Five of their eight vessels are sinking fast beneath the water.

Vulcan hears his breath being drawn in from a very long way away.

When Karragan hands him a long-seeing glass, he takes it mechanically, sets it to his eye, follows the line of Karragan's pointing finger.

It's aimed on the smallest boat – a tri-hulled voyager canoe that was mostly carrying supplies.

'Sol,' he whispers, hand to his mouth. 'How . . . how did . . .'

He sees Sol help a tall girl with coiled braids out of the water, and then a boy sporting long dreadlocks who Vulcan thinks he might recognise. The boy turns back to the water the second he's aboard and offers his hand to someone else . . .

The Chosen One. She is alive. The Chosen One did not die.

Vulcan feels his knees buckle as his head is hit with a volley of agonising throbs.

'Sire!' Karragan gasps. 'What's wrong?'

'Someone bring a boat!' Vulcan roars. 'BOAT! I NEED A BOAT!'

Etain

I'd never seen a trimaran before, not even in pictures in Old World books. It looks a bit like three canoes – one larger vessel in the middle, with two smaller ones either side, joined together by two curving beams at the front and back. An interlaced, basket-weave structure runs between each hull, providing a platform. The mast is front and centre and seems to be held there by nothing more than a few taut ropes. To me, it looks frighteningly basic and definitely unsuited to sailing five people out on open water, but Sol seems to relax as he climbs aboard. He strokes the planks and mainsail like it's an old friend, and I see an echo of what I would do when I walked into my forge.

Wise One, I miss that. I feel heavy and slow and broken, my shoulder still twingeing, my stomach keen to remind me it might have healed a little but not a lot. I'm breathing hard from the swim. Two weeks ago that wouldn't have been anything to me.

I have to sit and recover while the others store some of the extra food and clothes we brought with us in the middle hull.

'They'll spot us soon,' Sol says. 'Is everyone ready?'

'Let's go!' Aula cries from the water. We turn to see her cutting through the waves towards us. The last in the line of eight ships is shuddering in the water behind her. That's my girl. I can already see the first ship keeling. She hauls herself on to the boat, and I see her knuckles are bleeding badly from where she's punched through the ships' hulls. I tear strips from an old prophet robe and help her wrap them and she puts a palm on my side, where my half-healed burn is showing beneath the loose-fitting choli I'm wearing.

'You OK?' Aula asks.

I nod. She gives my hand a squeeze.

'Ow,' I say. 'Watch it.'

'Drama queen,' she mutters.

'Pot.'

'Kettle.'

'They're coming,' Taurus says, pointing in the direction of the shore. I shield my eyes and see a twin-hulled vessel similar to this one raising its sail. We always knew they'd chase us. We knew we'd have to be quick. Sol starts yelling what rope goes where and shouting at us to get moving. He snaps his fingers under my nose:

'Anassa. The lanyards on the mainsail. Undo them.'

I look in the direction he's pointing and hurry to undo

the small ropes securing the sail to the mast – there are only five of them, but they are so well tied my short nails only scrape against them and my fingertips go numb struggling to pull them apart.

'Weakling,' Aula says, light-hearted, and I step aside and let her try. Meanwhile Sol fumbles to undo a knot the size of two of my fists. I can't see what it's for or connected to but a second later Aula whoops and the sail unfurls. Sol hauls one rope and then another, moving so smooth and quick it looks like some kind of dance. He finishes with a jerk on a line, and the sail fills with the wind, the boat flings itself forward and we're skidding along the backs of the waves.

'Get that rope tied off!' he snaps, and we all have to look and scramble to know *which* rope he's talking about. He takes control of the rudder and screams at us to secure all the loose lines; tie off that thing, haul on that other thing. But the terminology doesn't stick and soon he gives up, leaving me manning the steering oar. He whips back and forth across the three hulls to do himself the jobs we'd been given.

I'm so busy watching him, trying to focus and not give in to the panic of getting out of here quickly, that I don't know it's happened until Joomia's curse resounds in my head.

I turn and spot Sol's brother immediately: his hair is streaming behind him like a pennant, his white robes filled with the wind, exactly the way I'd imagine a hero in an Old World story.

I clock four soldiers in the boat with him, and a smaller, blue-robed kid with a shaved head – I recognise him as the boy Sol disguised himself as. The kid is supporting the arm of a tall, thin, horribly familiar man standing at the bow.

Astor en't shrieking like before. His face is set, his mouth turned down, cheeks hollow like a death mask, looking right at me.

A high-pitched scream fires across the inside of my skull. What are they doing with him?

I see Vulcan twitch his hand on a line and the boat's bow turns toward us, catching up in seconds. Their sail, now it's got its wind, is larger than ours, plus they have the additional speed of two rowers in the back.

I don't look at Astor, but I can feel his attention on me. Joomia touches my shoulder, facing him. **I won't let him hurt you**, she says.

I can't even answer her. I'm rigid, frozen, my pulse skipping like a mouse.

Vulcan calls from the aft: 'Stop, Sol! Stop!'

Sol ignores him, leaning into a rope to give the sail more surface area for the wind.

Vulcan leaves the tiller in the hands of one of his soldiers, braces himself over the side and jumps. He's like a cat – one minute he's bunched, rolling, the next he's airborne, stretched out, reaching.

He lands feet from me, balancing neatly on the outrigger, as poised as any Metisian.

Aula was already running while he was in the air, and now she barrels into him, knocking them both backwards into the water.

I get about half a second to hope she's all right. Then Astor makes his own jump. He lets out a grunt and lands in our boat flat-footed but steady. When he moves his feet, I see smoke curling from under them and scorch marks on the wood beneath him. He stumbles towards me, eyes bulging, teeth bared, rimed with blood. He doesn't even know who he is any more, I can see it. He's just anger and heat. I force myself to inch back, feeling for the hatch in the canoe where we put our bags.

Taurus runs forward with a rope, darting out of reach of Astor's hands to loop it around his legs. But he's too slow. Astor's fist connects with Taurus's shoulder and he flinches back, the skin hissing fiercely as it burns.

'Not the rowing oars, we need them!' Sol roars as Joomia picks one up and levels it at Astor. Sol's still trying to wrangle the sail, holding hard to the lines, but I can tell he's too panicked to work it properly. His eyes pop as Joomia brings the paddle down in a swooping arc and the hard sheen of the wood mutates into branches exploding outwards. They attempt to wrap themselves around Astor's wrists, but the second they hit, the oar bursts into flames. Sol panics and the boat jerks as he moves the sail from the flames, forcing Joomia to totter backwards and fall into the water.

Astor blunders forward and wraps both his hands inside the sailcloth. Sol cries out, but his hands are seized by one of the two soldiers who've landed next to us. The other attempts to wrestle the smouldering oar from Taurus. I stand up, wielding my hammer that I've finally managed to pull from our bags, trying to ignore the shoulder pain as I throw my arm back. Astor's burning hands rip the blazing sailcloth clean from the rigging, the tearing noise dulling everything for a moment. Sol lunges for the sail, crying out, and the boat shudders to a halt as it's turned sideways by a rogue wave.

I sway, trying to keep my feet, but I fail. My head strikes wood as I go under, water surging over me like a closing fist.

The Chosen

There is a particular satisfaction to be had from smashing the Chosen One's head with a rock from the seabed, thinks Vulcan, rather like squashing a spider you thought you'd killed but hadn't. He waits for her eyes to roll back, for her to go limp. Then he drags her to the surface and throws her on the trimaran his soldiers had been unloading when he'd called for a boat. He surveys the scene: Sol and the dread-locked boy have been overtaken by his soldiers; the two other girls are nowhere to be seen. If they're overboard, they won't last long – it's unlikely either will have learned to swim very well growing up in one of Lore's bizarre cities.

Vulcan hauls himself back on to the trimaran and calls for Karragan – now steering – to pull alongside the stolen vessel. On it, Astor is still wreaking havoc, apparently unable to stop himself. Vulcan curses. He shouldn't have brought him, but he wasn't thinking straight. He beckons his soldiers to rejoin him. First they force their captives across before jumping over themselves. Vulcan spares Sol one icy glance before calling to Astor to stop, but the man seems to have come to the end of it at last by himself. He simply stands there, clutching the flaming sail. His hands blister, the wood around his feet blackening and shifting, until it simply collapses beneath him and he disappears. The water below boils fiercely as it takes his body; a pillar of steam rises in his wake.

Joomia watches Astor sink; it gives her an idea. She keeps herself as hidden as possible as she surfaces, drags in a few long breaths and swims down again.

Astor's eyes are almost blank. Bubbles pop intermittently from his mouth. She touches his face tentatively. His skin is still hot, even under the cool of the water, but it won't burn her. She swims around to inspect his neck and finds the lump she's looking for. It's dead centre, right at the base, slightly raised over his spinal column and radiating heat. Where is the knife Taurus gave her before they swam over? She feels desperately along her body and finds the sheath tucked into the inner waistband of her sirwal.

She draws out the blade, but no, it's no good – she'll have to surface.

She hurries up and down again, gripping Astor by the arm as soon as she's back and sinking the blade into the lump.

A cloud of blood oozes upwards. The lump *squirms*.

She cuts deeper and pulls at the wound. There. She can see the ant: swollen and bloated like a huge mosquito, dug into the flesh, its antennae wriggling, its legs scrabbling to dig itself further in.

She slips the flat of the blade under its body and levers up. It comes free with a thick jet of blood, the ant spinning madly as it attempts to swim through the water, the blood frothing as it meets the cold of the ocean. She makes a swipe for it, misses, swipes again, pins it against her knee. Its pincers made an audible *click* as it tries to sink them into her skin.

Try that all you like, she tells it. **I am reborn from the vishaal trees and vishaal trees don't burn.** Then she seizes its head and wrenches it hard from its abdomen. It hisses violently like a sword hot from the forge submerged in water, and then everything is still. She drops the ant parts, quickly trying to pull Astor to the surface with her, but he's too heavy. There are still bubbles rising slowly from his mouth. She swims up to breathe, and comes down once more.

Astor?

She puts her hands on either side of his flopping head and closes her eyes. She can feel him there, trembling at the edges of his own mind, weakened, unable to take back possession of his body. Yet he senses her, and a thought strays back along the thread of her magic.

It's over. You can use me . . . make the change.

No, she says, **it's all right, Astor. Come towards me.**

But he doesn't. A moment later, she feels him shudder and still.

Up she goes, though her heart feels heavy. One more breath. She listens for Vulcan, whose voice carries to her on the breeze. She sees Etain, clinging to the trimaran's outrigger, just out of Vulcan's sight. She's holding her hammer, fingers flexing, bracing herself.

Etain, Joomia says. **Don't look, but I'm behind you. Aula . . . can you hear me?** She feels a pulse from the emptiness – the space where Aula ought to be. **I've got a plan. Wait for my signal, then get them off the boat however you can.**

She doesn't have time to wait for an answer. She has to get back to Astor. She dives for his body once more. She's developed a knack for it now: transforming. She must hold in her head the idea that neither skin nor bark, blood or sap, are very different and both will reduce to soil in the end. She has to keep that in her mind, and then allow her magic to travel through the transforming body, and ask for the change.

It's different this time, of course, because they are surrounded by sea water, but the magic will adapt. On land, the transformation takes its cues from any nearby tree — pine, poplar or quercus; here, the magic reaches for something else . . . something more aqueous . . .

Vulcan watches the sinking outrigger, emotionless for a few more moments. Then he turns to the soldier holding his sibling and gestures.

The soldier releases Sol. Vulcan looks for a long time. 'You found a way to disguise yourself,' he says.

Sol shrugs. Vulcan reaches out and runs his hand over the many pendants. Sol stiffens.

'So one of these is flattening your chest,' he says. 'And another, perhaps, gives you a penis?'

The soldiers laugh.

'Talk to me, *sister*,' Vulcan says. 'Have you disguised your voice too?'

Sol's brown skin flushes darker.

Vulcan hits him in the stomach. At that moment, a wave rolls beneath them. Everyone adjusts their stance accordingly, but Sol stumbles, doubled over.

'That was a warning,' Vulcan says, business-like.

'A warning for *what*?' Taurus snarls, still in the grip of a soldier.

191

Sol spits.

Vulcan says, 'How did you do it? How did you escape?'

Sol only smiles.

Vulcan's eyes go to the pendants again. 'Who made them?'

'Mother,' Sol says.

'Liar.'

'No.'

Vulcan hits him again – and though it might not hurt Sol, the force of it throws him sprawling on the deck. '*Liar!*' Vulcan roars.

Sol picks himself up without a sound and merely looks at his brother.

Vulcan paces to the end of the trimaran and back, snapping his fingers as a thought occurs to him. 'Of course. *Her*. She sent you a bunch of spells, somehow? How were you communicating?'

Sol says nothing.

There is a kind of studied patience in the way Vulcan purses his lips. 'Were you going to live with her, Sol? Do you imagine she survived? Did you think she'd escaped? But where would she have gone?'

Sol's smile widens. Taurus looks between them, trying to guess what – or who – they might be talking about. Then he looks at Aula, who has an eye half open. Very, very slowly, she holds up a finger.

One.

'Well, where were you going with them if you weren't trying to find Domaga?'

It was only a year ago when it had happened.

Vulcan had had two siblings then. He'd found Sol and

192

Domaga crouching over his father's dead body, blood already drying in the creases of Sol's hands, under Domaga's fingernails.

Vulcan would have been next, probably. He was the heir.

He banished Domaga.

But Sol had been holding the knife. Sol had been the one to do it, he was sure.

Sol still says nothing.

Vulcan snatches at one of his necklaces. 'I'll break every one if I have to.'

'Do it,' Sol snarls, but he's afraid. He's very, very afraid.

Vulcan sorts through them. 'A rune for protection.' He smiles as he lifts one and snaps the leather cord as easily as a grass stem. The spell breaks in a whiplash of static. Then Vulcan hits Sol again. And again. And again.

Taurus glances at Aula. Is it time to act yet?

She hesitates, and then, *Two*.

'You ruined my ships,' Vulcan is saying. The blows go on. 'Tell me where you were going!'

'Stop it!' Taurus says, trying unsuccessfully to throw off his captor. 'Leave him alone!'

Vulcan turns his next swinging fist into Taurus's stomach.

Sol spits blood from his mouth. 'I was wondering when Father would appear. Liked to hit people . . . just cos he could . . . didn't he?'

Vulcan takes a deep breath and reaches for the pendants again, sorting through them roughly until he finds the one he's looking for and holds it up.

Sol's face breaks. 'No!' He smooths his face immediately, but the damage is done, and Taurus is shocked to see Sol's chin quivering.

'I will let you wear this when we return, Sol,' Vulcan whispers. 'We can go back to the land now, and I will drag the ships ashore myself and you will help me repair the damage you have done. Then we will take the harvest that Lore denied generations of our people, and when we sail back to Govinda with our people you will be by my side. But tell me how you escaped. Tell me where you were going.'

There is a war on Sol's face. The first tear falls silently; his throat works, but he is shaking his head. He says, 'No.'

Vulcan tugs the necklace.

The leather cord snaps—

Three.

Vulcan feels something snag his ankle. He looks down and sees a winding tangle of kelp looping itself around his leg. Slowly – too slowly – he realises what that means. He opens his mouth to shout orders but before he can make a sound the kelp yanks him off his feet—

Joomia swims hard for the boat, reaching it as Aula throws one of Vulcan's soldiers over her head and into the water. She sees Etain ducking the blows of the short, bald man – the real Karragan.

Taurus finally overpowers the soldier holding him and fights his way over to Joomia. He hauls her aboard in the same moment that Etain out-manoeuvres Karragan, kicking his legs out from under him. The Govindan topples backwards, and Joomia gestures . . .

And a thick kelp plant snatches Karragan's ankle and dangles him in the air – as it has done to all Govindans who were previously aboard the ship.

'Sol,' Etain says. 'Instructions?'

194

Every part of Vulcan screams in frustration. He cannot – will not – let Sol get away like this. 'MURDERER!' he roars as he hangs upside-down. 'MURDERER! COWARD!'

Sol's fingers go slack on the mainsheet. His face folds in pain. In guilt.

'SOL!' Etain bellows again. 'TELL US WHAT TO DO.'

She watches as Sol pulls himself together. He takes a deep breath, smooths his expression and readjusts his grip.

'Someone get the anchor,' he says clearly.

They move frantically, each to whatever task Sol asks of them. Joomia stays balanced on the aft, knotting the men tightly together with the kelp in one hand, battling Vulcan with the other. For each frond of kelp he manages to break, she conjures three more, knotting the tendrils so swiftly that his arms become crossed and tangled.

At first, Joomia finds herself fighting to keep him above the water but as Vulcan continues his verbal assault she gives up and simply holds him underneath, hoping he will exhaust himself and let her bring him up to breathe.

Aula, she snaps. If he gets loose before we're out of sight, he'll catch us. Get us moving.

Nodding, Aula plunges into the water, takes hold of the trimaran's aft and paddles frantically with her legs. It takes a few perilous seconds for her momentum to equalise, but then the craft picks up speed. Vulcan and his men wrestle against their kelp-frond anchors, roaring helplessly as the trimaran gets smaller with each passing wave.

Taurus

The second Aula gets us a good distance away, Etain collapses on to her knees and clutches her side.

'You've overdone it, sis.' I check her for any signs of bleeding. Her eyes try to focus on me. I grip her hand. 'Just stay here till you're steady,' I say, but she sits up, and turns to Sol.

'What did he mean, Sol?' she asks. 'What did he mean, *murderer?*'

Sol's crouched over by the mast, shaking. He says nothing.

'Sol?' I keep my voice gentle. 'What did he mean?'

'I killed our father.' Sol tries to snarl it, but his voice shakes. 'I killed our father. That's what he meant.'

Etain and Joomia look at me. Man, oh man.

Sol half turns his head. 'It's not what you think.'

'Maybe it's exactly what we think,' Etain says.

He glares at her. His nose is swollen, his eyes already pouchy with blood. 'My father, he . . . he was pretty close to evil, if you believe in that. He . . . was the leader of our people, before Vulcan. I haven't lied about anything, I promise. I haven't lied. I'll get us to Izanami. I'll find Kreywar's bones.'

This is not the cocky guy who got us aboard. This is a terrified kid. Somehow that's scarier than what he's saying.

Etain says, 'How can we trust you now?'

'I haven't lied about anything,' he says.

'It's done now,' I say, when Etain opens her mouth to say something else.

'Yeah, and he might've doomed us all,' she says, but she doesn't tell Aula to turn us round either.

Aula keeps up the pace for at least another hour. No one speaks. When she comes aboard, Sol gestures in the direction of the lines he wants us to mind and takes the steering oar. The sail is bigger on this one than the boat we meant to get, which Astor burned his way through. It means that we're still making a good clip against the waves. Joomia stays straight and still in the heel of the boat, face screwed up against the sun. I guess she's waiting for a sign of sails on the horizon, ready to fight again.

Eventually Sol stands up and says to her, 'He'll follow us, but not for a while. He'll need to repair the ships if he wants to survive at sea. You can sit down for a bit.' There's something different about his voice. It's higher, creaky. I already guessed that Vulcan was taunting him for being an *iphis* – a male born in a female body – but now it's more obvious. His face is rounder. His neck and shoulders are slimmer. The lump of cartilage in his throat is gone, his hips have widened. There are two definite bulges on his chest. I guess that's another thing those necklaces were disguising.

Sol glares at me as if it's all my fault. 'What?' he snaps.

'I was just gonna ask if you're all right—'

'Stop looking at me!' he says, mantling like a hawk.

'Hey, brother. It's OK—'

He hits me so hard I'm knocked backwards. Aula's there in a second and catches my head before it hits the lip of the canoe. I can tell she's ready to spit something vicious, but even before it occurs to me to tell her to leave it, I watch her

197

unclench her fist. She draws her breath in slowly and sets me back on my feet.

It's more embarrassment than anything which makes me say, 'What's his *problem*?'

'I'm guessing his people don't have the same attitudes to gender stuff as ours do,' Aula says. 'You heard all that nasty shit his brother was spewing – calling him *sister*?' She shakes her head in disgust.

I raise my eyebrow and spit blood. Etain's giving Aula an impressed look, and Aula shrugs. 'I didn't go through Ariadnis and come out with nothing, you know.'

She goes back to where she was sitting and I go back to nursing my pride. She's right. I should have sensed I was on dangerous ground sooner. Even with *my* people, you've gotta do your own investigating with people who are *iphis* (male in a female body), *orland* (female in a male body), *atlantiad* (someone with an ambiguously gendered body) or *shui* (someone who doesn't identify with a gender at all). Some people are happy to talk about it, other people not so much. Metisians were always encouraged to be happy in whatever body the nature lottery gave them and express themselves however they liked, with the pronouns they wanted.

I don't think Athenas was that different, though they did have an operation where their magi would tattoo a changing rune on to a person's pelvic bones that would make their nads change to match their gender. I know a few people in Metis snuck up to Athenas to have it done. Not that different from prophets going up to have prophecy taken out of them.

'T,' Etain says, blinking furiously to keep her eyes open. 'Find him some bandages.'

'Bandages? I don't think that's gonna help my mouth. Why, is anyone else hurt?'

I glance at Aula. She's got a cut on her forehead as well as the ones on her hands. She's leaning over the side now, hair whipped back and forth in the wind. Her eyes are closed. Why is that image so sexy to me?

'Taurus, put your eyes back in,' Etain says. 'Not for Aula – she'll heal quick enough – but for Sol. His chest.'

'Oh. Yeah. Of course.'

I decide to make an inventory of everything in the hulls while I look for bandages.

Dried fruit and some dried strips of what I guess is meat in small leather pouches. A few tools. Three baskets of fresh water. From the looks of things, most of the boat's cargo had been unloaded on to the island before Vulcan needed to use it to come after us. There's some ropey canvas too that will be good for repairing the sail if we run into bad weather. I don't find any bandages so I go into the stuff we brought with us. It's only been hurriedly wrapped in waxed cloth so some of the food's gotten wet or at least salty. The bread's no good, but all the extra clothes will be fine. I find a vest I can live without and tear it into strips before I hand it to Sol. He stares at me like I'm some kind of apparition.

'There's a bit of canvas you can stand behind to put them on,' I say. 'One of the girls will hold it up for you. Or I will, if you prefer.'

Joomia seems to come to herself then and finally turns away from the aft, looking around. **Oh**, she says, **I forgot. I caught it**. And she holds out her hand to him. The pendant's there. He looks so relieved I see his throat working to

199

swallow. He takes it from her without a word and reties the cord before stringing it over his neck again.

'Vulcan?' Sol asks Joomia, when his features have settled.

I don't know what he means until Joomia says, **Tell him he took a lungful of sea water, but I didn't kill him.**

I translate. His confused look tells me he doesn't know if he's relieved or not.

'You said he would follow us eventually,' Etain says.

Sol sniffs. 'Yeah, he'll follow. Can't let the escapee sister go. Especially one who had the audacity to become a brother and who had the nerve to kill the old man when no one else would.'

'You put us in serious danger,' Etain says.

'*You* wanted to come,' Sol snaps. 'I would've been faster on my own.' Etain sighs, and again he says, 'I'm not lying about it.'

'No, but you're not telling us everything, either,' she replies. He glares at her.

The island's about to disappear, Joomia says quietly. We all go to look.

It's so small from this far away, and so beautiful. For a minute, the silhouettes of the vishaal trees are still visible, and then even they fade.

The island's just a shape on the horizon.

And then it's gone.

Now is as good a time as any for your trick, Taurus, Joomia reminds me.

I try to stop myself from grinning. *They need me to do this. They need me!*

I brought the journal, Joomia says. She goes to the middle

200

hull and pulls out her bag.

Sol makes a sound of disbelief when he sees it. 'Oh, it's OK if *you* bring it?'

Aula says, '*She* found it. It's hers now.'

Sol rolls his eyes. Joomia hands it to me. **I thought the visual would help.**

'You know me well,' I say. She smiles at me. My best friend is back. And I get to help. They need me to point us in the right direction. Everything else – every bit of worry and nervousness – just shrinks compared to that.

I turn to the map pages at the back. There's magic here – I can almost *smell* the memories stored in each fibre. There's an old, tangy smell to it too – old magic. I hold one finger on the page with our island and press my thumb against the sketched shape of Izanami overleaf. I close my eyes.

It's nothing like anything I've ever looked for before. It's like I'm balancing on one leg. On a pole. In a storm. The focus I need is ridiculous.

They need you to do this.

As I waver and struggle for balance, I find there's a tip in my sense of forward, like I'm walking downhill. I open my eyes and my finger moves to point automatically.

'That way,' I say, trying not to grin.

My pulse is singing.

Purpose purpose purpose.

Etain

The first morning I'm woken by Joomia. With no sign of

Vulcan chasing us – not yet at least – we've anchored ourselves for a few hours, and everyone else is asleep while Joomia keeps watch. **You were crying**, she says. **Are you all right?**

'Nightmares,' I mutter. She hands me a cup of water and I sip at it, dozing in and out for a few minutes.

When I look up again, I see she's stripped to the waist and is hanging over the side of the trimaran, using a mash of soap nuts to wash. She lathers the soap nuts over her dark skin and uses a bone comb to tease through her ridiculous length of dark, wrinkled hair. It still surprises me that she can look so like Aula, yet nothing about her is similar. Aula would have counted the swim over to the trimaran as a wash, and her hair is knotted messily out of her face.

Joomia looks back at me. **Want a soap nut?**

'My arm feels really stiff.'

You've just done a lot of swimming, not to mention fighting. It's all right. I'll help.

There's a weird tension as I sit down beside her. I don't know why. She doesn't seem to notice anything strange about it.

I wriggle out of my tunic and she helps me lather soap nuts so I can dab gingerly at my burns and various scratches. Finally it feels as if I've washed off all the sweat and dirt of the last week.

When I try to rinse my hair, I get stuck. Astor's fire has burned the braids on the left side right back to my scalp. The rest of them appear to have adhered to my head, from blood or the sap Joomia put on them, I don't know. I think about trying to undo the braids, but as the sun comes up over the water, promising heat, I get a better idea.

'Joomia, did we bring any sharp knives?'

I sit with my feet in the water while she carefully cuts my hair away. The blade en't that sharp, so she has to angle it carefully, cutting as close to the skin as she dares. I find myself leaning into her hands as she turns my head and pulls my ear down to get at my hairline. When she finishes, it's like I'm coming out of a daze and I wonder if I'm tired again. When I look up at her, she's giving me a strange, absorbed look.

She shakes her head. **Sorry. It looks good.**

I shake my head. 'You were thinking of something else.'

She sighs. **Is it wrong to feel relieved?**

'About what?'

Relieved . . . that he split us again. That I'm me. That Aula's Aula.

We both look at Aula, snoring quietly.

'No,' I say. 'I'm . . . I'm glad too. That you're you. And Aula's Aula.'

There's that tension again. What is it?

But Joomia turns away again, and I'm left wondering.

Turns out we en't as atrocious at sailing when we en't being chased. Sol shows us all what he's doing, naming everything from prow to aft. He shows us how to read the sky rather than a map – in the day he shows us how to position ourselves against the sun. When darkness comes, he shows us which constellations to keep on our left and which star should sit in line with the prow at all times. For a few nights in a row we press on, wanting to keep ahead of Vulcan, fearing a sight of his sails on the horizon. I force myself to memorise everything Sol teaches us, and try to apply my forger skills to fix everything that might need it: a wonky pin on the mast; fraying fibres on the outrigger; a small tear in the sail that might get larger under high winds.

Occasionally, one of the others will look at me as if they're expecting me to take over leadership, but all calls about our navigation and the health of the ship are so obviously Sol's that my silence becomes complete. After a few days we can mostly anticipate when he needs the sail adjusting; and we all get good at watching the sun for when's a good time to start baiting the fishing net for our supper (we're trying to ration the dried food as much as we can – raw fish en't fun but it's better than nothing). I get used to the routine – the scar on my stomach peels badly, gathers a layer of sweat and stops feeling so separate from the rest of me. After three days Sol lets me take over for a few hours in calm sea while he tries to recover the hours and hours of sleep he's lost.

I torture myself with the knife edge I've set us on: if the fresh water runs out, we're dead; if the dried food runs out, we're dead. If we don't take it in turns to lie in the hull for at least some of the day, we'll end up using more water than we can ration: dead. If the wind drops, we're dead. If Vulcan finds us, we're dead. For three days I lie awake long after we've stopped sailing and Joomia's called up some tough plant from the ocean floor to act as our anchor.

Etain, Joomia says one night as we lie down, leaving Taurus on watch. **You're wearing yourself to a thread. Try to sleep.**

'Leave me alone, Joomia,' I say, but it comes out terse,

like a warning. She rolls over and goes quiet, and I stare at the sky, dazed by how cruel I can be. My dreams, when I do find sleep, are filled with salt water and the faces of my people, darkness and fire. Then I see my mother and Astor, and I hear the words that stripped me of my leadership.

It's not all bad. I try to remember what Aula said to me, back in the cave: *The prophecy said you were going to lead. It didn't say when or how. The way I see it, you're alive. And as long as you're alive, it en't too late to be the leader you were prophesied to be.*

It gets me on my feet every morning anyway. *Imagine,* I tell myself, *imagine if you come back with Kreywar's bones, and use them to buy back our people's freedom. They'll have to give you another chance then.* It's not really a happy thought, but it stops me focusing miserably on how I must have gone so wrong; on whether the prophecy mixed us up and it should have been Taurus leading us all along. He's got the compass thing after all . . .

The others talk regularly, but I find it hard – it's like it takes up too much space in my head to carry conversations – with Aula and Joomia, but Taurus too. *What if it should have been him?* I wonder, over and over, looking at him out of the corner of my eye as he helps Aula and Joomia fiddle with a lid from one of the water baskets, trying to make something to filter sea water, and prolong our chances out here. *Why do I feel like I can't talk to him about it?*

But a spell seems to come over us all soon enough, and I can't tell if it's cos we're hungry or tired or scared, but it feels like the sea has stolen our words.

The fifth day breaks the silence though. The dawn flares

205

blisteringly hot and airless. The sail sags limply on the mast. The sun beats us into holding a canvas over ourselves and weighing our options.

'Wise One,' Taurus pants, scraping his dreads into a tighter knot on his head and looking jealously at my bare scalp. 'If my powers weren't locked into my hair, I'd join you, baldy.'

I roll my eyes. 'Dunk your head again, it'll keep you cooler. What are we going to do now?'

'We have oars,' Taurus points out, pointing to the left-hand hull before leaning over the side to dangle his hair in the sea, 'but that's going to make us thirsty and we don't have much water.'

'I thought you got that saline filter to function yesterday,' Sol says.

We did, but it relies on the movement of the trimaran to push water through it, Joomia says. Taurus translates for Sol, who frowns and gestures at Aula. 'She dead or what? Get her to push!'

I'm sucking on my lower lip to prevent myself from saying something similar. I was fine when we were in sail, with the breeze to cool the sun's effect. But this is unbearable. The heat's so oppressive it's difficult to breathe, and every second we're still is a second we're not closing in on Izanami to find the bones and bring them back. Every second is a second in which Vulcan and his soldiers might appear. Without saying anything, I notice each one of us takes a turn at nervously scanning the horizon for ships.

I glance at Aula. Her skin, much lighter than anyone else's, has already blistered badly in the sun. 'I can push if you want,' she says, as if it's no big deal, but the pain and exhaustion in her face makes me feel for her hand.

'It can wait until the sun goes down a bit,' Taurus says, just as I open my mouth to ask her, *Well, if you wouldn't mind* . . .

'It can't if my brother catches up to us,' Sol says darkly.

'We just have to hope that doesn't happen,' Taurus adds firmly.

'What do we do until then?' Aula asks.

There's a long silence.

And then Joomia says: **Sol. Why the ants? How did Vulcan get to be in control of those ants? And how come they gave Astor fire?**

Aula translates this one.

Sol chews his lip. 'The ants are native to Govinda. They stay underground during the day and come out at night. The light they emit is a mating signal and a deterrent for predators. The fire . . . well, you saw what happened to your friend who went pyro on everything.'

'Astor?'

'Some of the subtypes of that ant colony are parasitic. If they manage to get under your skin they'll find a way to your spine and dull your brain capacity. It's basically an immobiliser for large prey – not meant for humans, I don't think. The fire only seems to happen when the chemicals they use to immobilise react with *skuld* blood. Makes the victim – well – pyrotechnic. It's *supposed* to break down your internal organs so the ants can lay their eggs in all your fleshy tissue, but for some reason, if it's put down in *skuld* blood it manifests as a kind of power. Clever, right?'

'Lovely,' Taurus says, looking nauseated.

Sol goes on. 'My brother puts the parasite ants inside his soldiers. That's how they move so uniform, so fast together.'

Now I feel sick. 'What about Astor? Why was he so badly affected?'

'Yeah. That can happen either if there's not enough *skuld* blood or if their body tries to reject the ant. Vulcan calls it survival of the fittest. He can control the ants because he can tap into hive-minded insects.'

We lapse into silence. Everyone looks as nauseated as me and Taurus now.

'Moral of the story: never let him near a beehive,' Aula says at last.

'Amen,' Sol mutters, inspecting his face with his fingertips. Wise One, does he look a mess. If there's a spot on his face that en't black from being punched, it's yellow or purple or blue. Not that any of us are looking pretty, not to mention the fact that this far into the journey, everyone smells like armpit.

I think Sol senses that Joomia wants to say something else cos he half turns toward her, looking shifty. 'What?'

I've just been thinking – Aula said your brother asked if you were going to . . . find Domaga? Who's that?

Aula translates. Sol chews harder on his lip. 'Domaga. My sister. She . . . she was blamed for my father's death because she told them she did it. Only Vulcan and I know the truth. I was imprisoned for being her accomplice. I really have no idea why. Maybe it was my brother's punishment to keep me with him in a place that I hated. Domaga was exiled.'

'Exiled?' Taurus says. 'Where?'

He's already shaking his head. 'Nowhere specific. Exile's really just a death sentence without the actual wording. You get put in a canoe with a week's worth of food and water, your hands and feet are tied, you get one oar. They tow you out to open ocean and leave you there. If they see you coming in to shore again, well . . .' He mimes nocking an arrow and makes a creaking sound out the side of his mouth for the strain of the bow. He looks back at us and shrugs. 'Some people – if they manage to break their bonds – row right back just to get it over with quickly.'

'Wise One,' Taurus says quietly.

'But you think your sister survived?' I ask.

'I don't know. I want to believe she did. But I don't know.' He turns away. 'I think . . . perhaps, she may be on Izanami.'

Taurus

Hours later, as the afternoon relents, Aula stretches and stands up. 'I need a dip. I'll catch supper. Gotta be fish down there somewhere.'

No one argues. She's not as fast in deep water, but the bonus of having bark-tough skin is that she can withstand the pressure of the water further down. She's our best bet for food out here.

She comes back up a few minutes later, panting. 'There's a school that way,' she says, pointing. 'But I need someone to hold the basket up while I fish. Easier than keeping one or

209

two in my hands while I grab the others.'

'I'll do it,' I say.

Joomia flashes me a look that's somewhere between teasing and warning. I think of that conversation with Nine before the ants:

What is this?' I ask. 'What's going on here, between you and me?'

She snatches her hand back like I've burned her. For a second I can see her eyes flicking backwards and forwards, confused. 'Aula's still in here,' she says.

As we swim out, I look back a few times to check on the boat. The sun's setting, its rays flaring against the water. Aula dives before I can catch up with her. When she comes up, she slowly puts a fish in the basket I'm holding. The basket has been waxed to keep out water and bugs, so it's floating at our head height like a buoy.

'Can you get more?' I ask.

'Yeah,' she says.

But instead of diving down again, she takes the rope trailing from the basket and pulls it so it's shielding us from view of the boat. I meet her eyes. There's a flash between us in the water, like a current of electric. Then we're kissing. She grabs my face. I wrap her legs around me. We both hold on to the basket and kiss harder. I don't know for how long.

We break apart, breathing heavy.

'OK,' she says. 'OK. So that's still a thing.'

Then she dives again. My heart, Wise One.

She comes up again, puts two more fish in the basket. I pull her to me. The skin across her nose is so badly sunburned it's peeling. Her eyes are squinted against the remnants of

210

the sun. I check the basket is still shielding us from view.

'This is so not the right time,' I say, tucking my boner into the waistband of my sarong. She laughs. And then . . . something strange happens to her face. A cloud moves above and I squint against the light in my eyes. It's not Aula looking at me now. It's Sol.

He smiles slowly.

And then I wake up.

Sol is leaning over me with a water skin. 'Morning, Bull,' he says. 'Pleasant dreams?'

I still have a boner, don't I? I sit up to hide it. He snorts and hands me the water skin. The air is cooler, I notice, and the sky is darker.

'We're moving,' I say, and it's true – the sails have filled again, and the sea spits gently in the trimaran's wake; the breeze feels good on my face.

'We are,' he agrees. 'Wind started about halfway through the night, but Aula got us going before that. You slept a long time, huh?'

I look for Aula. She's on the steering oar. She's the only one who can hold it properly steady in the water. She's squinting at the horizon, hair stuffed up under a headscarf, adjusting the steering oar the way Sol's showed us all how to. I follow the direction of her gaze and see the clouds livid black on the horizon. There's no sign of Vulcan, but this storm is just as much of a threat.

'We're going to need everyone awake,' Sol says. He takes a drawstring bag filled with dried fruit from the middle hull and gives everyone a handful. The wind gusts like it's been seeking us, tasting for our presence. It sings over the sails.

211

The trimaran skids slightly over the next wave.

'Damn it,' Sol says. 'We should have reefed it earlier. Leafy, lower the mainsail like I showed you, yeah?'

Joomia nods and moves quickly to it.

None of us say anything to each other as we get ready. I stuff the blankets back into the hatch in the main hull and go to help Etain secure the jib. Joomia calls to Aula to adjust the direction; Sol rolls the mainsail to keep its surface area smaller. I tie my dreads more securely and don't look at Aula.

Sol calls, 'Look starboard – do you see the rain coming down over that way?'

We nod.

'We want to try and sail around the weather, yeah?'

Everyone nods.

'Good. I'll keep Rusty on the oar here, then I want Anassa and Bull on mainsail. Leafy, I want you to keep watch for any heeling. If you do, you take the weights in the main hull and get us balanced again, got it?'

'When did he give you two nicknames?' I ask Aula.

'About the time I decided to call him Shithead,' she replies brightly.

We go on carefully, trying not to look up, but the clouds gather darkness like paper absorbing an ink spill. The wind squalls and shoves us off balance. The waves chitter and hiss. They slip under the boat and buoy us up before dropping out again, leaving us to skid down the other side.

We're going like that for half an hour, fighting the wind that wants to turn us right into the storm. At some point I look left and see a grey smudge on the horizon. I stare, wobbling. As I look, another shape comes into view: blurry, but there.

I look around: another. And another. Probably nothing. Just low-hanging clouds, right? But half an hour later I look again. There's no mistaking the sails now.

'Sol?' I call. 'Sol?'

'What?'

'Your brother,' I say. 'I think he found us.'

He swivels backwards, sees the ships and turns back. 'Ah,' he says.

How'd they catch up to us so quickly?

'I hit those boats with everything I had.'

'It doesn't matter,' Sol says. 'His ants can repair anything. At least he's only brought three.'

There's a silence, and then, almost comically, the stuttering stone-crack of thunder, and rain, falling in handfuls of hard pinpricks.

'Are you sure he's not here to . . . I dunno . . . help us out?' I ask.

Sol laughs. A gallows laugh.

Etain shields her eyes against the rain. I'm pretty sure she's calculating how badly they'll cut us up if we keep heading away from the storm clouds. 'We're going to have to go through it, aren't we?'

Sol spits over the side and squares his shoulders. 'Trial by water,' he says, staring right into the blackest part of the sky. 'Everyone ready?'

We're soaked in seconds but it sure gets us moving: scrabbling only to keep us steady.

'Sol!' Taurus yells. 'Tell us what to do!'

'Leafy, hold the sail! Keep your compass thing going, Bull. You all right with that oar, Rusty?'

Aula gives him a sarcastic thumbs up and he laughs. 'That's the way. Now, Anassa? Get that rope in the main hull and tie us all down.'

For minutes, we're just a mess of limbs and panicked, lashing movements, and then, like in the battle with the mindless, I feel a kind of forced calm shutting down my instincts. Water sloshes over my feet. He showed me this before. Safety lines. I'm halfway through the job before I let myself look back. That's a mistake. The first of the three ships is already much, much closer than before. I can see a blurry silhouette at the prow of the closest one. He's too far away to see properly, but his attention is clearly fixed on us. My foot slips.

Sol catches my elbow. 'Don't look back, Anassa,' he says.

'What will happen if he catches us?' I have to shout to be heard over the wind and the rain.

'He'll kill me, to prove a point. Or enslave me with one of the parasite ants, like your friend Astor.'

'What about us?'

'I don't know. I don't think he'll take chances with Rusty and Leafy now that he has *twice* failed to defeat the Chosen One.'

'What about us?'

214

'If he lets you live it'll only be so he can kill you in front of your people.'

There's a long moment where I just stare at him. Then I open my mouth to confirm what my face is saying, but he speaks before I can.

'I know what you have to do if it comes down to it,' he says, reading me correctly. 'I know you're tempted just to do it now. But please – I'd rather you got Rusty to break my neck before that happens. Please.'

'You know I can't promise that,' I say. 'I'll save them first. I always will.'

'And you think you're done being their leader,' he says, but he doesn't seem surprised or angered by my answer. 'You need to talk to your br—'

FWWAP!

The wind gets knocked out of me as Aula flattens us both against the deck. I hear the whine of something passing, lightning-fast somewhere over us. I look up to see the arrow shoot past the prow and straight into the water.

'Shit!' Aula shouts. She makes a running grab for the steering oar where's she's left it, but it slips through the clip holding it in place and disappears into the water. 'Shit! Shit!'

She throws herself in after it. Her safety line – I forgot—

Another volley of arrows, but only one makes a definite hit – thunking into the deck.

'Bull!' Sol calls. 'Reef the mainsail all the way! Let out the storm jib!'

I rush to help him. The canvas is heavy with water and it takes both our strength to keep the cloth folded long

215

enough for him to lash it down. He unhooks a lanyard on the jib and—

'Argh!'

An arrow clips his arm. A second lands in the wood a few feet away.

Down! Joomia yells.

We hit the deck. I feel the swell of a wave beneath us turn the trimaran sideways into the wind. It scatters the next round of arrows but we have to pay for it when the wave crashes over the deck. I hold tight to the boards beneath me, look up gasping—

I grab Taurus's hand. 'You OK?' I ask.

He checks his arm. He looks ill. 'It doesn't matter,' he says.

'Taurus—'

Another burst of arrows peppers the deck. Then another heavier clatter as Aula throws the sailing oar back up. I squint and see her paddling furiously alongside us—

'Anassa! The oar! We need to get it into the water!' Sol bellows.

It takes the three of us to haul it back to its place at the aft.

There's a pause. I imagine Vulcan's crew scrambling for arrows. 'On my count!' Sol says as we slot the oar back into its circular holder. 'One – Two—'

Move! Joomia says. I'm knocked sideways as she throws herself forward.

There's a rushing *thunk-thunk-thunk* and we only just manage to keep hold of the oar.

Then Joomia stumbles back. My mind can't comprehend

it at first: there are three arrows jutting horribly from her arm, her shoulder, her back.

'JOOMIA!' Taurus bellows.

We both drop the oar and Sol lets out an indignant sound.

I'm fine, Joomia manages weakly. **I can heal it . . . you help Aula.**

Taurus ignores Joomia, examining where the arrows have struck her.

'SOMEONE GET THE STORM JIB UNFURLED!' Sol shouts.

Aula! Joomia insists.

I look around wildly. Aula's made it over but she's only just about clinging to the starboard hull as the trimaran dips into the valley of a wave. I drop to my belly and grab her by the scruff of her tunic. She manages to get a foot aboard. Her other foot slips—

I grit my teeth and wedge my knee into the latticed structure of the outrigger, anchoring us, pulling her up. She's barely got her feet planted before she's up again, stumbling toward Sol where he's struggling with the oar on his own.

Out of the corner of my eye, a huge wave yawns over us. There's a teetering second before it hits and I manage to cry, 'HOLD ON!'

For a second, the trimaran is under – well and truly under – and when I open my eyes, spitting brine and coughing, it feels like a miracle that it's still in one piece.

Aula and Sol are still fighting to keep the oar in place.

Another flurry of arrows, but the wave has scattered

their aim. Aula's far tougher skin means that when one catches her arm, it just bounces off. Another buries its head in the steering oar. Aula breaks the shaft with no more effort than snapping off a twig and, with a grunt, plunges the oar's blade into the water.

Three things happen then:

First, Taurus finally manages to let out the storm jib.

Second, Aula and Sol turn the oar, and by proxy, the trimaran, so that when the next wave threatens, we're poised to ride along its length rather than cower beneath it. It's smart but it brings us, for a few seconds, closer to the nose of Vulcan's ship.

And third: I see a rain-smudged archer at the prow nock an arrow and take aim.

It's a strange, time-slipping moment. I don't know how I know, but I do: that arrow en't like the others they've been raining on us. It's a bolt. And that bow en't a longbow. We sweep along the wave—

I fill my lungs. Yell a warning—

And Aula dives for Sol, but she can't let go of the oar quick enough.

I'm slipping and sliding toward them on the deck's slick surface—

But the bolt hits Sol—

I don't see where—

His body convulses with the force of it—

And he goes to his knees—

The ocean . . . it shudders. A colossal, pulse-halting tremor. The trimaran quails in the water, and frothing white foam erupts in fierce, gurgling fountains all around us—

Then the storm jib fills and we're swept out of range of the archer's second bolt. We're all rushing to help Sol and keep the sail steady and the steering oar neutral—

WAVE! Joomia gasps. **WAVE!**

I jerk round to look.

It's swelled out of nowhere: nearly three times the size of the other waves buffeting us and frothing white with spray. The face of it is impossible. The boat drags in the wake of its gathering bulk – it towers over us like the lip of a foaming mouth.

I can only gaze up at it in horror as it rushes us, cresting as it comes.

It falls.

The seconds warp strangely before it hits us. The underside of the wave glistens like a wrinkled skin. Joomia's hand shifts, sticky with salt, against my wrist.

Then it hits.

The force of it rips the air out of my lungs in one long stream. Some part of the boat – the mast or the rudder or something – catches my jaw as the water shoves us under, punching us deep below the surface. Joomia's hand is gone immediately – the current's just too strong and she doesn't have Aula's power.

The pressure is hard against my sinuses; my body's going deep. My ears ache.

Etain!

I struggle, and push and try to steady myself, but it just spins me out more. I don't know which way is up. I don't know anything.

219

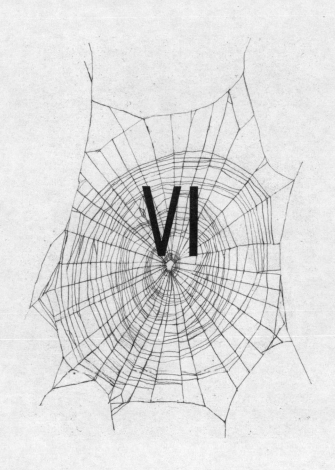

The Chosen

It's cool and dark and muffled beneath the surface. Aula lets the wave push her under as far as it can, and then she opens her eyes and immediately begins to look for Etain – she knows it was only the two of them left untethered, so as long as the safety lines have held, the others should still be aboard.

It's murky, but she sees the trimaran bobbing on the surface, dazed like a fighter downed by a single hit. The port hull and outrigger are in ruins, the mast snapped, hanging by splinters. The sail billows in the water like a strange plant.

Then she sees Etain, thrashing her way forward, seemingly unsure of which way is up.

Aula swims for her, beating her legs hard against the churning water, and grabs her, pulling her towards the surface while being mindful not to yank her arm out of its socket.

Their heads break the skin in time to watch another wave yawn over them. Aula ducks, kicks against the pull of the undertow and resurfaces, spotting the trimaran some twenty yards off. Behind it, two of Vulcan's ships have fallen back, but the larger ship has weathered the wave better than they did – it's knocked them off course but they appear to be turning.

Aula ploughs through the angry white water, hauling Etain up with her. She reaches the trimaran and rolls Etain aboard. Etain pushes herself on to her hands and knees, coughs hard and forces herself to her feet.

Taurus is crawling over to Sol. Joomia is halfway through pulling the last arrow out of her back. She catches sight of Aula and tries for a weak smile.

I was wondering if you were going to make me jump in after you.

'You still full of holes?' Aula asks. Joomia grunts and the arrow comes out at last. Joomia's skin has changed to wood around the wounds the arrows have made, as Aula expected. Without the protection of Aula's hardened skin, the magic in her found a different way of slowing the arrow's path. It's strange; Aula knows what it's like to heal herself now, though she hasn't retained the power since they split anew – she can almost feel it as Joomia's skin knits itself back together.

Get us out of here, Aula, Joomia says as another wave surges beneath them.

Aula looks back at Vulcan's ship. 'If I rip out a good chunk of the hull now . . .'

No time, Joomia gasps. **We need to get out from under these clouds.** She looks at Sol. The arrows Joomia picked out are nothing compared to the bolt stuck in his chest.

But Aula doesn't look away from the ships: through the wall of rain she can just make out Vulcan's crew darting about, attempting to turn them port and come after the trimaran again.

Wavelets slap at her. The current worries her legs. She grits her teeth and takes a firm hold of the aft. 'Fine,' Aula says. She presses down so the nose of the middlemost hull clears the water and paddles hard.

Karragan calls the people of Chloris back to their tents for the evening. It's been a good day, he supposes – fifty trees cut down and prepared for transport. Govinda will have more boats, more housing. But the success feels empty.

The Chlorisians tried to rebel last night. Stupid. Useless. The soldiers turned fire on them. The dead and the injured now lie in the medici's tent. None of them are from Govinda. He thinks of their scorched bodies and stares at the work done today: at the tree stumps glowing white as bone in the twilight. As the Chlorisians form silent queues to their tent, passing Karragan, he schools his face to mirror Vulcan's: someone who knows he has power, and uses this alone to intimidate. But the Chlorisians return his gaze without expression. There's something absent in them today. A kind of stunned disbelief.

It makes him feel sick.

Karragan feels the ant Vulcan implanted in himself squirm in the back of his neck. A hot shiver of pain cuts down his spine. Sweat beads beneath his tunic, the material clings in the small of his back. He glances around to make sure no one else is in sight before allowing himself to kneel and retch.

Acid, hot and burning, rasps his throat. The branches of blue veins on the inside of his wrists have turned bloody red, glowing like coals beneath his skin.

He should be beyond this stage by now. The sickness should have passed. But it's still hurting him.

'Sir?' says a lingering soldier, on the edge of camp.

'I'll be along in a moment,' Karragan says. He lies down

where he is. It'll just be for a moment. A moment, and then he'll go back.

He wakes hours later, drenched in sweat. Karragan knows with cold certainty that he's dying. He'd never have thought himself unequal to infestation. He'd never have guessed it would do this to him. He should have warned someone. Then another soldier could have taken his place.

Surely Vulcan will feel his death and know of his failure. It makes Karragan ache to think of it. Yet he has been feeling ... very strange over the last few days. An idea has begun to invade him, taking a firmer hold the longer they've been here:

Could he ... Vulcan ... Govinda ... could they be wrong?

This island ... yes, there has been conflict, but to Karragan, from what he's been able to glean from these people, the conflict seems a much gentler, safer kind than any he knew growing up on Govinda.

He can't move now, even if he wanted to. The pain is too great, and his grip on his sanity feels slippery.

Ade finds him like this. She has slipped her captors. She has work to do.

She turns him on to his stomach and he protests only with a feeble hiss of protest. 'Out,' she murmurs, and brandishes a knife.

She reopens the wound without a murmur from Karragan. She plucks out the struggling insect and squashes its body against the ground. Acid leaks thinly from its ruined exoskeleton, blistering Ade's fingers.

Then Karragan wakes, feeling the wound on his neck dribbling blood. He is still not convinced he isn't dying. His mouth is dry and rank. His insides feel sour and scalded. Slowly, he pushes himself on to his hands and knees and looks up at his rescuer.

He's seen the Chosen One – *Ones* – now, and in her he sees an older version of them. They have her freckles. One of them has her dark olive skin. The other has her reddish brown hair. Time has worn her like old sandstone. She is thin, but not fragile – like a birch tree.

'You can sail,' she says, without any preamble.

'What?' he says hoarsely.

'You can sail.'

'Y . . . yes?'

'Eat this,' she says, handing him a long tubular fruit he doesn't recognise. He obeys.

'Drink this.' She hands him a water skin. He drinks.

'In an hour you . . . better. In two you . . . have a . . . change.'

She taps the left side of her chest and, after a few moments, he connects the gesture with her words. *A change of heart*.

He laughs. It's relief, but something else too. 'About what?' he asks.

'Everything.'

He drinks from the water skin and nearly gags. 'What *is* this?'

'Nutrients. Medicine. Spelled – to get you on your feet.'

He stares at her. 'And then what?'

She chews her lip. 'Then we sail.'

Taurus

The waves get mercifully smaller. Whenever I look back, Vulcan's ship is still there like a stain on the horizon. It doesn't get any bigger but it doesn't get any smaller either.

'Taurus! I need you to give us a direction!' Sis is at the steering oar.

'Give me a second.'

I crouch over Sol as he clenches his teeth and tries to keep still. Stoic as hell. If it were me I'd be screaming and absolutely everyone would know about it.

I can't think of anything to say but, 'Hold on, Sol. Hold on.'

Like that's any help at all.

I hear the familiar sound of creaking wood. Joomia's already up and mending the mast. The sharp green smell of her magic hits me. Wow. I'd forgotten there were smells other than unwashed bodies and salt. She's reanimating the wood and joining the cracks – making knots form and knitting fibres tight on themselves. I put my hand on her shoulder.

'I know that's urgent, but can you help me with Sol?' I say. 'He's not in a good way, and I don't want to take out the bolt, but I think you might be able to—'

'There en't time for that, Taurus!' Etain interrupts. 'We need the sail. You need to give us a direction!' Her face is screwed up against the rain.

'Yeah, yeah, I know, sis, but he's not in good shape—'

'Joomia can see to him in a second.'

'OK, I'm gonna pretend I didn't hear that,' I say. 'Joo—'

'Joomia can see to him in a second, Taurus,' Etain repeats, like I haven't heard her.

'He's *dying*, Etain!'

'We'll all die if we don't keep moving and you don't give us a direction!'

Etain! Joomia says, looking alarmed. **We can spare a few seconds.** She comes to kneel next to me, eyeing the bolt sticking out of Sol's chest. **Shall I take it out or . . .**

But I'm not really listening. I'm trembling with rage. How could Etain say that? How *could* she? I can't even look at her.

Taurus, Joomia says gently.

I shake myself. 'Sorry. I don't know. Maybe . . . leave it in? We might damage something inside more if we try to take it out.'

Sol opens his eyes then and glares up at us. 'My necklaces,' he says.

I don't get it, but Joomia does.

His necklaces only work when they're in contact with his body, she says. **It's Athenasian – *oluwaseyi* – magic; it'll be feeding off his energy.**

Together we lift Sol's head and gently pull each necklace away. I only vaguely recognise the symbols on them. 'Want to know what you look like as a bloke, Bull?' he whispers.

'You're hilarious.' I mutter, but I'm genuinely stunned that he has the capacity for a joke left in him. I give him a grim smile as Joomia lays her hands on the shaft of the bolt and starts murmuring to herself. **I think I've got an idea,** she says. She uses her power to turn the wood brittle as kindling. Fraction by fraction, she pulls the shaft out of his chest. **OK,** she says. **The head will have to stay in for now. I don't think I hit anything vital.**

Sol jerks with suppressed laughter when I tell him what she said. 'Nah,' he says. 'Right as rain.' He bites his lip. His face twists in pain. Joomia goes digging in the main hull, looking relieved when she pulls out a handful of green, scalloped leaves. I help her chew them methodically to make a paste.

'Boswellia,' I tell Sol, when he raises an eyebrow. We feed it to him bit by bit. His face goes slack. His breathing slows. I get a sympathetic twinge in my own chest as he closes his eyes. All his hard, bitter lines smooth. It leaves a sad, upward flick to his eyebrows. That does something funny to my heart. I guess you can't see how tough someone is until they're vulnerable.

OK, Joomia says. **Now the sail.**

I get up and help her rerig the sail to the mended mast. It's closer to a tree trunk now than anything else and particularly gnarled in the places she's fixed the crack. When the sail flares, Aula climbs aboard at last, and collapses on to the deck.

I go to her.

'Mmm, fine,' she murmurs. 'Just need . . . sleep.'

Joomia's not far behind her: they curl up together, like they've only just come out of the tree. I reach for her hand, and she squeezes it. **Lore's journal's still in my bag if you want to . . . to pick a direction.** She yawns.

'It's still dry?'

I made the cloth waterproof. Vishaal sap's good for everything. She barely stays awake long enough to finish that sentence.

230

But I'm not ready to compass yet. I'm too angry at Etain, too pent up with leftover adrenaline.

I go to the sail. Etain stays on the oar. We don't look at each other.

'I can't see it any more,' she says. 'Vulcan's ship.'

I'm too tired to even be glad about that. For a while we're silent.

Then she says, 'How's your arm?'

I'd honestly totally forgotten about it. 'It's still bleeding a bit but I'll be all right,' I say.

She lashes the oar so it stays in place and comes over. When she touches my arm, it's like she's asking permission. I shrug. She finds a strip of cloth, wraps the arrow wound tight and tucks in the ends. I've never seen her look so tired. Is she still afraid to sleep? When she's done, she sways.

'What am I doing, Taurus?' she whispers. 'What am I trying to prove?'

'I dunno what you mean,' I say. I do, though.

She looks up at me so slowly it's like her eyes are too heavy to lift. 'Do you think it *should* have been me leading? Honestly?'

Wow. She said it. I'm so surprised I almost forget to be angry with her. 'Yes, Etain, of course I do,' I say, because it's safer than the real answer: *I don't know*.

'You don't think I could have done anything different?' she asks.

I don't say anything. She carries on, almost to herself, 'What could I have done differently? Where did it start to go wrong?' I can tell she's been thinking that for days on end. I guess exhaustion has worn thin the place where she keeps these things.

I shake my head. 'You didn't do anything wrong, Etain.'

But I don't think she's listening. 'I just . . . I just wanted them to get along. That was my *purpose*. Like Aula and Joomia had a purpose. Like you have a purpose.'

I burst out laughing. It's an ugly sound. 'What purpose is that, Etain?'

She blinks at me. 'You're the compass.'

'The boy who would be her compass,' I say. 'Yep. That's me. The guide. The helper.'

She purses her lips and sighs. 'Do you wish it was the other way round?'

I goldfish a few times cos the answer isn't as simple as *no*.

Etain puts her head in her hands. 'How could she have expected this of me . . . of us? How could she have expected us to succeed? Did she want us to fail?'

'Who? Lore?' I ask.

She blinks. 'No, not Lore – *Ma*.'

I pause. 'Ma just . . . just did what the prophecy told her to do, Etain. You know that.'

'And what did the prophecy tell *her* to do, Taurus? Separate us? Send you to live in a different city? Build us a brick corridor, put blinkers on us so there was only one option? What are we *doing* here, Taurus? Who tells a three-year-old girl who knows nothing about anything that she has to be in charge of all the people left on Erthe? Who tells a little boy that he has nothing to do in this life but help her?' She points at Aula and Joomia. 'Who tells two kids their destiny is to unite all people so the fuck-ups of everyone in *history* are forgotten?'

'I don't know,' I say. I'm about to cry, and I'm not even sure why.

'I do.'

This is Sol. He's staring straight upwards, listening to us. I think the Boswellia's still having some effect, cos he looks peaceful.

'This is a new time,' he says. 'A young time. The Erthe is picking itself up from its own ashes. It must be led by the young, so it can make mistakes as the young do, so it can grow into itself.' He sighs.

'But I was deposed,' Etain says, and there's something so childlike about her voice that it makes me say the thing I've had two hands clamped down over too:

'And I wasn't meant for anything.'

Sol sighs, exasperated. 'Can't you see that it doesn't matter? Look, I'm not prophesied to be anyone's saviour, but I'm gonna try to save mine anyway. And if I can help you save yours, even better.'

He stops abruptly, and closes his eyes. I wait for him to go on, but after a while I realise he's gone to sleep. I wonder about Sol. What kind of person does something that selfless? Is it selfless? Or is it just that there's nothing left for him without his sister?

Etain goes back to the oar. 'Taurus,' she says, 'I'm sorry. We need a heading.'

I go back to the sail and take a really deep breath.

It takes most of the strength I have left to do it. I sink into that feeling of wobbling, precarious—

Wait. Shit.

It's different this time. I'm still teetering, but the almost uncontrollable swinging point of direction isn't all over the place any more. It's firm – almost directly ahead, a little to the left.

'Etain,' I say.

'What?'

'I think . . . I think we're nearly there.'

Etain

We sail through the night.

Joomia gets up to take over from Taurus but I let Aula sleep – she's done a hell of a lot of paddling.

When the dawn comes, Izanami sketches itself on to the sky.

It's surprisingly underwhelming to see it there, high enough for the peak to be wreathed in cloud – but *Athenas* was high enough for that. It's also more of an island than I was giving it credit for. I mean, the majority of it *is* a volcano, but there are stubby green trees around the mountain, the base is wide and flat – and as we get closer, I can see a thin strip of sand along the shore that will work for our landing.

No sign of habitation, Joomia says, echoing my thoughts. **I don't know whether to be relieved by that or not.**

I'm too tired to think anything much. We just need to find those bones. I look over at Sol, and guilt greases my stomach at how I acted just after the storm.

His breathing is even enough. You should sleep, Joomia says. Damn her for being a mind reader.

234

'I'm too tired to sleep,' I say, which is true. I look down at myself, at all my scrapes and scratches. I can feel every direction the ocean's pulled me in. My neck is stiff and sore from whiplash. My lungs feel watery. It's gross, but I'm still basically wearing the clothes Joomia gave me after Astor burned me. That means there's sap under my fingernails, dried blood – brown, going orange – still on the front of the button-up tunic Joomia put me in. 'Wise One, I'm a mess.'

You're not, Joomia says.

I roll my eyes, feeling irritated. 'Joomia. Do you ever stop?'

Stop what?

'Being so damn nice all the time!'

What's wrong with it?

Nothing's wrong with it. Nothing *at all* is wrong with it. Why is it so hard for me *not* to be such a bitch?

Gently she says, **What would it cost you, Etain, if you were damn nice all the time?**

'No one was ever nice to me when I grew up.'

She snorts. **I don't think that's true.**

She's right; it's not. I open my mouth to take some of it back, but it sticks in my throat. A few minutes later, Joomia rouses the others.

We're here, she says. **Wake up.**

I think about Joomia darting forward to take arrows that were meant for me. I think about her fixing the sail. I think about how her fingers felt when she turned my head and cut my hair away.

As we draw nearer, Joomia, Taurus and I get out and start kicking us shorewards, but we struggle in the shallows. Finally, Aula finds her feet on the sea floor, *lifts the entire trimaran into the air* and drops it neatly on to dry land. A few of the planks snap, the ropes sag, the sail withers.

We swim the rest of the way to the shore and fall down on the sand, panting. It's a different texture from our beaches: gritty and grey and—

'Why is it *warm?*' Aula asks, sounding almost offended.

Hot springs underneath, Joomia says.

That explains the familiar smell too. A hot, wet, damp smell. Sulphur and minerals and something metallic, similar to blood. Our water supply in Athenas was fed by hot springs, a little like this, but never as strong.

'Maybe we should start looking for Sol's sister. If she really is here,' Taurus says, 'she might be able to help him.'

'In a minute,' Aula says. 'Just . . . just rest here a minute.'

No one argues.

My thoughts spin out. My gums ache. My eyes itch. I get that swampy feeling of being on the edge of sleep—

In my dream, spiders come out of a small cave at the base of Izanami and flow down the beach toward us. They crawl all over the trimaran and all over our faces, our bodies; all different shapes, sizes, species. They do bite, a little, but just to taste, just to gain an understanding of what's washed up on their shores.

Etheling, they say to each other as they trail over Sol. *Voyager*, they murmur over Aula. *Chosen*, they say about Joomia.

They reach Taurus. *Compass*, they think. *Lost compass*.

Then they get to me, legs scampering over my limbs, fangs finding a place on my wrist.

'What?' I whisper. 'What am I? Was my mother right?'
But they don't answer. They're silent. It's like I don't exist.

The Chosen

Deep inside the caves of Izanami, Domaga watches as the
spiders work their way into the centre of the massive web,
carefully adjusting threads, tiptoeing backwards on their
tightropes to inspect a disturbance in one corner, then
resuming their work. It has taken a lot of patience and
cooperation to get the spiders to work in tandem like this.
Unsurprisingly, they are very hard to communicate
effectively with. Domaga has never made the mistake of
thinking that she is having real conversations with them, but
since she gave up trying to translate the frustratingly specific
nature of human language to the frighteningly abstract
nature of spider language, she has found a way of working
alongside them.

The progress of the web is slow – it may still be many
weeks before it is finished, but Domaga knows it is pointless
to rush them.

The volcano rumbles then. Something tugs on her
attention, and a spider on a different web alerts her to
something about to happen.

'Now?' she asks incredulously, but to no one in particular.

In a frenzy she hurries to shoulder a large sack – prepared
for this eventuality – and breaks into a limping run that
takes her through a long, ascending passage and out toward
the shore.

The wind hits her first, whipping back her thick black head of curls, then the sheeting rain, stinging her face. She pauses, panting, to tie back her hair and squint at the shoreline. The sea writhes restlessly before her. But if there is anyone or anything out there, being tossed by the waves, she cannot make them out. She hurries along the beach, her feet sinking and slipping in the sand.

'Damn leg!' she barks, stopping briefly to bend over her left shin, where a mottled, splat-shaped scar stretches itself from knee to ankle. If you were to look objectively, you might notice that this leg is shorter than her right, and at the slightest angle, as if it had been broken and healed in the wrong position. She straightens up and once again looks left and right for wreckage, debris or floating bodies.

There.

A battered trimaran, beached on the sand like a weary animal. Four people are scattered around it. One lies on top.

'Sol,' she whispers. 'Sol . . .'

She brings Sol first and lays him out in the cave. Gently she detaches her best weavers from their webs and places them over the wound on his chest. His breaths are shallow. The spiders do not understand urgency in matters like this, perhaps because they always work alone. The web, even when it's broken, will take as long as it will take. But the spiders of this cave – of this island – are used to Domaga's strange requests. In healing wounds, as they have done before, each will work on her piece of the overall crafting before linking them together.

Let it work, she thinks. *Please let it work.*

She brings the others back to the cave one by one. It-is hard work, especially with her leg, but with a makeshift stretcher of patched-together fabric, she manages. None of them wake, and no wonder – when Domaga's canoe finally shifted against the sands of this shore, she did not wake from sleep for a good few days. She lays them out carefully and goes back out again.

The hulls of the trimaran mostly contain clothes, but there's a handful of half-dried tomatoes in the bottom of a jar, a spoonful of goat curd in a paper wrapper, a square inch of fruit loaf. She crams them greedily into her mouth, checks to make sure there's nothing else that needs unloading, and starts digging.

If one of her brothers is here, she muses, it may well be that the other isn't far behind. Though would he ever find his way to the island? She decides to err on the side of caution. It takes her hours, delayed again by her handicap, but when she grows weary she crawls on her hands and knees and shoves handfuls of sand on to the deck. Bit by bit, the trimaran is buried until only its strange, knobbly mast is visible, so similar to some of the sapling trees that have dared to grow on Izanami's flanks that its camouflage is complete.

Then, because she cannot bear to go back to the cave and see how well the spiders have been able to work on her brother, she decides to pick through the bags.

There really are an inordinate amount of clothes, but there are also things that she will find useful: a hammer, several different knives, paper (paper!), sail canvas, waxed storage baskets and . . .

A book wrapped tight in waxed paper, waxed cloth, then waxed canvas, tumbles out into her lap. Slowly, she opens it. She frowns. A dead language. She can make out *Year One*, and then . . . and then . . . and then a name.

Her mouth goes slack. She presses her palms together to stop them from shaking and looks again.

But it says the same thing: *Lore Sumati, Year One*.

Taurus

I get woken up when something hits me in the face. Something hard. With corners.

'*So*,' says a voice.

I open my eyes. Lore's journal is lying askew on my chest. Where the hell am I? I try to bring everything into focus. I'm in a dark . . . a dark room? Sand underneath us. The smell of the sea. Wise One, it's hot in here—

I jump, finally spotting that there's a woman standing over me, panting. She's tall and fat and I guess you could say she wears both of those things well. I'm guessing she's the one who threw the book. 'Lady, do you know how old this is?!' I pick up the journal and fold it shut.

She snorts. 'Not as old as this volcano!'

'Who's shouting?' Aula sits up next to me. She sees the woman and squints. Even only half awake, she gives her the most obvious up-down I've ever seen. 'Right. Sol's sister. I'm so glad we made it,' she says. She lies back down and closes her eyes.

'Where did you get that book?' the woman says. Aula's

right. She does look like Sol. Better fed, though. I can't tell if she's wild with anger or with excitement. 'Where did you get it?'

Aula doesn't move an inch but Etain and Joomia – on either side of us – do. They blink awake like they're emerging from cocoons.

'We found it,' I say.

'Have you read it? Can you translate it?'

I glance at Joomia. 'Er . . . she can . . . a bit.'

The woman whirls on her. 'Does it say anything about Kreywar's bones? Does it say where she put them?'

Joomia blinks. **Um . . . not that I—**

'She hasn't been able to translate all of it yet,' Etain says.

The woman makes a snarling noise of frustration.

And then comes Sol's voice, strained but better than he sounded last I heard him speak. 'Domaga, we don't need the journal. I've found something better. Or some*one*.' He adds, with a glance at me.

Her face changes. She hurries over to Sol. He's lying in what used be a long, thin canoe. The dried leaves and sand filling it make a kind of mattress. I guess that's her bed. I remember what Sol said. So his sister was banished, and she paddled here – in that? OK, I'm impressed.

I look around for more details. We're in some kind of cave, but not like one I've seen before. The walls around us are mottled grey, wrinkled and pitted like a lizard's skin. We've been sleeping on a kind of carpet made from feathers; I wonder if she made it herself. In a corner, there's a seriously dilapidated barrel which looks like it's full of water.

Then I glance behind me. The cave goes back further

than I can see — and I can't see much. The way is covered — floor to ceiling — in spider webs. Every size, shape and pattern, like a many-layered lace. Not one of them is empty either. Spinners of every size, shape, species. They're moving quickly, tapping threads, racing back and forth over the silks as if testing their strength. I take a few paces back. It feels a bit too much like coincidence to find spiders here, of all things.

'Like arachnids, huh?' I ask.

'What on Erthe—' Etain murmurs. 'What are they all doing here?'

'Guarding this place — the volcano, the tiny shore around it,' Domaga says. 'They've been here far longer than me. I have them to thank for guiding me here.'

'*Guiding you?*' Etain asks.

Domaga grunts. 'I have enough *skuld* blood in me to communicate with them. I was stranded out at sea, banished, nowhere to go, when I heard them calling me. You can imagine my disappointment when I got here and found out the call was not from any person.' She snorts at our faces, but I don't see any self-pity in her, just steeliness. 'Spiders like prophets. They like our energy the way moths enjoy light. They are drawn to it. I was never much of a prophet until the spiders found me. They have helped me with my visions.' She has her hands on Sol's chest, and I see spiders crawling up her wrist. 'And my wounds,' she adds, and I notice for the first time the splattered scar up her left leg and how she seems to be leaning on it as little as possible.

Domaga meets my eyes as I raise them hastily to her face. 'Sol says *you're* going to find the bones. You have a gift?'

'Yeah, he does,' Etain says, before I can answer. 'And speaking of those bones, I think we need to discuss what happens now.'

Aula grumbles and shuffles to her feet as if we've made her get up. 'Not without more sleep.'

Domaga gives her an approving look. 'I'm sorry I woke you,' she says gruffly. 'I was . . . excited. It has been a long time since I spoke to anyone. And I have been waiting to hold Lore's book for . . .' She takes a deep breath. 'It has been a long time. We . . . we can talk later. For now, sleep. Or wash, if you like. There are hot springs in the cave on the other side of this beach. It opens out on to the sea so the ones at the entrance are mixed with cooler water. Don't use the others. They'll be too hot.' From her strained expression, I'm guessing she thinks that we stink.

'What about Vulcan?' I ask. 'What if he finds us here?'

'My spiders will watch for him. They are always watching that horizon.'

I glance back at them. Are these the same type that I found crawling all over Ade? 'How do they do that?' I ask uncertainly.

'The same way a prophet might scry for someone they can't find. They are sensitive to the presence of magic, and anything that has it. There'll be time for more explanations later. Go on, now.'

Etain says, 'Your brother followed us here. Back on our island, my people are enslaved, being forced to cut down the trees of our island and harvest food we can't spare. We don't have time to wash. Or sleep.'

Aula mutters, 'Speak for yourself,' and I agree.

'You're the Anassa, then,' Domaga says.

Etain lowers her gaze. 'Not any more. But still I—'

'I know what you want, girl. It's written all over you. It's all right, I hear you. But give yourselves an hour or two to recover at least. Your friends look like they need it, even if you don't.'

Etain opens her mouth. And closes it. Wow. I haven't seen that happen in a long time.

'Is there food?' Aula asks hopefully.

Domaga looks amused as she says, 'There's some sweet root growing further up the cliffs. If you're fast enough, I suppose you might catch one of the cliff birds, or the lizards that like to swim further down the island . . .'

Aula smacks her hands together. 'Got it,' she declares. 'Come on, Taurus. Etain and Joomia can have their baths first.'

I trail after Aula. This place. It doesn't feel real. Or maybe I don't feel real. I'm the sort of tired that you need a week to get over.

Aula isn't. She scampers up the cliffs like a kid who drank too much sugar syrup. The birds Domaga mentioned are some kind of massive pelican with beady eyes and sleek grey feathers. Aula scares off the first few with her scrambling, but they come back when she investigates their nests, swinging at her with sharp beaks.

She climbs down looking put out, but not grumpy. 'I can't kill them. Never could, really,' she says. 'En't that cowardly? I always ate the sausages they made in Athenas. I never really thought about where they came from. Guess

the birds are gonna live another day. Do some more laying.'
She shrugs, holding out her bunched-up tunic to show me
twelve big blue eggs.

We walk a bit further along and Aula recognises the
lizards perching on the rocks some distance out. 'Marine
iguanas.' She leaves me with the eggs so she can get a closer
look. They're blotchy red except for their fat forelegs which
have a verdigris green to them. Even when she swims close,
the lizards aren't in the least bit interested in her.

I doze off on the sand for a bit, and only wake up when
she stands over me, grinning, water dripping generously
off her hair.

'How do you have all this energy?' I ask.

She dumps herself on the sand next to me and starts
to unwind the tangle of her hair from the back of her
head. 'I . . . I dunno for sure – Joomia and I haven't talked
about it yet, but I don't think we really need to eat that
much any more. Since we came out of the tree, even as
Nine. We still have to eat, but as long as we've got a lot of
sunlight and water . . .' She pulls a face. She knows how
weird it sounds.

'You're happy, being yourself again,' I say.

'Yeah. For however long it lasts.' She shrugs. 'I know
that's selfish. Cos of what's happening to our people. But I
reckon I have to enjoy the time I've got before Joomia and
me figure out how to put ourselves back together.'

I frown. 'Wait, what? Put yourselves back together?
Why?'

'Because of the prophecy, Taurus. *Unite* or there will be
nothing left to save.'

I shake my head. 'Aula, you've already fulfilled that prophecy. It's done. The trees are one, and they didn't split again just because you did.'

She shakes her head. 'But the *people* aren't united.'

I laugh. 'Did you expect the people to magically discover they liked each other?'

She chews her lip. 'No, I didn't. But I thought . . . I thought that us being Nine would help. I thought we'd end up being the symbol of unity they needed.' She pauses, and makes a face. 'I guess I thought we'd inspire them.' She sighs again, and begins to comb out her hair with her fingers.

I stare at the clouds. 'You did inspire them, Aula.'

She snorts.

'You *did*. But as far as I could tell, no one knew what to do with you two as Nine. I really think they felt guilty that you both had to give up who you were to save them. It would have almost been easier for them to process it if you'd died.'

She looks at me hopefully, and I'm glad I told her the truth rather than saying they missed her or some bullshit like that. She stares a little too long though.

'What?'

'Nothing. Are *you* happy that I'm myself again?'

'I've missed you.' Saying it feels like finally getting to lie down after standing up all day. I put my hand on her bare shoulder.

She leans to me, and I sit up. The air, just air before, goes supple and smooth between us. Her mouth is hot. I want that to be enough. It's not. My senses just about explode.

I want us both to be naked. I want to feel all my skin against all of hers. It's good to know that she's like me, that she wants that just as much as I—

'No,' she says and pulls away. She's not angry or anything. The *no* is like I've asked her if she needs salt on her food. My body aches.

'You don't want me?' I ask, trying not to sound hurt.

She laughs. 'Yeah, I do. But you're tired, and it doesn't matter to you who you have sex with right now. You just want a distraction from all the shit bubbling away in there.' She presses her finger between my eyebrows.

'I thought . . . I thought *you* needed distracting,' I say. I hear the pleading note in my voice and sit up, feeling disgusted with myself. We're silent for a while. The lizards aren't as charming to watch this side of her kiss.

'Aula,' I say. 'I don't know who I am.'

She picks up my hand and holds it in both of hers. 'Yeah. I know how that feels.'

'Is that why you like me?'

She pulls a face. 'Not just that.'

I think about that. 'But you hardly spoke to me. When you were Nine. And on the boat, you never touched me.'

'You wanted us to have sex on the boat in front of Joomia and Etain and Sol?'

'You know what I mean.'

'I wasn't *me* when I was Nine. The feelings were kind of curdled. And the boat . . . we were all just trying to get here, you know? We all needed our own head space.'

'I felt calm,' I say. 'Not all the time, obviously. Mainly the ocean's worn something away, washed something out.'

'Yes,' she says sadly.

'Aula. I don't want you and Joomia to become Nine again. I want you to be you. And her to be her.'

'Don't, Taurus,' she says. 'You'll ruin my happiness.'

'Well, you're *my* happiness.'

She looks at me stonily. 'Don't do that, Taurus. Don't turn me into your one thing.'

'I'm not.'

'You are. Listen, if I had my way I'd have stocked up on my maps the second Vulcan split us, and I'd have taken my own boat and been heading for anywhere else. You don't know what it's like. To have been two-as-one . . . this *relief* at being myself again.' She stares out toward the horizon. 'When we get out of this latest catastrophe, if I get the chance . . . I just want to be on my own for a while. Sail the Erthe. See if anything's left.'

'Why shouldn't you? Let's save the island. And then let's go away; you and me on a boat we build ourselves. I'll be your compass and you can be mine,' I say.

We both look at each other.

Do you need a compass, Aula?

She twines our fingers together. 'It sounds nice,' she says.

'But . . .' I say, because I can hear one.

'But . . . maybe it's time we learned to be our own.'

Etain

The island has a heavy heat. Perhaps it's the lack of trees taller than my hip, or the abundance of hot springs, or the

248

plain heat of the magma rising from beneath the earth, but it feels hard to breathe. We find the cave with the rock pools easily enough. When we step inside, the steam is so thick I can't see my hand.

Joomia sighs in relief, but I back out quickly, seeing smoke, seeing flames, feeling fire.

Etain?

To my horror, tears needle at the back of my eyes, a lump rising in my throat. I see the bodies of my people laid out before the council tent. The steam follows me. I break into a run and don't stop until I feel the sea washing against my ankles.

Etain, are you all right?

I look back at her. 'I'm fine,' I say, but my voice wavers and my knees don't want to straighten out. 'I just think . . . I'll just wash in the sea. You go on.'

She puts her hand on my shoulder. I know that she's going to say she'll stay with me. Without warning, my memory pushes up an image of her washing on the trimaran: the smooth winged movements of her shoulder blades as she lathered the soap nuts. My face and chest heat.

I feel her hand on my neck. **Etain.**

I pull away. 'Honestly, Joomia. I'm fine. You go on.'

She looks a little hurt, but she nods. **OK.**

I take off my clothes and wade into the surf. My muscles stiffen in the cold, but that's fine. Anything but heat. I scoop handfuls of sand from the bottom and scrub my body. Even after I've washed away the grime of the last two weeks, I don't feel clean. My skin is a battlefield. Years and years of smithing burns all over my hands, the messy knot of scar tissue where one of the mindless's arrows went into my arm. Now this handprint across my stomach.

I never used to care. I still have bracelets I made to show off my burns scars. Even though the arrow wound cost me my hammer arm, I was still a little proud of it. I thought it could be my badge: I *earned* the right to be their leader. Here was my scar. I *fought* for *all* my people. I had so much confidence in who Ma told me I was going to be.

Who was that girl? I wonder. I think about what Sol said: *You think you're done being their leader* . . .

It's time to decide. I'm awake, and we survived the storm, and we're here. So who will I become? Someone who'll do anything to save her people? Or someone who'll do anything to claim a role I thought was meant for me, but might not have been?

I wait for Joomia on the sand, and then we walk back to the cave together.

How are you feeling? she asks, looking better for the wash.

The choli she wears covers her upper body, but I know she's got her own scars there. Her arm and shoulder blade have taken arrows that would have poured out my life. When I meet her eyes, I find myself wishing I were the kind of person who could burst into tears and sob on her shoulder.

'Better. Clearer.'

She smiles. **It's always good to be clean.**

'Thank you, Joomia,' I say. 'I'm sorry.'

She smiles tiredly. **You don't have to apologise.**

'You saved my life.'

She snorts.

'What?'

Come on, Etain. I would have done that for anyone. *You* would have done that for anyone. If you want to say sorry, say sorry for being angry with me when I was trying to help you. For trying to speed us along when we were trying to help Sol. For spending the last two weeks . . . She pauses. She's said it all gently, quietly. What she says en't barbed with resentment or bitterness. She's just being . . . honest.

'For spending the last two weeks being a self-pitying brat?' I say forcefully, trying to make it sound bracing. 'It's all right, I understand. I apologise.'

But she's already shaking her head. Don't be the Anassa with me. Be my friend. You *are* my friend, aren't you?

I stare at her. 'I'm sorry, Joomia,' I say at last.

She sighs. I know you are, Etain. It's not your fault. You were just built that way.

For some reason, that stings the worst. *You were just built that way.* It's not wrong, I was. But—

'I didn't want to be,' I say. 'I *don't* want to be—'

'Hey, Chosen One.' Domaga is limping towards us. 'Is it true you're the girl to come to if I need a healer?'

While Joomia goes to look at Sol, I sit with Domaga in the entrance of the cave and rest my eyes for a moment. She doesn't say anything, only hands me a bowl of cloudy-looking juice. I sip it. It's sharp and summery, fragrant. I watch Taurus and Aula wander towards us from the other side of the beach.

Domaga turns to me. 'You said my brother was close.'

I glance at the horizon. 'He didn't have Taurus as a guide, and we lost him during a storm.'

She shakes her head. 'Vulcan is a good navigator. I assume you've seen what else he can do.'

I know what he can do; I just don't want to think of it that much. I hope Domaga's spiders are doing a good job of watching for any sign of him.

Aula comes to sit next to me, and Taurus goes to make something with the eggs they brought back. Domaga looks about to protest, in politeness or protectiveness, I'm not sure. Aula says, 'Let him do it, you won't regret it. Can I have some of that juice?'

Domaga nods without looking away from me. 'Sol told me he came here for the bones,' she says. 'But that is beyond him for now. Is it your intention to go in his place?'

My heart dithers on a beat. A part of me insists I haven't thought about it. Another says that I was always intending to go, with or without Sol.

'Yeah, I am,' I say.

Aula eyeballs me, but I don't look at her. She sighs and says, 'We're all going.'

'How fortunate that one of you is a compass who can point to anything you want, then,' Domaga continues. 'The last time I tried, I got this for my trouble.' She gestures at the bulbous scar on her leg. 'Now I can't even walk properly. I was lost in the tunnels for days – I nearly starved to death.'

'How did you get out?' Aula asks.

'The spiders guided me,' she says.

I say, 'The spiders on my island. They seemed to . . . take possession of someone I know. Was that you?'

'Oh, your prophet with the scattered mind,' Domaga says. 'Yes, that was me. My spiders had detected such a powerful disturbance; I thought I had to investigate. I don't absolutely understand *how* I managed to project myself through her – I think we were both trying to scry and it seems our magics collided. She told me your cities had united. She told me Lore's spell protecting Chloris had broken.'

'She knew about it?'

'She was aware of it, yes. She managed to convince your island's spiders to protect those incredible trees Lore planted, didn't she? And covered them with impenetrable vines?'

'Can't even cut through the vines with an axe,' Taurus says.

She smiles wryly. 'Do you understand why she did it now? Have you seen what Vulcan's ants can do to trees?'

Aula glances at me. How often has Ade proved she shouldn't be underestimated? How long will it be before I finally get the message?

'Could you see the island *now* if you wanted to?' I ask. 'Could you see what's happening?'

She nods. 'I looked while you were asleep. Your people are still being held and being made to work. I can't give you specifics about their individual wellbeing. The spiders are not the best spies with Vulcan's ants running around.'

'I don't get it,' Aula says. 'You can communicate with spiders because you're a prophet? You en't an Etheling as well?'

Domaga smiles, showing a gap in her teeth. 'Bless you, no. Nor is Vulcan. There hasn't been a true Etheling on Govinda for a long time.'

'*What?* So how can he do the things he does?'

'You didn't see his arm? When our family realised that

it might not be *us* who produced the next Etheling for the island, it threatened our power. We stole from our ancestors' graves and implanted the bones in ourselves. And the bones kind of got . . . passed down.'

I wrinkle my nose. 'To you as well?'

She laughs. 'No, no. Not under my grandfather and then my father's reign. That honour was for the eldest son. Certainly not for a girl.'

'What do you mean?'

She stares at me wonderingly. 'You have no idea, do you? No idea. Do you know what people in the Old World thought about women?'

'Yes,' I say uncomfortably. No one likes to talk about it much, the same way no one likes to talk about what the Old World people thought about race, back when race meant something different, segregated. I used to have nightmares about it when I was little. But that's all. Nightmares. Not *real*.

Only, I see in this woman's face it is real, and I think of Sol and how suspicious he was at our reaction – or, I guess, lack of reaction – when we found out he was an *iphis*.

'There were some people in Athenas who still had those ideas,' Aula says glumly. 'It's a sticky thing to shake, I guess.'

Domaga holds out her left hand to show me a scar on her middle finger. 'I slipped a knuckle bone from my great-grandmother's grave, just after Sol killed our father and I took the blame.'

'You *gave yourself* a bone implant?' Aula asks incredulously. 'On your *hand*?'

Domaga shrugs. 'I certainly tried to. I thought it would be my escape. If I had Vulcan's power, I could have had those volcanic ants build me a ship. Oh, yes – they live here too. They live anywhere where there is volcanic activity. But the implant didn't work. It just wasn't the right shape for my hand, and obviously the pain was . . .' She licks her lips and lets out a long breath. 'I didn't get very far with it, in the end. Enough to give myself this scar but no further.'

'So how does your thing with the spiders work?' Taurus asks.

'Like I said, I can't command them, as Vulcan would,' she says. 'His influence is directly through the ant queen – he controls her, she controls them. But with the spiders – through the *skuld* magic that gives me prophecy – I connect to them individually. I can speak to them. We have an understanding . . . I got them to trust me. My cooking and my body heat brings in their prey. Spiders don't have a hive mind – nothing like that – but they are connected. The ones on this island and the ones on yours. They have a kind of natural *skuld* magic.'

The trees have that too, Joomia says, still tending to Sol.

Domaga goes on. 'Their webs helped me to see what was happening on your island – and on mine. It takes a lot of practice to read the webs correctly, but I've gotten the basics down. It is a little like scrying in water.'

Taurus brings out the food then. It's delicious, as usual. I can never figure out where his instincts come from to put all those elements together. Domaga gives him an appraising look.

'This finding ability of yours . . .'

255

Taurus looks up from shovelling eggs into his mouth. 'Sorry, what?'

'Your compass power. How does it work?'

He swallows. 'Oh. I don't know, really. I wasn't really conscious of it until Ade showed me how.'

'You didn't tell me that,' I say, surprised. I assumed he'd taught himself.

He shrugs. 'You had leader stuff to do.' Which means I wasn't paying attention.

Domaga says, 'But to look for Kreywar's bones – am I right in thinking you will need a heading?'

Taurus chews his lip. 'Maybe. Lore's map helped me to guide us here. I'm better at finding people if I know them already. If it's an object it helps if I've handled it a bit.' He tilts his head, thinking. 'I reckon I know quite a lot about Lore now, and she's the one who put the bones there—'

Sol lets out a yell.

There's a sudden, grinding noise from deep in the earth, like two giant molars scraping together.

'Move,' Domaga says. 'Move! Get off the sand!'

I don't even get to ask what she means before the ground starts shaking.

The Chosen

Instinctively, Joomia shoots out her hand and lifts the others into the curls of the vines at the entrance. She braces one hand against Sol's cot and a foot against the wall of the cave—

The next moment, Aula is at her side. She throws an arm

over Joomia's head, another over Sol's collarbones and holds them still as the cave rattles. Joomia takes a deep breath, reshapes her grip on the vine-hook she'd been using to dislodge the arrowhead, and pulls the sharp stone the rest of the way out.

It's a few minutes before everything is still again. Aula and Joomia unfold themselves from the brace of the wall and, while Aula hastens to pick everything up that's fallen on the floor of the cave, Joomia rinses her hands and resumes her mini-surgery.

'What do you think of her?' Aula asks, nodding toward Domaga at the cave door.

Joomia bites her lip, and begins to sew the wound together swiftly, making room for the spiders working on the web magic (or, she thinks ruefully, whatever the hell kind of magic it is) inside to climb out. **There's something strange going on,** Joomia says reluctantly. **There's a distractedness about her. A yearning, and not necessarily a healthy one. I don't know what it means.**

'What the hell was that?!' yells Taurus, and Aula shoots a hasty look over her shoulder. 'Joomia, we're all right – you can let us down now!'

'You mean . . .' Aula muses, 'you don't think she wants to help us?'

Joomia's reply is measured. **She wants to help us. But there's something hurting inside her. She's like Taurus. She's angry that she has no power to change the world around her.**

'Er . . . Joomia? Can you let us down?' calls Etain now.

Aula makes a scoffing noise. 'That sounds a bit grand for Taurus, don't you think?'

257

Joomia smirks. **Well, you ought to know.**

Aula flushes, but she should have known. Sharing a brain, sharing a body, has removed all secrecy between them. 'Shut up. But seriously.'

Joomia snaps the thread with her teeth and gestures for the vines to unload their captors. **I don't know, Aula. It's hard to tell with him. He's good at hiding himself. Just . . . just keep an eye on him, I guess.**

'Gotcha,' Aula murmurs.

OK, I'm done, I think. I hope it heals properly.

'I think it will,' Aula says. 'There's a deep magic in this place. Do you know what I mean?'

Joomia does. It is almost as if the island is just as aware of them as they of it, though perhaps she and Aula are more sensitive to it than the others.

Aula goes on: 'I feel like it's sunk into everything. Maybe that's what's made the spiders take on a kind of prophet power, and talk to Domaga. It's like—'

Like the vishaal trees, Joomia says, nodding.

'Yes! Exactly like that!'

A magic source, Joomia says, contemplating what that means. **Well, we'll see. I still think we should ask Domaga for alcohol, or honey to bathe the wound. Just in case.**

'Waste of good drink,' Aula mutters, but she still raises her voice to shout: 'Domaga!'

Etain

In the night, Sol wakes up.

I'm closest to him, so I take the water skin Domaga left us and help him drink.

He manages a few sips before he starts to cough and splutter.

'You're tipping the skin wrong,' he says. 'You have to go slower.'

I pull in my lips and hold it steady until he holds up a hand. Somehow, I still manage to spill it all over him.

'You're no good at this, are you?'

'At what?'

'Looking after sick people.'

I'm a bit ashamed it's that obvious. Sick people make me nervous, since Ma.

'I thought you'd be heading into the volcano by now to find the bones,' he says.

A nervous, hot feeling of shame creeps over my back. This was Sol's plan, and instead I'm using it selfishly. But he's in no state to go anywhere. Before the rest of us went to sleep we agreed we'd get a few hours' rest and then leave to find them. We can't wait much longer – Vulcan could still turn up any time. 'I'm sorry. I know it was supposed to be you.'

He shrugs. 'Like I said, my ma didn't See *me* doing it. Just getting here. As long as we get the bones, I'm happy.' His eyes are a lot brighter now, less bloodshot. Someone's put his necklaces back on.

'I'm sorry I was such a bitch on the boat,' I say.

'You put getting away from my brother ahead of my life,' he says. 'That's nothing to be sorry for. That's just weighing one life against four. You need to start owning

259

your decisions, Anassa.'

I fold my arms. 'How do *you* do it?'

'Stop listening to other people. Stop letting them tell you what to do. I mean, take advice, of course, but you have to realise you don't have to listen to everyone's emotional undercurrent. You just have to let them hate you sometimes.'

'How do *you* know all this?'

He smiles. 'My mother knew about good leadership. She kept the Govindan prophets strong. She let me know I wasn't alone. She raised Domaga and me. But she knew when to let go. She knew when to batten down the hatches of herself and just do what needed to be done.'

I press my lips together. He sees.

'Your problem is, you don't know when to open the hatches. Can I tell you something?'

'I think we both know you're going to anyway,' I say.

He grins. 'See what I mean? You're clever, and you're good at observing people – maybe too good, cos it seems to have given you a bit of a blind eye to yourself. So here's my little observation. Call it a gift – you do what you like with it.'

I raise an eyebrow. 'Um . . . thanks?'

He leans in. 'Your friend Joomia over there?' We both look at her, sleeping on her side, her breathing as soft and even as Aula's is loud and irregular. 'You're in love with her.'

Maybe it's cos I'm tired, but I don't fend off the assertion as I'd usually do. Those words go echoing deep beneath my skin. They ring for a long time, like they're looking for somewhere to lodge. And then I feel a place somewhere inside me – somewhere I don't usually go to – open up, and reply.

It just says, *Yeah, I know*, but I feel as if I've managed to pick out a splinter that's wedged in deep and swelling everything around it. And I let out a little sigh of relief.

Sol nods, watching my face. But I won't reply – that part of me is private, not for him, even if he brought it to the fore. I say, 'Are you in love, Sol?'

He smiles. 'On Govinda, there is someone who loves me. He helped me escape. He made me the necklaces that disguised me as various people along the journey over to your island. But I will not see him again if we don't find those bones. If we can't make more land.'

I take the opportunity to admit something. 'That's been worrying me, Sol.'

'What has?'

'Well, now I know about the bone magic your people have been using – now I know the powers Vulcan has aren't even naturally his . . . I thought I could trade the bones for my people's freedom. Would he leave peacefully then?'

His expression hardens.

I hurry on: 'But if I give them to him, you can't use them to make more land. How will we both have the outcome we want?'

As I'm saying it I realise I'm being slow. Of *course* the most obvious answer would be to split the bones between us. I'm about to say it too, but something about his hesitation makes me bite it back. Something curdles in my stomach.

'I should've guessed,' I say softly. 'You were going to

trick us, weren't you? Have you been working with your brother the whole time?'

Sol raises an eyebrow. 'I know you were in the water for a lot of the time, but I assume you *heard* what my brother thinks of me? He'd as likely work with me as—' I stare at him and he lets out his breath sharply. 'Fine. Yes. I was going to trick you. My people need more land. They deserve the chance Lore gave your people. They deserve the chance to start again.'

'And that chance is worth my people's freedom? Worth the cost of our lives and our homes?'

I can see in his face that the answer is yes. I let out my breath heavily. 'I guess I'd do the same in your situation.'

We're silent for a minute or two. I imagine the cogs turning slick as oil in his head. Then he says, 'Well. I won't pretend I wasn't nervous about double-crossing you. Especially with your titans there.' He eyes Aula and Joomia. Then he says, 'Do you have an alternative?'

I decide to say it. 'Well . . . we could split the bones? I'm sure there will be more than enough.'

He looks uncertain. 'It's crossed my mind before now,' he says. 'And perhaps it would work . . . but what happens then, Etain? Vulcan already has control of your people – why would he give that up just for bones that *you* say are Kreywar's?'

'He could test them,' I point out.

'Yeah, and then he's got bones that can make land, *and* your island, *and* mine.' He grimaces. 'I've been an idiot. I kept imagining that I'd return to Govinda with a land-making bone in my arm or my leg and everyone would

262

follow me instead of him. But it's not that simple, I can see that now.' His sigh is ragged. 'You can't trade with him, Etain. It wouldn't work. If you'd met my father, if you'd lived with my people, you'd see. Men like him see compromise as weakness.' He pinches the bridge of his nose and exhales hard. 'I think . . . I think we're going to have to fight him. I think we'll have to, one way or another, or a lot more of your people will end up like Astor and a lot more of your trees will get cut down.'

It comes to me before I've really considered the implications. 'What if I brought you all over to Chloris?' I ask. 'There's space and resources. I'm not saying it would be comfortable – or easy to get your people over under your brother's nose – but if you're so determined to save them I'm guessing they can't all be as bad as him. Would you do that? Would you help me fight him then?'

He looks at me long and hard. 'Are you sure you've thought that through, Anassa? Your people certainly wouldn't like it. What if mine tried to impose their patriarchal ideas on you? You would not last long as their leader then.'

'I didn't last long anyway,' I point out. It's the truth, but it hurts to say it. 'My people might not have a patriarchy, but we do have our own shit. We will find a way.'

He shakes his head. 'You are in grave danger of becoming an idealist.'

'Look who's talking,' I snap. 'What was it you said? *I'm not prophesied to be anyone's saviour, but I'm gonna try to save mine anyway; and if I can help you save yours, even better?*'

He laughs. 'Even with an arrow wound, I'm a good actor.'

263

I don't believe that, though.

'What do you think?' he continues. 'Can we work together?' He shifts, adjusting his position on the pallet. 'Can you trust *me*?'

I bite my lip, thinking. The silence goes on and on. 'I'll try,' I say at last.

'Come here, then.'

I hesitate and he laughs.

'It is our custom, to seal a deal. I'm not going to cut your hand off.'

I have to lean over him. He grips the back of my head and grasps my hand. Then he brings our faces together.

'What are you doing?'

'Keep still! This is our gesture – you must stare into my eyes, and I yours, until our tears mix.'

I snort. 'For a culture obsessed with masculinity, that seems a very emotional way to seal the deal.'

'That is the point. It symbolises vulnerability.'

That shuts me up. The word *vulnerability* often makes me think of Taurus, and how tender and emotional he tends to be. At least, when he's not with me and I'm pushing him away when he starts with his questions about Ma. The tears fall then, and I'm not sure if they're real or because my eyes are still open.

When it's done, I sit on the edge of the canoe-bed for a while, just to think. Sol doesn't seem to mind. Eventually, his breathing evens. I'm about to go and lie back down when he whispers, 'You should say something to her.'

Joomia. 'I thought you said I could do what I liked with that,' I say. But he doesn't answer.

My eyes find Joomia. She rolls on to her back and for a moment, her eyes flutter, and she's looking up at me. She smiles, and then closes her eyes again.

Taurus

The compass point is jittery when I reach for it, like a kid waiting for someone to shout *go*.

I'm still clawing my way to properly awake. As a kind of practice-run I ask, sleepily, for the compass to show me something that will make land. It points straight at Sol. He's still lying on Domaga's boat-bed and at that moment is making a tiny sand island in the centre of a bowl of the same tangy fruit juice Domaga served us yesterday.

I shake myself. I didn't know the compass had my sense of humour. OK, so more specific.

Bones. I'm looking for Kreywar's bones.

'So the legend is they're *under* the volcano?' I ask.

'Yes,' Domaga and Sol say at the same time. Sol looks a lot better this morning than he did before that weird earthquake. Domaga said casually that they happen every now and then. My estimation of her went up a couple of notches.

'Do you ever worry about what happens if the volcano erupts?' I ask.

'It does, sometimes. But the eruptions are small, and it's never got me.'

'Don't you worry it might?'

'In a few hours, I won't have to,' she points out.

'What are you going to do when we trade the bones with your brother?'

'Hope the effort of using them will kill him stone dead or instead I'll lead my people in a revolution against him. I haven't decided yet.'

'You don't like answering questions.'

Domaga just smiles, then looks beyond me, to Etain, fastening on her tool belt. It's been a while since I saw her wearing it, but it reminds me of a happier version of her.

'Are you planning on some smith work while you're in there?' Domaga asks.

Etain shrugs. 'You never know. What if the bones are buried under rock?' She obviously hasn't slept, but she looks determined. 'Are you ready?' she asks me.

She, Aula and Joomia all turn to look at me. Am I ready? Like I haven't been waiting for such a moment for ever.

I take a deep breath. I sink inside myself. *Bones*, I think, trying to imagine Lore with them in her hands. For a moment, it's like I really do see her. She's walking along this shore. Thin and sea-washed and gritty with sand. Her face is blank with grief. The bones are in a sack slung across her torso. She's walking towards—

I open my eyes.

'This way,' I say. I realise my finger's pointing right at the wall of spider webs.

Domaga frowns. 'That way's blocked. There was a cave-in a little while back. It happens sometimes. Well – you felt the ground shake yesterday.'

Aula cracks her knuckles. 'No problem,' she says. 'But I don't want to hurt the spiders. Can you ask them to move?'

266

Domaga looks a bit scandalised, but after a minute she nods. She hobbles to the wall of webs and murmurs something. The spiders shudder like the earth is shaking again. There's a pause. And then they scatter, shooting silk to get to the ground or else flitting along the walls of the cave, too fast to track. 'I warned the spiders about Vulcan's ants,' she murmurs. 'Good luck in there.'

She isn't coming with us? Joomia says.

At the same time Aula asks, 'You aren't coming with us too?'

Domaga pats her bad leg wryly. 'I've learned my lesson there. Someone must stay with Sol. And I trust you'll want a warning should my brother show up?'

'I was going to mention that,' Etain acknowledges, nodding. 'Thank you. But I can't help wondering why you're trusting us to do this.'

Domaga shrugs. 'I don't know yet. But someone has to make the first move, don't they?'

Etain gives her a small smile.

'Thank me when you bring out the bones,' Domaga says. 'Now go on. Look after each other. And watch out for holes in the floor, unless you want to come out with a leg like mine.'

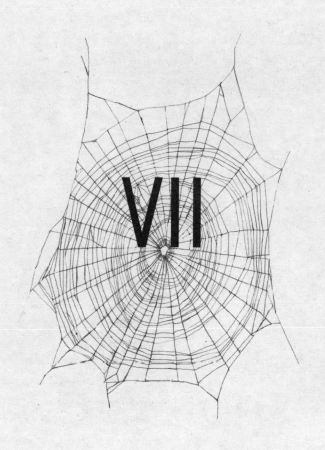

Etain

Once we've ducked under the cobwebs, taking quite a few of them with us, the way opens out on to a long, low passage. It gets darker the further we walk, but once we've made a few turns the walls take on a faint luminescence.

I find myself smiling at the veins of glowing, phosphorescent mineral embedded in the rock – just like those inside the passages to Ariadnis. It's so familiar that for the first time since we left the island, I feel a *rightness* about what we're doing.

We come to the cave-in that Domaga was talking about: a spectacular cascade of sharp, porous rock. There's no visible gap in the boulders. Aula scampers up and down them, muttering to herself, knocking on rocks and the wall itself. Joomia casts seeds at her feet, creating thin leafless vines to grow rapidly into the cracks around the boulders and feel out the air flow, testing for weaknesses. These two can get us past anything.

Eventually Aula says, 'I think I should move the rocks right at the top, if I can.'

Joomia's vines wilt, shrivelling back into the seeds she cast. She picks them up, eyes them and puts them back in her bag. **Still good for a few more growths,** she says to herself. **Yeah, I think you're right, Aula.** A moment later Aula is grunting from the top of the pile of boulders and hefting some of the smaller ones out of the way.

While we're waiting, Joomia moves back a few paces to stand next to me. She's probably only doing it to get out of the way of any falling rock, but it makes Sol's words about her rise in my mind; further up than I've allowed them since I woke.

My hand moves before I've decided if it's a good idea. I rest the tips of my fingers on Joomia's left elbow. It's an innocent place to touch her – not her shoulder, which would be too friendly, or her hand, which would be too intimate. But it's definitely an *unnecessary* place. For a long time, I resist looking up at her.

When I do, her face is burning with something. I hold her gaze. My heart gallops. Her lips part.

Then Taurus shouts as Aula shifts a much larger rock and it rolls down towards us, breaking the moment, even though it gets nowhere near us.

My pulse is still humming when Aula says, 'I don't wanna move too many more. It'll be a squeeze, but I reckon that's as good a space as we're gonna get.'

Stupid. I scold myself. *Concentrate. This is what you're supposed to be doing.*

One by one, we manoeuvre our way up the rocks and scramble through. On the other side, the air is closer, hotter.

The tunnel looks pretty much the same, though it's narrower, and the walls slope at strange angles, but it's eerie to think that no one has walked along here for a long time, possibly since Lore herself.

We reach a fork in the tunnel about half an hour later. Taurus strides confidently ahead, turning left. I can see now how easy it must have been for Domaga to get lost in here.

It's a labyrinth: passages lead only to more passages, turning this way and that. But Taurus isn't hesitant. He knows. It gets a little darker, the minerals more sporadic. When I raise a hand to my forehead, it comes away damp.

Another fork. Left, right and forwards. This time, Taurus hesitates a moment and closes his eyes, breathing deeply. He holds out his hand, like he's dowsing for water. 'Straight on,' he mutters. 'Is there any water left?'

No one answers.

I chew my lip. I drank the last of mine just after we climbed the rocks.

Joomia puts her hand on the cave wall, as if to steady herself. **It will be all right. We can go back now, if we want to.**

No one says anything to that either.

'There's less light further on,' Taurus says. 'Careful of the floor. It's rougher too, I think.'

Domaga said there might be holes, Joomia reminds us. **Be careful, Taurus.**

We walk on in silence.

Taurus's prediction comes true at once: the mineral in the walls grows fainter. Minutes later, Taurus lets out a strangled cry that's cut off as Aula darts forward and yanks him back by the scruff of his neck. It sounds like Joomia's warning has come true too.

We shuffle forward carefully as Taurus points at the floor. The hole in front of us is the kind of black that swallows colour and sound.

'It might only be a couple of feet down,' Taurus says, but he doesn't sound convinced.

'Yeah, or a hundred,' Aula says. 'Look, there's the other side. It's not far.'

And without more warning than that, she swings Taurus into her arms like she's holding a baby, backs up a few paces, and takes a running leap.

'I could have made that myself,' we hear him muttering on the other side. 'I'm *Metisian*.'

Aula says something disparaging, and Joomia's hand finds mine in the dark.

'Watch out!' Aula calls. 'I'm coming back!'

I free my hand and fold my arms. *Concentrate, Etain.*

Aula lands close by. 'Who's next?'

Taurus steps more carefully after that. There are a few more holes in the floor, but none of them are too vast to cross alone. I lose count of the forks in the tunnel. Without Taurus, we'll never find our way out. How long have we been down here? An hour? Ten?

My belly shrinks with nervous fear.

'This is just *classic* Lore,' Aula says abruptly. 'What *is* it with her and dark caves?'

She's trying to lighten the mood, but her voice sounds strange and isolated, and the humour doesn't quite stretch to cover us. We walk on. And on. And on.

I don't realise how hot it's got until a dribble of sweat runs down from between my shoulder blades to the small of my back. My mouth feels dry and papery. The tunnel's been narrowing for a while now, and we've been forced to go single file, Taurus in front, then me, Aula and Joomia.

I put my hand on Taurus's shoulder and he's just as sweaty as I am.

'T?'

'Nearly there,' Taurus says. 'I think we're nearly there – they're somewhere along this corridor.'

Light flares in the gloom, just as Taurus swears and jumps back. I try to catch him, but the heat makes me slow. He slips through my hands and cracks his head on the floor.

'Taurus! Are you—'

'Fine,' he mutters, sitting up and rubbing his head vigorously. 'It sounded worse than it feels.'

Ants, Joomia says, squinting at the ground warily. **Like Vulcan's ants.**

I worm around Taurus and hobble forward in a squat to look. They're brilliant red, but light shines beneath their hard exoskeleton, brighter even than the minerals. It makes my eyes hurt just looking at them, even with only a few, trailing in a line from one tiny hole in the tunnel wall to another huge hole in the floor. They're carrying large pieces of rock on their backs, at least twenty times their size. 'Strong, en't they?' I say. I take another shuffling step forward and peer down into the hole. 'I think . . . I think there's lava down there. I can almost see it. Be careful coming forward. It's a big gap, but if we—'

Joomia screams. **Etain! Get back!**

Something bright bursts over my head in an arc of heat and thunder. Aula yanks Taurus out of the way, and I stumble to my feet— Obviously, *obviously* the smart thing to do is to retreat. But for some reason, my split-second reaction tells me there's no time. No time to go back.

I don't have a choice.

I jump.

Taurus

Lava.

The white-hot molten rock hits Aula's arm and covers the left side of her body. She shrieks. I don't see Etain at all.

No no no no no—

There's three of us screaming:

'ETAIN!'

'Etain!'

ETAIN!

I grab Aula's hand and pull her towards me, staring at the lavafall, looking for Etain – praying Aula's all right – praying that somehow Etain isn't beneath that swirling, smoking rock.

Taurus! Back up, back up down here—

'But – Etain! We have to find her!'

Aula lets out a feeble snarl. I stare at her left side, trying to see how badly she's hurt through the soot. But . . . but there's nothing. No hideous burn. No injury. She's a Chosen One, and she's fine.

We stumble backwards down the tunnel.

And then – just as quickly as it came in waves over us – the lava stops, as if a tap above has been shut off.

I stand up and risk one step forward again. 'Etain!'

Now the pouring lava has cleared, I can see her – just

— on the other side of the hole in the floor. She grunts, heaves herself up.

'I'm – I'm OK,' Etain says hoarsely. 'It didn't get me.'

I start to shake. Aula gasps. A strange, strangled sound shudders out of her. She's *laughing*. I see something dripping from her arm. What *was* – what *should* be – lava, isn't lava any more.

It's . . .

Sap, Joomia gasps. **It's *sap*.**

'It didn't *feel* like sap,' Aula says. 'It *felt* like it should hurt . . . but it didn't.'

I start to laugh too, in relief, I think. Though I could just be hysterical.

Are you really all right, Etain? Joomia calls.

'Yeah,' Etain says, sounding like she's also on the edge of hysteria. 'I jumped. I didn't think. I just . . . jumped.' She looks herself over, as if she can't believe it. 'I'm not hurt.'

'So . . . so it's not really lava?' I ask, looking at Aula again.

'Oh no. It's real,' Aula says. She squints back at it. The heat's still there, but nowhere near what it was. 'It just . . . didn't burn me.'

The vishaal tree, Joomia says suddenly. **It was the vishaal trees. We came out of them, and the vishaal trees—**

'Don't burn,' Aula says. 'Lore's guarding her hubby's bones pretty fiercely, isn't she? What a bitch.' But she sounds approving.

We just sit there for a while, then Etain gets to her feet. 'Taurus. Shall I carry on along this way?'

'I guess I'll have to find another way around,' I say.

Etain looks surprised. 'Why?'

'Well, you can't go *on*.'

'Why not? I'm fine, look.'

'Yeah, but how will you find your way back?'

Joomia steps hesitantly up to the precipice of the hole, right where Etain was standing before the lava came.

Seconds later, the lavafall yawns into life, once more arcing over us, flooding into the hole between us and Etain. To my surprise, Joomia reaches out toward it. I shout to warn her – I can't help it – but when she touches it, she only grimaces. When she takes her hand away, her hand is dripping sap, just like Aula.

After another minute, Joomia comes back along the tunnel and the lava stops. She swings around and considers the hole. **Etain's standing right on the edge on the other side. Surely, if Lore wanted to trap her *on* that side, there would be a trigger for the lava there too. But it seems to only be here. Even then, there's a few seconds before it comes, and Aula only got hit because she was reaching for Etain.** She pauses. **I think, if you take it at a run, Etain, you should be all right. You can get back. Aula and I can stay on this side to catch you.**

Aula lets out a morose noise. We all turn to look at her. 'But we're so close,' she says with an impish look.

They are. And Joomia and Aula can get across without being hurt. It's just me that's stuck here. I don't have a choice. I have to let them go on without me. I stare at them. Then at Etain. 'I thought . . . I thought you were . . .'

'I know,' Etain says. 'But I'm all right.'

She's still trembling, but there's tight, panicked fervour in her eyes. The same look that made her tell Joomia to leave Sol when we were out of the storm. She's fixated:

there's one goal and no obstacle's too great.

'I can find another way,' I say again. 'I'm the *compass*.' But it sounds weak. There *is* no other way. Sometimes the compass thing shows more than one way. Not this time.

The look Etain gives me. For a second, I hate her. I really hate her.

I shrug. 'Guess I've served my purpose, huh?'

'Don't do that, Taurus,' she says. 'It's not like that.'

'What am I supposed to do?' I ask. 'Sit here? *Wait* here, worrying that you might fall into *another* lavafall?'

Etain shakes her head. 'If there's anything more I can't handle, I'll come back, and Aula or Joomia can—'

'Right. Sure. Sure,' I say. 'So you're all going. And I'll wait for you. Be my own compass, right, Aula?'

'Stop being an idiot,' Etain snaps.

She doesn't get it. I don't get it either. I've done what the prophecy says I'll do. I've guided her. My part's over. But it feels like it's too soon. It's not enough.

'I just thought—' I begin, but she cuts across me.

'We're here for our people, not so you can feel useful.'

A little explosion pops in my chest. 'But when exactly *am* I useful, Etain? When we were kids and you were pissed off with Ma and needed someone to take it out on? When Joomia was too scared to act cos of something she couldn't control when she was a kid? Or when Aula needed the reassurance of me taking her to bed?'

Hard silence. Aula kisses her teeth. 'Firstly, you're one to talk. Secondly, this en't the time for you to have an identity crisis. We all have our stuff. We can hash this out all you like, but not right now.'

'We all have our stuff,' I say. 'Right. Like when you poisoned my mother.'

I've never seen a person's face fall so quickly. Aula looks like I've slapped her. I'm relieved. The second someone says something ugly and true you can let anything out into the air.

Joomia puts her face in her hands. **We're here for our people, Taurus.**

'Really? Are you sure we're not here so Etain can feel like a real leader again?' I say.

You *have* purpose, Taurus, Joomia says. **You're my best friend. You—**

'I'm *trying* to *save* our people, Taurus,' Etain says throatily. 'Just like Sol said on the boat.'

'Oh, whatever. You'd do anything you could to become the person Ma wanted you to be,' I sneer.

'Yeah, I would. At least Ma wanted me to be *something*!'

I stare at her.

I get to my feet.

I walk back down the tunnel. My footsteps echo.

They don't call for me.

They don't come after me.

Why would they?

Taurus isn't destined to do anything.

Etain

None of us say anything after he leaves.

I find I'm shivering despite the heat.

What did you say that for? I'm screaming at myself. *What the hell did you say that for? You could see he was upset!*

I look at Aula. She's staring at the floor. There are tears in her eyes.

Like when you poisoned my mother.

'Aula. *Nadrik* poisoned Ashir. Not you.'

She nods. 'Yeah. Yeah, I know. That just . . . well, ow.'

He didn't mean it, Joomia says. **He's just** . . . But she trails off. I get why. It's difficult to recover when someone you love – someone who's supposed to love you – acts like such a—

Are you sure we're not here so Etain can feel like a real leader again?

At least Ma wanted me to be something!

The memories flood me – old and new.

Etain, Joomia says. **You're still shaking. Do you want to come back now?**

Astor's foot catches me across the jaw, and I collapse back—

'*SHE LED HER PEOPLE TO DESPAIR,*' *he screams.*

I raise my hand and watch it tremble. I'm so afraid.

'No . . . I'll . . . I'll go on.'

'Do you want us to come with you?' Aula asks.

'I'd rather you were on *that* side waiting for me in case, um . . . in case I need to jump back really fast.'

Aula nods.

At least Ma wanted me to be something!

I push it away; take a shaky breath. I look forward, along the tunnel ahead of me. I take a step. I look back. 'Taurus . . .'

Joomia's obviously thinking the same thing. **One of us will go and look for him. The other will stay here, waiting. You . . . you'll go on?**

281

'Yeah. I guess so.'

I look the other way. Forward. The bones are somewhere along this corridor, Taurus said. Oh Wise One, why did I have to open my mouth to him?

Be careful.

I shake myself and start walking.

Taurus

The gaps in the floor seem bigger on my own. I jump one and barely make it across. I overbalance once, and catch myself clumsily on the edge. My feet dangle. I scrabble up, and the rock opens gashes in my legs where I'm too hasty.

I lie there afterwards. I'm crying.

The things I said come screaming back to me. I get up, and start walking again. The effort of keeping Etain's words out of my head makes me dizzy, and I stub my toes a lot. I lose track of time. The need to keep going is desperate. If I keep going I don't have to think, don't have to direct, don't have to—

Wait.

Wait. I don't remember this part of the tunnel. The mineral in the wall is dimmer than anywhere we were before. Shit. I sit down on the floor to clear my head out. Or at least push all the crap to the sides. Breathe. Breathe. The way out. I need the way out.

I open my eyes and see my finger pointing back the way I just came. I must have taken a wrong turn. Wise One, how many wrong turns?

Something about that makes me laugh. It makes me think of what Lear said to me.

You can guide other people, but you don't even know where to begin directing yourself.

I can find direction. But the want in me to *do something*, to have purpose . . . I can feel it, but I can't point it toward anything.

I think, *What's the good of being a compass if you can't even direct yourself?*

And a second later, the minerals in the walls stop glowing.

I didn't know how much I needed the light until it's gone. I hold my hand in front of my face, so I can feel my breath bouncing back off it, but I can't see it. There's nothing but blackness.

A sluggish dread rolls under my ribs.

I use the wall of the tunnel to feel my way to my feet. *It doesn't matter*, I think. *Use the compass.*

But when I fumble inside myself for that calm, purposeful guide, it's gone – like walking towards a room where you can hear people talking, but when you open the door, there's no one there.

I wait for it to return, but the room's still empty.

The light doesn't come back.

The compass is gone.

Elwin

The mineral in the walls flickers out about ten steps further down the tunnel.

283

Panic thuds in my throat. I swallow. I really, really hope Taurus hasn't gone much further back along the route we came, with those gaps in the floor. I hope he waits.

What have I done to him? Why did I have to say *that*?

I should go back.

Joomia will find him, I tell myself. I have to go on.

And I *can* go on, cos by now my eyes have adjusted, and I realise I can see by the light of a much dimmer, but nonetheless illuminating, source.

The insects aren't giving off the same brilliance as before, but as I watch, they grow brighter again, the ants forming a wriggling procession along the ceiling of the cave. As I walk, they're joined by more of their brethren, the light brighter, glowing, moving. The clicking is soft at first, but it builds ominously, an orchestra of insects on rock that almost beat as one. The light still grows, but it's not just them now. It's coming from somewhere up ahead – a bloody light. More lava. More magma. Recognisable now I've come so close to being doused in it.

The tunnel widens. There are gentle rumblings beneath my feet, reminding me of Old World stories. Of dragons in caves. I feel like a dragon now, breathing fire and smoke rather than air. The clicking is near-deafening. I put my hands over my ears.

And then the tunnel ends.

Before me is a wide, dome-shaped cavern, bright with that same strange, bloody, molten light. The walls are *moving*, glittering like the facets of a jewel. Almost vibrating. I blink, but I'm not imagining it. I take a step inside, and everything stills at once. Too late, I realise how wrong I was. The light en't lava at all, but more ants. On every inch of the curved wall. Millions and millions of them. This is their nest.

I've just announced myself to the entire colony.

Taurus

I don't know how long I've been feeling my way in the dark.

I'm not crying now, but I want to. I remember the singing magic that broke Nadrik's jewel and released the memories. I try it, but nothing happens. Maybe all the magic in my blood went with the thought that banished my compass. I sing anyway, until it hurts to carry on.

I'm so hungry my stomach feels like it's turning itself inside out. I don't even want to think about thirst. I feel thin and hollow, like a paper lantern without any of the light. My lips started cracking who knows when; they're properly bleeding now. My eyes chafe against my eyelids every time I blink, like there's sand in them. I try to go slowly, but my limbs are beginning to give out. Give up.

Only . . . only . . . what's that sound?

Footsteps in the dark, moving quickly in a passage close by.

'Etain!' I try to shout, but my voice is barely a croak. 'Joomia? Aula? I'm here!'

No one answers. But the footsteps get louder . . . they're coming from behind me, for sure they are. But if it were Etain or Aula or Joomia, they should be coming from the other way.

'Hello? Etain?'

They're close now. My heart is heavy. I said some shitty things. Maybe they're not replying cos they're still angry. I would be too.

Now the footsteps run. I turn – waiting to hear their voices.

Instead, someone's hand catches the back of my head. It's gentle.

'You are thirsty,' says a voice. 'Open your mouth.'

I *am* thirsty.

The second the liquid hits my tongue I know that it isn't water. I choke and try to gag, but the hands clamp across my mouth.

'Swallow.'

I'm too weak not to.

My knees give out.

'Sleep,' a voice says. 'Sleep.'

I know that voice—

Who—

—

Etain

I stay absolutely still. I don't even breathe. The ants are static now too. Slowly, I let out my breath. Slowly, they go back to scurrying over each other.

I can hear my pulse thump in my ears. If I move again, will they attack me? Sink themselves into the back of my neck, like they did to Astor? I take another breath in. Let it out.

I look around. The bones have to be here somewhere – they *have* to be – Taurus's compass has never been wrong. Not that I know of. But the ants are too thickly spread, moving too often . . . How can I search for the bones in this?

I need to do something to make them scatter. It'll only give me seconds, but hopefully that's all I'll need. Wise One, I wish Aula were here to do it for me.

Never mind.

Gradually, like I'm moving in water, I fumble for my tool belt – for my largest hammer.

I undo the loop holding it in place.

I bring it up over my head.

Now.

I slam the head hard into the rock floor.

Instantly, the ants flood toward the ceiling, clearing the floor – leaving—

Yes.

The remains of a casket, long since disintegrated, and bones – worn and brown, but definitely human – the skull is bored through in several places but mostly intact.

I jump forwards and pick up whichever pieces my hands find first. The ants are already swarming back, one latching on to my arm, but I swat it hard, crushing its body flat against me. It comes away—

And I turn—

I'm running—

But the clicks tell me they're following me, faster than I am, dropping on to me from above as I reach the tunnel and stumble back along it.

Pincers jam the nerves in my wrist, making my grip

slack on my hammer, but I thrust the bones into my tool belt before I drop them.

The hammer clatters to the floor.

My skin en't hard like Aula's, not self-healing like Joomia's, and the pincers sink deep. They're all over me, the clicking like shears held next to my head. One slices into my ankle and I go sprawling.

NO! I scream at myself. *UP! Get UP!*

There's Joomia, up ahead, across the hole, and I wrench myself to my feet and break into a shambling run. The ants swarm to get ahead of me, jumping at me, clicking, biting, and I'm sticky with blood – my blood and their poison.

I'm failing now. Failing.

I call for Joomia, but my breath rasps in my throat.

An ant crawls up my spine—

No.

It bites deep into my neck.

I scream. Joomia hears. But she can't go near the hole and risk setting off the lava.

Etain! Come on! Come towards me! Jump, and I'll carry you over.

Help me—

My sight blurs, turns red. My neck screams with pain. There's fire in my mouth.

I dredge the last of my strength from somewhere. The hole's just there. I can make it.

Three yards—

Two—

One—

I let out a roar and leap—

The Chosen

It's lucky Joomia's there, but it's unlucky that Aula was the one to go look for Taurus. As Etain leaps, her descent goes awry, and her eyes widen as she realises she isn't going to clear the gap.

With a wild gasp, Joomia lunges for her, catching hold of her tool belt, Etain's weight threatening to pull them both down. In a split-second, Joomia closes her eyes and channels her power. She doesn't look, but she can feel a sudden heat as her feet turn, briefly, to roots, anchoring her to the floor of the tunnel. She roars, grits her teeth and hauls them both backwards, slamming into the rocky ground just as the lavafall flares once again in a white-hot surge above them.

'I got the bones,' Etain says weakly.

Great, Joomia says weakly. Etain droops, spent, her head lolling against Joomia's chest. That's when Joomia sees the ants. And the blood. She rolls out from under Etain's body and relieves her of the chisel on her tool belt. Carefully, trying not to panic, she pinches each insect free of Etain's skin and smashes each over-sized head with the blunt end of the chisel.

She finds the ant on the back of Etain's neck last and picks it free with a shudder, just as the sound of footsteps start to echo toward her from somewhere down the tunnel.

Maybe Aula's managed to find Taurus. She hopes so. She turns Etain over and drags her back, away from the heat of the lava.

'Water,' Etain mumbles. 'Please.'

I'd like some too, Joomia says, with a feeble laugh. **Can you stand?**

'No.'

We need Aula then. She closes her eyes again and feels for the emptiness inside her, the place where she and Aula join.

She's back. I've got her, but she can't walk. She's exhausted. She's got the bones.

Aula can't answer, but Joomia feels a kind of echoing throb along the emptiness, and knows Aula heard.

The footsteps get louder and soon there's a silhouette in the tunnel ahead – but the minerals in the walls are no longer illuminating anything. Even so, Joomia frowns. That's not Aula . . .

Domaga comes shuffling into view. I realise now why the footsteps sounded so lop-sided.

'Are you all right?' she calls.

Joomia nods, knowing Domaga won't hear her. Unconsciously, Joomia puts a hand on Etain's shoulder. Something doesn't feel right.

Domaga stops a foot away to pant, hands on her thighs. She's leaning on a stick, Joomia sees. 'Did she get the bones?' Domaga asks.

Joomia hesitates, then indicates Etain's tool belt.

Domaga nods. 'That damn lavafall and the gap in the floor. I didn't find this place until after I fell' – she indicates her leg – 'and by then I was too crippled to have made it over the gap where the lavafall is. I started to study *every* passage after that. Looking for another way. I know the labyrinth now. I know every way in and every way out. And there's no other way round that gap . . .'

290

Joomia nods uncertainly. Why does this feel wrong? Domaga said she would be looking after Sol. So why is she here . . . what is she doing?

In answer, Domaga punches her – one hard jab that cracks Joomia's skull back against the tunnel wall. She sags, dazed and cringing with pain, though feeling for the mutative healing in her power as a reflex.

Domaga bends down and snatches the bones from Etain's belt, which rouses her.

'What are you doing?'

Domaga smashes her in the face with her stick.

Joomia gestures wildly, but the seeds in her pocket sprout only yellow and brown, spindly and ineffective.

Domaga says, 'If you try to follow, I'll kill your brother.'

Joomia tries to focus on her retreating figure in the dark, but her vision is melting, and her head spasms with pain.

Taurus

Half awake, I feel the wind moving over me in my sleep, and the ground beneath me rises and falls.

It takes me a while to realise why.

I raise my head. Sails above me. The sea – the sea all around—

I'm on the trimaran.

What?

I make an attempt to sit up and everything screams in protest. Spiders scatter off me.

'About time. I was going to wake you.'

I look round. Domaga is at the steering oar, and Sol lies beside me, still asleep.

I try to make sense of it. There's the shape of Izanami, getting smaller. I open my mouth to speak, but my throat can't even force out a rasp.

Water.

Domaga crosses to the hatch in the main hull and draws out the water skin, bringing it to me. My hands can't stop trembling enough to hold it, but she cups the back of my head and helps me drink.

I remember the feel of that hand, in the tunnel. The memories start returning.

'Slowly,' she says sternly as I try to gulp it. When I'm finished she says, 'Do you need food?'

I shake my head, although I do. But I need answers first. 'The others . . . did they get out OK? Are they . . . are they following?' I look around, my vision swinging wildly. But there's nothing and no one else out here but us.

'Easy,' she says.

'Domaga . . . no. They're not . . . they're not . . .'

'No, they're not dead.'

'Then . . . what are you doing?'

She takes a deep breath, like she's steeling herself. 'What must be done.'

The Chosen

Aula has had just about enough of this island.

She had been aimlessly looking for Taurus in the dark,

calling out for him, when Joomia called to her:

She's back. I've got her, but she can't walk. She's exhausted. She's got the bones.

The urgency in Joomia's voice disarmed her, Aula reasons now. *That* was the reason she didn't hear the footsteps in the dark. *That* was the reason she didn't notice the hole in the floor.

Someone's palms in the small of her back.

She fell, flailing into the gloom, reaching out for something, anything.

She'd managed to catch herself, her knees slamming into a ledge, pulling herself up – blind, disorientated. But she'd fallen far, *far* down and now her foot is stuck in some crack.

As she works her ankle free, she puts two and two together.

Sol's a little shit but she doesn't think it was him. He had a young, hopeful, decent look about him that she associates with Taurus. But Domaga? She was brought up in a repressed, poverty-ridden hell hole for most of her life, then got banished to starve out on the sea to wash ashore on a dangerous volcanic island with only spiders for company. Who has all that happen to them and *doesn't* go a little rotten? *Nadrik* had even less reason to turn out the way he did.

The thought seems to loosen something at her foot, and she can finally ascend out of the hole, gripping by only her fingers, swinging herself from wall to wall – less than the width of her arm span – and eventually hauling herself out.

She sees Joomia within sight, at the other end of this corridor, healing her own injuries. As Aula rushes to her, she spots Etain holding a hand over a bloody nose. Both of them are trying to pick themselves up and aren't able to rise to more than a crouch.

'She got you too, huh?'

'She has the bones,' Etain says.

'Of course she does. More of those fire ants, huh?' Aula says, eyeing the ant corpses littered on the floor.

'Lore buried the bones *in the ants' nest*,' Etain says, her voice shaking with exhaustion. 'Aula, Joomia thinks Domaga has Taurus too.'

'What? What does she need Taurus for?'

'Compass, probably,' Etain mutters, attempting to use the wall to stand up but only overbalancing. 'Also, ransom. She said she'd kill him if we tried to follow her.'

'Damn it. Where the hell does she think she's going? Get on my back, Joomia. Etain, come here.' She scoops Etain up into her arms like a bride.

With her passengers loaded, Aula springs back along the tunnel. 'I have no idea where we're going – before I was just taking guesses, only guided by the sort of ache that links me to you, Joomia.'

I grew moss along the wall to mark the route we used, Joomia says. Put your right hand out – feel it?

'Oh, yeah!' Aula says, touching at it with delight.

I also grew it thick on the precipice of all the gaps. So you'd know when to jump.

'You're so clever.'

Thanks. I think you're very brawny.

Aula allows herself a grim laugh. 'What I want to know is: how the hell did that . . . that . . .'

294

Turncoat? Gannet?

'*Bitch* . . . find us in the dark? And turncoat? *Gannet?* Joomia, what's wrong with you?'

Sorry.

'She's been here . . . how long?' Etain murmurs. 'She's definitely had time to explore, and explore well. With those spiders, she could have been watching us the whole time, couldn't she?'

'I guess so. Hold on, you two. I'm going to jump now.'

She makes that jump, but the moss suddenly disappears. Aula can only guess Domaga saw Joomia's moss and scraped it away as much as she could. Aula has to feel to find it again, but it's a hurried job, and it's not hugely effective, disorientating Aula enough for her to take two wrong turnings – no joke with two people on her back, even with her strength.

Aula is shocked to finally reach the pile of boulders again, but it's not as easy as that – the path she cleared is blocked by a criss-cross of thick, gummy cables: a mesh of woven spider web. Etain and Joomia have to get down to help Aula fight her way through them. The fibres are only as thick as grass stems, but stronger than wire, and Etain goes through every tool on her belt before Aula finds an effective way to tear them – with her teeth.

'Go!' Etain croaks when the way is clear. 'Stop them!'

'Yep,' Aula says, jumping nimbly down the rocks and disappearing out toward the cave.

'Joomia—'

Don't strain yourself.

'We can't let Domaga leave with them – those bones.

They're our only chance.'

I know, Etain.

Etain scrambles out the other side, Joomia right behind her, hovering in case she takes a bad step on unsteady legs. But there's no need.

When they emerge, blinking in the sunlight, they find Aula kicking the grey sand, staring at the hole the boat left in the sand – and the empty sea.

'Too late,' Etain whispers. 'We're too late.'

Taurus

I try to stand up, but my legs won't hold me. I remember the hand in the dark again.

'You drugged me,' I realise.

'Yes. Do not worry, it will wear off.'

'Domaga, what are you doing?'

'I need you to point me toward Govinda. I stole the journal from your friend. That's enough, isn't it? You can still give me my heading?'

Oh, shit. 'I don't understand,' I hedge.

'I need you to *direct* me.'

'But . . . why?'

'With my brother gone from Govinda,' Domaga says, 'there is no one strong enough to hold his place. I will implant the bones inside me, and with this power I will lead the revolution. I will give them an Etheling they can stand behind. I will give them more land, more hope.'

As she says it, I see two long human bones wedged under the sash around her waist.

'But we need them too, Domaga,' I plead. She has to see reason. 'We need them to trade our people's freedom with your brother.' I don't say anything about the fact that Vulcan and his men could run into us at sea any time, but I think it. Maybe he's gone back to our island. Maybe not. But we're in serious shit either way, floating about on the sea with no protection.

299

'If you give my brother the bones, you are doing deals with a dictator. I will help your island, but *my* island comes first.'

'Domaga – come on – be reasonable. There are *two* bones there – you can spare one.'

'NO,' she snaps so hard I jump. 'No,' she says more calmly. 'You don't understand. Vulcan will not have them. I will not let that happen.'

'Why?' But it hits me before she replies. If Vulcan has a bone, he won't need her. No one will need her. 'And Sol?' I change tack. 'Did you ask him what he thinks of this?'

She glances protectively at him. 'Sol is my family. Govinda is his home. We are going to save it.'

'Domaga?' comes Sol's voice.

We both look at him. He blinks a few times and frowns at the sky over his head. Slowly, he sits up. His eyes widen as he takes in the trimaran, the sea, the sail in full wind. And me.

'What are you doing?' Sol says. 'Domaga, what are you doing?'

Etain

'I can *just* see them,' Aula says, squinting at the horizon. 'I think that's them. But it would take me ages to catch up.'

I turn round and head right back into the cave.

I start off walking, but then my feet get ahead of me. Soon I'm running back along the passage, past the spider webs, back towards the tumble of boulders, out of breath and raw with a pain that's just about everywhere.

'Where the hell do you think *you're* going?' Aula says, jogging to catch up with me.

'I'm going back,' I say.

'Why?'

'I need more bones.'

It's such a simple answer, and I'm furious with myself. *Why* didn't I take more when I had the chance?

Aula laughs. 'I know you're joking because you *just* had a very near brush with death by fire ant. Not to mention Lore's friendly little lava booby-trap.'

'It doesn't matter. I have to try.' What else can I do?

I reach the boulders and start to climb.

Aula skips around me easily and blocks my way. 'You *want* to end up like Astor? Blood gushing out of his nose and flames from his mouth?'

'Aula,' I say carefully, 'this en't about me. It's about my people.'

'OK, and how is it you think getting yourself killed in an ants' nest is going to help your people?'

'*We need those bones*,' I shout. '*We need them to trade with Vulcan!* What part of that don't you understand?'

'Who says you have to trade with Vulcan? Could you *try* something else?'

'What else do you want me to try, Aula?'

'How about *being* our leader?'

'What was I supposed to do? *Force them* to follow me? I can't be leader unless . . .' But I trail off. I'm too dizzy. I have to sit down.

'Unless what, Etain?' Aula's not giving up. 'What do you

need to do to prove you're the leader? This wasn't even your quest. It was *Sol's*. And you came because it was a nice little detour that went alongside yours. Do you even *want* to lead?'

'I'm supposed to—'

'Fuck *supposed to*. Do you *want* to?'

I stumble to find the words. 'You don't understand. Ma said I was *destined*. Ma said it had to be me.'

She rolls her eyes. 'Yeah, OK. Cos I know nothing about the expectations of Head Prophet Ashir.'

'You *don't* know—'

'I don't? The Chosen One of Athenas can never understand?'

'No, you *can't*. Because *I* took all the shit, Aula! *I* took all her crap about responsibility and destiny and expectations. You? You got encouragement and hugs and support and you threw it all in her face on a daily basis. What the hell would you know about me and her?'

'That is such *bullshit*, Etain. How can you not know how much she loved you?'

The answer rushes up into my mouth, crowding behind my teeth like vomit. I try to hold it in, but it comes out anyway:

'Because she's not here!'

It echoes around the cave, an ugly shout.

There's a horrible silence. Aula stares at me like I've slapped her. 'She's not here,' I say again, My voice cracks. I'm shaking.

Slowly, Aula folds herself to sit in front of me. I take a few deep breaths and look around at the gloomy cave, the fallen rocks, the lacework of spider webs and, finally, at her.

'I just . . . I just wish . . . she could tell me what to do now.'

Aula gives me a watery smile. 'What, she didn't put this in your leader lessons? How to deal with a strange spider-speaking woman who's kidnapped your brother and the ransom for your island?'

I laugh weakly, but another surge of sadness rises over it. 'I failed her,' I say. 'Even before all this. I couldn't find a way. I don't . . . I don't know how to . . .'

'To do this without her,' Aula finishes. 'Yeah, I know.' She sighs, and pulls me into her arms. 'You know, it's taken me a while to figure it out too, but maybe it en't that great to focus on a parent's expectations of yourself. It can make things pretty boring.'

I think about Taurus. Ma hurt me with expectation, but she hurt *him* – and *I* hurt him – just as much with a total lack of expectation. By expecting him to feel like he was enough without doing anything to help.

Perhaps I *do* know what to do.

'We have to go after them,' I say.

'Well, *yeah*,' Aula says, letting me go. 'We just got to find a boat. I was thinking we could make something of that boat bed Domaga put Sol in.'

'Her old canoe?'

'Yeah. Whatever it's called. Water first though, eh?'

We're just finished cupping handfuls of water from the barrel in the cave when we hear Joomia calling.

Etain! Aula!

We get shakily to our feet, but Joomia's already running to meet us.

303

'What is it?'

Come! Come with me! Come outside!

She's . . . she's *grinning*, grabbing my hand and pulling me along in her wake.

'No need to wait for *me*,' Aula calls from behind us, but Joomia's not listening. She's running, feet kicking up sand, and it's all I can do to keep up with her. At the steam pools, she stops and points.

Look! she whispers. **Look!**

I shade my eyes and squint.

I clutch her hand.

Bobbing towards us, with a little triangular sail, is a boat.

'That's . . . that's one of the island's fishing boats,' Aula says incredulously.

It is. But that's not what has my mouth open in awe. It's who's *in* the boat. A memory floats to the front of my brain like a soap bubble and pops. Ade, grabbing my arm, and her under-eye scars going white.

I find you on an island. I find you in a boat.

Taurus

'Sol. This is for *us*. This is for all the years we suffered with him. Father, and then Vulcan. This is for the way they treated you when they found out you were different—'

'So you're *giving* him our island?' I interrupt.

Sol winces as he sits up. 'I don't want it to be like this, Domaga. I made a deal with Etain.'

'You did?' I ask, half a hope stirring in me.

Domaga snorts. 'That girl is no leader.' She turns to me. 'Even *you* know that, boy.'

'No, I don't,' I say.

She laughs.

Sol doesn't. 'She's destined,' he says. 'Lore Saw it, Domaga. She's destined to lead her people.'

Domaga spits to the side. 'Like Vulcan was destined, Sol? And Father, before him?'

'That isn't the point,' Sol says. 'She's not like them. And even if the prophecy's a load of shit – the *reality* is that her people believe it.'

Domaga raises an eyebrow. 'Her people deposed her.'

Sol shakes his head. 'You didn't see their faces, Domaga. I talked to them when I was looking for someone who might know where Lore's book was. They knew she hadn't been captured. They *believed* in her ability to save them. And you've just left her on that island. You could have at least brought her along to do that.'

'And face tussling with their Ethelings?' Domaga says. 'I don't think so.'

I sigh. I guess I can see her point there.

'Anyway, where would it leave us if she put *our* best chance to save *our* land in the hands of our brother?' Sol doesn't answer and she nods. 'It is not people with destinies who change the world, Sol. It is people who have no choice.'

'Like you?' I say.

'I would have thought you'd be in sympathy with me. I know who you are, boy. My spiders were always watching. They *tasted* you.'

I'm about to ask what she means, but then I remember.

It strikes fast, with a pinch of pain, sinking its fangs into the muscle between my thumb and my wrist. I flinch, a second too slow, and it drops to the ground and scuttles away. The bite's still visible on my hand.

I feel sick at the thought that she's watched me – that she might know something only *I* could. All the want in me. All the bitterness.

I'm lost.

'I know that well,' Domaga says. Her voice is surprisingly soft. 'When everyone around you is Chosen for something and you are left to rub their shoulders and wash their feet when their courage fails them. Yeah, I know about that.'

'I never minded that,' I say quietly, surprising myself with the truth. 'I *wanted* to help. I just . . . I just wanted there to be space for me to do something great as well.'

I swallow. Outside of the echo chamber that is my head, I can hear how ridiculous that sounds now. How childish.

I look at Sol. *I'm not prophesied to be anyone's saviour, but I'm gonna try to save mine anyway. And if I can help you save yours, even better.*

Why didn't I open my ears?

That's why you'll never be destined for anything. If you weren't so selfish . . . if you weren't so— But I shut down that thought before it can go any further. A kinder, wiser part of me replies, *You understand, then.*

'You're right, Domaga,' I say aloud.

She looks at me askance. 'Yeah?'

'Yeah. Sometimes destiny doesn't have anything to do with it. But when it does . . . maybe it's there to get the person it refers to off their arse and actually *do something* that matters. So . . .'

I look at Sol. His necklaces catch the sun's rays and throw them at me.

'Er . . . so it's *more powerful* when you do something of your own accord.'

And more remarkable that Aula and Joomia came with us, even though technically their 'destiny' was finished.

And it's more remarkable that Sol decided to come here and—

Again, his necklaces flash at me. I remember something. Oh. *Shit*. I put a hand over my mouth. 'Kreywar's mark . . . those earthquakes.'

'What?' Sol says. 'What is it?'

I shake myself, force myself to keep talking.

'That's what I'm saying – you're *right*, Domaga, it *is* more powerful that you're trying to do something for your people, Domaga, of your own accord. I just . . . just wish you could find a way that helps both of us.'

I glance at her. Her face hasn't changed.

At last she sighs. 'You have a kind heart. I admire you for trying to change my mind . . .'

'But . . .' I say heavily.

'But,' she agrees, 'I have been on that island a long time. Perhaps I moved too hastily, but I have only so much courage left in me.' She looks at me openly then, and I see all the places I reflect her. She looks old, bitterness and disappointment in every line of her face. This is who I could become. 'Please,' she says. 'Show me my way home.'

Do something.

I close my eyes and grope for the compass. As certain I was that it was gone in the tunnel, I know it's there now. And I'm ready to direct myself. Whoever it takes us to face.

Make a choice, Taurus.

I lift my finger and point.

Etain

Ade hugs Aula and Joomia as she climbs colt-legged and unsteady from the little sailing boat. She looks at them, smiles and says, 'My girls.'

I can tell that something's changed about her, but I can't put my finger on what until she looks at me. Her face is as scarred as ever, and she looks battered and windswept and blistered by the sun, but her eyes have more focus in them.

Trying, girl. Trying to get better.

She looks shy and nervous and hopeful all at once. 'Prophecy. You needed a boat,' she says, and turns to look back over her shoulder. For the first time, I notice the *other* person in the boat. The man who Sol disguised himself as.

'This is . . .' Ade begins, apparently trying to remember.

'Karragan,' he says in a small voice.

'Sailor,' says Ade.

'She saved me,' says Karragan.

'He . . . helped. Me,' Ade says.

'He's Vulcan's deputy,' Aula says, narrowing her eyes.

Karragan screws up his face. 'I was. Now I . . .' He casts around for the words and finishes, 'I want to help.'

Ade nods enthusiastically, but I've barely heard him. For

some reason, I'm tearing up again. Ade's here, and I somehow know that she did it for me.

'Girl?' she whispers. 'What's wrong?'

I wish it was you. I wish it was you who'd died.

I open my mouth to say something, but my breath only shudders traitorously in and out again.

'I'm – I'm sor—'

She shakes her head. 'No. No, girl. It's all right.' She sighs. 'I miss . . . her . . . as well.'

'I'm sorry.'

She shakes her head again and cups her hands around my shoulders. 'Heavy,' she says. 'I understand.'

We watch as Aula and Joomia come running back from the cave, bringing supplies. I hadn't realised they'd gone. 'I am sorry too,' she murmurs. 'For . . . for the . . . vines.' She seizes my hand. 'Let's put it right.'

Taurus

It takes another day for the strange drug Domaga gave me to wear off entirely. She's wary of me as I regain my legs, but once that's over, she seems to feel reassured that I'm not going to throw her off course or jump off the boat.

On the second day, she lets me help her sail. This is better. It distracts me from the path I've put us on. It stops me from worrying that maybe I'm wrong.

I can tell Sol wants to help too. The wound in his chest looks better, but he tires easy and Domaga won't let him walk around for more than a circuit of the three hulls. While he sleeps, her spiders probe his wound carefully, and spin more webs across it.

'Will you miss your spiders, Domaga?' I ask.

She shakes her head. 'They do not have personalities. Not individuals, like you and me.'

'I thought you said they weren't a hive mind?' I say.

'Not that either,' she agrees. 'They are one, but they are different. It is the same with many animals. Their high mind never really arises to take control, as ours does. They live still with their instincts.' She notices my expression and asks, 'What?'

'Nothing. Just . . . no wonder you wanted to get away from there.' How did she live so long with no human company?

I catch Sol looking at me, but he doesn't say anything. I wonder if he's suspicious of our direction. His wound is healing, and he's obviously getting better, but even small movements seem to cost him a lot and I think mainly he's too exhausted to question what's going on too much – especially now that I look like I've given in to Domaga's orders. Still, I start to use the journal more, even though I don't need the map for where we're headed.

The skies stay clear, the wind fills the sails. We're making good time. I keep the dot on the horizon behind us in our sights. The dot that's been there ever since the first day, so small it could be a bird, or a rock. But I know who it is.

I try to make a plan. Even if it works, I'm going to be cutting things close. Every day makes me doubt myself more. I have no idea where Vulcan's ships are, what threat they might cause. But I have to try.

Is this right? I ask the compass. *Is this what I'm supposed to do?*

Sometimes the compass point dithers, like it's as unsure as I am. But mostly it points me where I've asked, and no more.

I guess this one's on me.

On the fifth day, I wake up to hear Domaga swearing. I leap to my feet, thinking, *This is it. It's happening. She's seen the island. Or Vulcan.* I look over at her, but she's not where I thought she'd be – she's craning out to look behind us, not in front.

I follow her gaze. I begin to shake.

The tiny but unmistakable silhouette of a single-sailed vessel is behind us.

'Your sister and her friends found a boat,' Domaga snarls, launching herself at me. 'How did she follow? What haven't you told me?'

'Nothing,' I say, but she's not convinced.

I wipe my tears away. She slaps me. 'Tell me! Is your sister a compass too as well as a leader? Is that it?'

'They've been following us for days, Domaga,' Sol says lazily from where he's lying on the hull. 'Probably, they've been following us the whole time. Keeping their distance.'

'I didn't see—'

'Because you've been driving yourself and Bull to the brink every moment you're awake. You're sleep-deprived.'

'Why didn't you say anything?'

'I *told* you,' Sol says. 'I made a promise.'

She puts her hands over her mouth to muffle a frustrated scream. 'Sol, don't be naive. Etain can't trade the bones, not like this. *Think* what Vulcan will do with the bones if he has them.'

'I won't have to soon, will I, Bull?' Sol says, looking at me.

'What do you mean, Sol?' I wonder what he's talking about too.

'Because,' Sol continues, 'unless there's another island left on Erthe that makes ships like ours, Vulcan's little fleet is right over there.'

Domaga looks in horror towards the opposite horizon.

I hadn't seen them yet, either. For once, my attention had been drawn away – just at the crucial moment. I knew this would come – confronting Vulcan again, but damn it, I wanted to have a head start on him. Domaga's yelling distracted me. Sleep-deprived too; Sol isn't wrong about that. And he's not wrong about the ships either.

Their proud, distinct shapes turn rapidly towards us.

'Where are we? Are they guarding the way to Govinda?' Domaga murmurs.

'Nah,' Sol says wearily. 'I don't think so. Either he's gone mad, or this is part of some really bad plan, but unless I'm wrong, Bull here's used his compass to lead us right to them.'

Etain

Aula lets out a guttural stream of swear words.

'What's Domaga doing? Giving the bones to Vulcan herself? I thought she hated him!'

No, Joomia says. **No, look – she's turning the trimaran!**

'It won't make any difference,' Karragan says, but he stands to adjust our little sail, swinging us round so we'll follow in Domaga's wake.

Etain, what do we do? Joomia asks. **They've seen us and we'll never be able to outrun them.**

I have a sick feeling she's right. Already, Vulcan's middlemost ship has cut out from the other two and is making a beeline for the trimaran.

I flick through the possibilities. What does Vulcan *want*? To punish Sol for embarrassing him by sneaking away and on to the volcanic island? Everything Sol's told us about Vulcan and Govinda suggests that his ego is fragile enough to justify him going to such extremes. But maybe he wants what Sol wants in his own way . . . another chance for his people. I en't gonna give him more chances than he deserves but I decide right then and there that if there's *any* chance to reason with him before a fight like the one Sol predicted happens, then maybe the first thing I need to do is to weaken him.

'The ant queen,' I say slowly. 'We need to kill the ant queen. That's where a lot of his power is coming from, right?'

Yes, Joomia says. **Remember, Domaga said . . .**

Karragan looks astonished. Nervously, he raises a hand to the back of his neck.

'Wondering if you've chosen the wrong side?' Aula says pointedly.

For some reason he looks at Ade. 'No,' he says softly. And then: 'Yes. Destroying the ant queen would definitely swing the odds for you.'

'But where do we find her?' Aula says.

We all look at Ade, and she laughs and points to the trimaran. 'Ask them.'

My stomach churns nervously. 'OK . . . so we go closer. All agreed?'

Everyone nods.

Joomia turns the rudder; I swing the sail right into the wind. Aula jumps over the side, grabs the nose of the boat and starts to swim hard.

The Chosen

Vulcan had almost given up. When he'd lost the trimaran in the storm, he probably should have given up. Instead, he waited.

He could not use his ants, though they murmured unhappily in the belly of his ship. They wanted to be back in the forest eating, or else back where they belonged in deep burrows beneath the ground, where lava flowed nearby them like a lazy river. He drew kelp from the sea and speared fish for them. They ate everything he laid in their midst. But they were not happy.

So Vulcan had chosen then to punish the archer who'd shot the bolt at Sol.

'WHAT PART OF "I WANT HIM ALIVE" DO YOU NOT UNDERSTAND, CRETIN?' he'd roared over the screams, as the ants sucked the archer's flesh until it peeled from his bones.

The punishment had refreshed him. He decided to

invade the minds of more hive-minded sea creatures, but they could not tell him much. So he decided to wait, forcing his ships to sail back and forth along the same latitude. Vulcan had learned this from the ants: waiting could be useful. Waiting could be made to serve you. Sometimes it was a long game, sometimes a short one.

This time it was a short one.

He had been about to send one of the ships back to Chloris for supplies when the trimaran had reappeared in the water – though not, he saw through the long glass, with the passengers he had expected.

'Domaga,' he now murmurs in wonder, watching as she frantically turns the trimaran away from his approach.

'We're going after them, sire?' asks one of his men.

'Of course,' he replies. 'No one needs reminding that there is one person the archers should not hit, under any circumstances?'

'No, sire.'

'Good.'

Taurus

Domaga weeps silently as she turns us. She twitches on a line and leans hard on the steering oar. Her grace is gone. She's stiff and mechanical. She doesn't ask me to do anything. She doesn't look at me.

I didn't expect her to be terrified.

I should have.

I've delivered her into the hands of her brother. Sure,

she's desperate to overthrow him, but it's clear that without the implant of the bones – presumably not something she's going to try to do without help – she had no intention of facing him alone. I dunno what it means to be that afraid.

'Domaga. I'm sorry.'

'You don't know what you've done,' she says.

'Why, Taurus?' Sol growls. 'You think Vulcan's going to reward you for our capture?'

'This was your idea?' Domaga jumps. We all swivel starboard to see Aula powering through the water and hauling herself aboard one-handed. I stare at her. I can hear everything I said to her in the echo of the tunnel like I'm still there. She glares at Domaga. 'I'm really pissed off with Sol, but this is partly your fault.'

Domaga's lip trembles.

Aula turns to me. 'I'm really pissed off with you too.'

'I know.'

'You said some shitty things.'

'Yeah. I know. I'm sorry.'

'You left us in the tunnel.'

'I know, Aula.'

'You're a stupid idiot.'

'Yeah.'

'OK. Good. That's settled.'

Aula flicks her eyes to Vulcan's ships, pressing closer. 'We don't have much time, and I dunno what you're planning, but whatever it is, does it help you if Vulcan doesn't have his ants?'

'Obviously. Anything that immobilises him helps.'

316

'That's what I like to hear. Domaga. Sol!' Aula's voice is laced with urgency.

They snap to look at her.

'Vulcan's ant queen! Where does he keep it?'

'In a box,' Sol says. 'It's er . . . wooden?'

Domaga nods. 'And it has metal finishings. And a leather strap.'

'If I kill the queen—'

'How? Her blood is pure fire.'

Aula laughs. 'Don't worry about that. What happens if I kill her?' she says quickly.

'The ants will find another queen. But not until they're back on land.'

'But killing her severs his ties to the ants?'

'Yes,' Domaga says breathlessly. 'Yes, I think so. But his soldiers—'

Aula cracks her knuckles. 'Don't worry about them either. Once their ships are sinking and they're in the water, Joomia can take it from there.' She grabs my hand. 'Can you point me to where it is?'

'Not without seeing the chest myself.'

'It will be on whichever ship Vulcan's on,' Sol says. 'Can you find him?'

'Yes.' My finger ends up pointing straight at the foremost of Vulcan's ships coming for us.

Aula nods. 'Don't die, OK?' She jumps back into the water.

'Where were we?' I ask weakly.

'You were about to tell us you're joking with all of this,' Sol says.

I take a deep breath. 'I'm not. I pointed us this way.'

'Why?' Sol asks. 'If this was part of your plan, then what's the rest of it?'

I shake my head. I have to focus. 'My plan is *you*, Sol.'

Etain

We meet Aula as close to Vulcan's ship as we can, staying outside shooting distance.

Aula, between us and it, looks back at Joomia. 'Ready?'

Joomia looks back at me. **What will you do?**

'Try not to get in the way,' I say. 'Here. Use me.'

I hold out my hands for her to step on to. She touches my cheek. When she kisses me, my pulse gives a strange wobble. 'What was that for?' I murmur.

Luck, she whispers back. **Whatever you want.**

'Kissing is for later!' Aula yells.

Fine! Joomia snaps. She squeezes my shoulder once, steps on to my cupped hands and dives into the water. For a few moments, I see nothing but a faint trace of two frothing lines in the ocean, heading straight for Vulcan's ship. What if they get sucked down in the boat's undercurrent? What if they strike the enormous rudder?

But Aula guides Joomia, and I soon see their heads bobbing beside the ship, too close for Vulcan's soldiers to spot them. Joomia gestures, and vines burst from her pocket, thick and whip-fast, snaking over the porthole windows before they disappear over the barrier.

They climb.

I can only watch them and hope. Of course it's then that Vulcan's men start shooting at us.

Taurus

'Sol,' I say. 'I don't think your mother gave you that necklace by accident.'

He frowned. 'What do you mean?'

I glance at Domaga, wondering if she's following me.

'What do you mean, Taurus?' Sol presses.

'I mean, what if the point of sending you to Izanami wasn't about getting something out? What if the point was to show you what you already can do?'

Sol looks at Domaga. She's staring at me, her hand slack on the steering oar. I hope she's still concentrating enough to keep us out of shooting distance of Vulcan. Sol laughs. 'Come on, Taurus. Stop talking in riddles.'

'Whenever you've been in serious pain . . . I guess you haven't been as conscious of it, but we have. I think it was you who made those quakes out at sea – just like it was you causing them back on Izanami when Joomia was trying to pull out that arrowhead.'

He shakes his head. 'Taurus, you're mad.'

'No. I'm not.' I grip his hand. 'When I asked the compass for something that would make land, Sol. Before we went into the volcano. Well, it pointed at *you*.'

He shakes his head and looks across to Vulcan's ship. Then he sits up sharply. 'Domaga! We're drifting!'

But she doesn't move. She's staring at him, and I wonder

319

if she's connecting dots in her memory. Maybe Sol's been causing earthquakes for quite a while without knowing. Maybe she's always known, deep down.

'Sol,' she whispers. 'Sol, I think he's right.'

The Chosen

Vulcan's men move fast. Just a moment after Joomia's swung her leg over the barrier to come aboard, a soldier whips her on to her back on the deck. He attempts to roll her over, to pin her arms, but his hands are frozen, fingers fused together, skin hardening into swirling patterns, bark climbing over his wrists.

Joomia wriggles out from beneath him and ducks just as Aula throws the first man stupid enough to touch her head-first across the width of the ship. He sinks into the water.

Ordinarily, Aula supposes, this would put a normal enemy off, but these men have parasite ants controlling them – they will not be deterred. In a few minutes, many more men are swarming the deck, vying for position to fight.

Look at their hands, Joomia says, watching as a few of the men come forward, palms up, the air around their fingers rippling with heat. **They're infested**, Joomia says, spotting swollen points on each individual's neck. **Like Astor . . . only it's worked on them. They've got enough** *skuld* **blood for it to—**

One soldier gestures suddenly in their direction and a wave of scalding air blasts at them. The full force of it misses only because Aula yanks both herself and Joomia out of the way in time, but she curses as it catches her side.

'Shit. What now?'

Try to put as many of them in the water as possible?

'Got it.'

So they do, Joomia with her vines, occasionally turning limbs here or there to wood, rendering soldiers motionless; Aula with pure brute strength.

'We need to get inside,' Aula says, panting.

Joomia looks around for a hatch.

There, she says, spotting the opening roughly ten feet away. **Cover me.**

She turns and ducks through the outstretched hands of the first man to come for her, and makes a sprint for it. Aula follows swiftly, throwing men – literally throwing them – away from her at random: into the sea, shoving them back, as swift and ruthless as Nadrik taught her to be.

While Aula fights, Joomia fumbles with the lock by hand, and when that doesn't work, summons an insidious, curling ivy that can strangle trees whole. It worms its way inside the lock and breaks it open. Joomia lets out a breath, pulls up the hatch—

But someone else slams it shut.

'I thought I'd killed you,' Vulcan says. 'Now you are two. You are like worms. Is that the gift of the Chosen One of Chloris?'

But he doesn't wait for an answer.

Aula hears the clang of skull against deck, but she doesn't understand until she turns to see Vulcan holding Joomia by the throat, like a limp doll. Joomia's eyes are unfocused.

321

Blood drips down her face from her scalp, dark as lava.

'One down,' he says. And casually he throws Joomia's body into the sea, nothing more to him than an ant.

Taurus

Sol looks down at his hands, panicking.

'I don't understand. It doesn't make any sense. How can I have had power I didn't know about?'

'Very easily,' I say. 'I've had this compass thing since I was born, but I just . . . I used to think I was just pretty good at finding stuff. Intuitive or something.'

'It makes sense,' Domaga says. There's reluctance in her voice, but at least she says it. 'Ma told me you were going to be our salvation.'

Sol shudders. 'No. No, I'm no one's saviour.'

Someone on Vulcan's ship screams. I don't turn. I don't look. If I do, I'll break.

'Sol,' I say. I take both his hands in mine. He looks at me. 'Think about what you told me. *I'm not prophesied to be anyone's saviour, but I'm gonna try to save my people anyway. And if I can help you save yours, even better*.'

'It was an act,' he mumbles. 'I was going to trick you if Domaga hadn't.'

'No you weren't.' I don't believe it. Sol's different from her. 'You said you made a deal with Etain.'

He shakes his head. A tear emerges. He throws my hands off. 'Even if I could do it, where am I supposed to begin? You want me to make an island right here?'

322

'If you like, but that's not the point – at least, not at first. The point is to scare Vulcan. The point is to show him who has the power now.'

Sol puts his face in his hands.

'Listen to me. Joomia didn't really begin using her power until about a year ago. It's inside you, Sol, waiting to come out.'

'TAURUS!'

I turn round. Etain's little boat's coming up fast on us – and beside her – I've only got a moment to take it in – is that Ade? And *Karragan*?! Then I focus on Etain's face. Drained. Like death.

'What? What is it?'

She can't speak. She points.

A body in the water. It's face down. Blood clouds like ominous smoke in the water around it. Long dark hair floats like seaweed.

Joomia.

I don't think. I jump in after her.

Etain

Ade saw Joomia first.

The men Aula and Joomia had managed to knock into the water were already swimming towards us. I twitched the sail to move us out of their range.

I only saw the splash, up ahead. I didn't understand. Ade did, though. She started scrambling around in the boat.

'Ade, what are you doing?' Karragan spluttered.

She was throwing everything out into the sea. Clothes. Food. Water baskets.

'Faster!' she screamed. 'We must go faster!'

'What? Why?'

'My girl!' she cried, pointing. 'MY GIRL!'

And I saw.

Now I watch as Taurus splashes towards her.

'Domaga! Stop the boat! Bring in the sail!' Sol yells, jumping up from where he was sitting.

'But we need to stay away from Vulcan's ship. We'll get hit!'

'Just do it!'

As our boat pulls alongside them, I turn and jump across. My foot goes through the left outrigger, but I just wrench it out and stagger across to the other side, holding out my hands to pull Taurus up, to pull Joomia up—

My mind goes blank when I see the damage. Blood seeps out of her hair on to my hands, dark as ink.

'Her skull is fractured,' Domaga says.

'Joomia?' Taurus moans. 'Joomia?'

'It is no good,' Domaga says.

'She can heal,' Sol says.

'Not this.'

'Domaga, shut up,' Sol snaps. 'I've seen her do it. I've seen her heal herself.'

There's a splash. Ade. She barges Domaga out of the way, shaking. I let her pull Joomia from my lap and into her arms. She begins to sing softly under her breath.

As my mind begins to shut down, as Taurus begins to cry, I look across at Vulcan's ship. With everyone sailing it either knocked down, in the water or still fighting, the boat is slowing down too. I can just make out the shape of two figures, darting back and forth across the deck. Aula and Vulcan. Still fighting. The soldiers are leaving Vulcan to that fight for now and have turned their attention – and their bows – at us. Beyond them, another Govindan ship is arriving to help.

My eyes catch on a vine, trailing from the starboard side. I reach for my tool belt. I'm still wearing it. I run my fingers along my tools. Pick. Chisel. The two smaller hammers. An awl.

'Taurus,' I say.

He looks up, eyes red. 'What?'

'Come with me.'

And I get up and dive into the water.

Taurus

We climb up Joomia's vine to Vulcan's ship. On deck, the damage is catastrophic. There are broken beams, random sheets of metal, soldiers sprawled at every edge. Aula and Vulcan are still locked in battle, limbs blurred, bodies flipping and racing, too fast for my eyes to follow. On the other side of the deck from us, the second of Vulcan's ships has pulled alongside and frantic figures are setting up planks to cross over and help their master. They haven't noticed us. Yet.

Etain completely ignores them. She looks around and heads straight for a hatch, far down on the deck.

'Etain . . . what about Aula?'

'She'll be fine,' she says mechanically.

'You can't know that,' I say.

'I can,' she says. 'Because of Joomia.'

She pauses. The hatch is speckled with blood. A curl of thick ivy lies in pieces next to a shattered lock. She pulls the door open and drops down without a sound. I follow her.

Three men come at us almost at once. I'm not ready for them, but Etain is. She has two hammers in her hands so fast I swear they appeared by magic.

I panic, looking around for something – anything – to defend myself with. I lock on to Etain's tool belt and pluck out the closest thing to my hand. An awl. I duck, roll and jam the spike into the first shin I can see. The man grunts and drops. A second plants his foot against my ear, slamming my head into the floor, and twists. I howl in pain, lashing out wildly.

He kicks me in the shoulder. I nearly drop the awl.

Etain's hammer finds his thigh. He cries out. For a second, I'm free.

I roll backwards, take a firmer grip on my weapon and draw my arm back. I look up. He's looking back at me. For a second, I just see a human. A person. I hesitate.

Etain doesn't. Her hammer shatters his shoulder. He drops with the others. Three men moaning on the floor.

'Quick,' Etain says, panting. 'The ant queen. Find the ant queen.'

I shuffle like a drunk to my feet and close my eyes. I don't need calm any more. The inside of me is hollow enough, like a husk. A cave that someone used to live in.

The ant queen, I say to the compass. Show me the ant queen.

'This way,' I say to Etain.

Etain

Taurus walks hands out, like a sleepwalker, down a tight, twisting corridor to a room at the back of the ship. It's larger than the others. Vulcan's quarters, I'm guessing.

It's lavish inside, rich in fabrics and glittering metals and engraved wood. Dark floorboards, a bunk with white sheets, a tiny staircase in the corner that leads down to a lower level.

Taurus walks straight over to a small table. The box sits upon it, like an old-fashioned treasure chest. It's about the length of my forearm, compact, with a leather strap nailed to either end and a starburst design decorating the top.

A familiar chorus of clicking from beneath us sets my nerves on edge. Not as loud as I've ever heard it, but still . . . it's there. I look nervously towards the tiny staircase. I hiss to Taurus to make him look back at me. 'I think he's keeping the nest beneath us. Or at least, part of the nest,' I whisper.

Taurus nods and points at a hefty padlock that holds it shut. 'Got something for this?'

I put one of my hammers back and take out the chisel just as a heavy thud resounds overhead.

I raise my hammer.

BOOM.

The whole boat, the floor beneath my feet, judders like we've just been hit with a tsunami. Both of us – and the box – go flying. I hit the floor hard, but sit up immediately, pulling the box towards me as the boat continues to rock, the walls shaking.

Taurus scrambles over and hands me the chisel.

'What's going on?' I say.

For a second he looks as dazed as I do. Then his face brightens with understanding. 'Sol!' he says. 'Sol. I think he's—'

He cuts off as the clicking grows louder.

I look at the box, but it's not coming from there. It's coming from the tiny staircase.

'Let's get out of here.'

I take the leather strap and shoulder the ant queen's box and we run back the way we came. As we climb out of the hatch, I chance a look over my shoulder. The clicking rises to a roar, and at the end of the corridor the floor of Vulcan's room floods and swarms with hundreds of insects. They gather for a moment, swelling like a wave, and then they rush toward us – towards *me*.

'Go, Taurus! Quick!'

On deck, some of the men from the second ship have managed to cross. Each one of them is in golden armour and carrying a sword the length of my arm. They're crowding around Vulcan and Aula, trying to distract Aula long enough for their master to incapacitate her, but with the ship still shaking, they're struggling to help at all. It's not just the ship – it's like the *ocean* is shaking and bubbling

328

around us, like someone put acid in the water.

'Taurus. What—'

But he's pointing out toward the trimaran.

The men Aula and Joomia threw off the ship are converging on the trimaran now, with only Ade and Domaga to hold them back. Up front, Sol stands with his head thrown back, braced like he's about to lift a great weight. His hands are slowly lifting toward the sky, his mouth open in a scream of pure exertion.

And out in front of us, in front of the ships, some dark shape is massing beneath the brine like an oil spill, swirling like the beginnings of a maelstrom in the broiling water. Before I can comprehend any of it, Aula roars my name.

I crick my neck as I turn to look at her. And Vulcan. He's staring at us. At the box. If he notices his ants flooding the deck from the hatch, he doesn't show it.

We've run out of time.

Taurus holds the box for me as I fumble to position the chisel against the padlock. The ants swarm over me again, but I ignore them. I try to slam my hammer arm down, but my shoulder pulls tight—

Damn arrow wound.

I miss. I nearly hit my fingers.

'Etain—' Taurus says breathlessly.

'I know,' I say. I flick a glance: Aula is holding Vulcan back from us, but only just. I can almost feel him escaping Aula's grip. I can imagine him picking off her fingers one by one. I aim the chisel, lift the hammer.

Wham.

The padlock scuffs, but it's not good enough. Taurus grimaces in pain as the ants begin to bite, but he doesn't drop the box.

'One more,' I say.

'ETAIN!' Aula screams.

I position the chisel again. I lift my arm.

With a yell, Vulcan reaches us.

I bring the hammer down.

And at the same moment, the ocean explodes in a shower of black mass.

The Chosen

Vulcan stops in his tracks.

The sea is boiling – a magnified version of water in a pan over flames. From the bubbles, steam rises in thick white clouds. There's a pause. And then another explosion. Great black swathes of . . . of *something* arc into the air along with the spray. *So this is what made the ocean shake so*, thinks Vulcan. But what could be causing it?

He searches, he *feels* through his ants for the cause. Their voices nag him about trouble, but he does not listen. What is causing the sea to combust? The ants are more than a little blind without land beneath them, but their antennae still taste the air, and on the breeze they can taste magic. *Etheling* magic. True *etheling* magic—

And then Vulcan looks from the broiling sea to Sol, arms spread wide at the front of the trimaran. The pose of a god.

'Sol,' Vulcan whispers. 'How can it be? Sol . . .'

The queen, the ant's voices clamour. *The queen is in trouble*.

But Vulcan is transfixed by his sibling, by his power and his stance, and so he does not notice what's happening right before him.

The boy lifts the ant queen out of her box and pinions her squirming body on the deck.

Vulcan does not see the girl take the awl and position it over the ant queen's head.

THE QUEEN IS IN TROUBLE.

At the last second, Vulcan snaps out of it. 'What?' Vulcan says. 'NO!'

Etain

My hammer saves me from being snapped in two. As Vulcan raises his fist to break me, I lift it over my head in defence. The handle is longer than I'd usually make them, and the extra metal gives me just enough time to roll out of his way before the handle *snaps*.

The next thing I know, Vulcan has two hands wrapped around Taurus's neck.

'Stop!' I say desperately as Taurus's eyes bulge and he drops the box.

'Stop!' I yell. 'We'll put her back!'

But Vulcan's not listening. He carries on squeezing. As his muscles flex, the faint outline of a scar appears on his outer forearm.

331

'TAURUS!' Aula screams, but the soldiers have surrounded her, swords pointed at her from all sides. My mind slows, like water.

One soldier feints a jab at Aula's shoulder, but she calls it, catches his arm and swings it backwards. His sword clatters along the deck toward me.

Taurus makes a faint whining noise.

Do something, Etain.

I dive for the sword, fumble for its grip, crawl forward on my hands and knees. Vulcan's staring at Taurus, at his death grip, and doesn't see me, not even as I swing the blade up over my head.

'Sire!' one of the soldiers screams. 'Look out!'

Vulcan turns. But not before I bring the sword down.

The Chosen

Vulcan is not used to things not being in his control.

Just before his father died, he told Vulcan a secret: his abomination of a sister, who shaved her head and presumed to wear men's clothes, who professed to be a man herself, *she* was an Etheling. A real one. After hundreds of years had passed without.

His father reminded Vulcan of when Sol had been a child, and the strange months in which the ground had shaken and groaned like a giant lived beneath them. The earth had shook when things were not to Sol's liking.

Vulcan felt sick. 'Is *she* to be your heir, Father? Is that what you are telling me?'

332

'Of course not!' his father snapped. 'Do you think I would have taken that chance? As soon as we knew, I had a magi construct a dampener. For many years, a person in the kitchens has been adding a special seasoning to her food.'

'So *that* is why you have not banished her for . . . for *gender treason*.'

'Yes,' his father said gravely. 'You must keep her close, my son.'

'Why do we not harvest her bones?'

'Oh, we *will*. But look: she is not yet fifteen. Our experts believe Ethelings reach their full strength around eighteen or twenty, when they are fully grown. We will wait. And then, my son, we will harvest her bones.'

And so Vulcan had done as his father had said. Even after their traitorous sister, Domaga, had killed their father, Vulcan had kept Sol safe.

Frightened, black thoughts have been growing in his mind since Sol stole that boat and escaped.

Now, seeing Sol out there, calling up land mass, Vulcan has no doubt his power is being challenged again.

Vulcan could snap the neck of the boy in his grasp. He could squeeze the air out of him in an instant, but this day has already terrified him enough for him to need to do *something* to feel like he's in control again. So when Vulcan presses his thumbs into the boy's throat, he does it carefully, almost gently, savouring the moment, the feeling of the boy's passivity against his strength.

When the light in his head – his connection to the ants – blackens, Vulcan does not understand it. The power wastes from his hands, yet he cannot comprehend it.

Then he sees the blood. He sees an arm – an *arm* of all things – fall to the deck beside him. *His* arm. He begins to gasp like a fish, adrenaline telling him to do something – do *something*!

The boy gasps, coughing, working his legs hard to shuffle away from him.

And then Vulcan sees the girl with the sword, tall and muscular, her head bare, her black skin shining with sweat, her shoulders slumped in fatigue. His vision swims. She picks up her hammer and her awl and she crosses to the ant queen, who is crawling away much slower than her workers. The girl wants to make sure the job is finished. She pinions the ant with the heel of her left hand and uses her fingers to position the awl.

As the girl raises her hammer, Vulcan begins to laugh. No, he won't say anything. No, he won't. He carries on laughing as she brings the hammer down.

A column of white fire blasts high into the air, blasting everyone on deck backwards. Vulcan peers through his eyelids to watch the damage: the girl twisting in pain as the flames taste her.

'A queen for a queen!' Vulcan shouts. 'A queen for a queen!'

'Girl. My girl. Wake up. Wake up.'

Joomia blinks, and opens her eyes. The simple movement is excruciatingly painful. Someone – she thinks maybe it's Ade – is leaning over her.

She tries to move, but pain explodes like a starburst in front of her eyes and she nearly blacks out. Far off she can

334

hear yelling, screaming, splashing. She can't seem to see properly; everything's blurred, spinning in every direction and strangely coloured: a saturated blue.

I'm going to be sick, she thinks, as the colour continues to swirl. **What happened?** she asks.

Ade sighs in relief to hear her. 'Heal, girl. Skull hurt. Heal.'

Joomia remembers then. Vulcan's hands on her. The deck meeting her head.

'Skull crack. Skull crack,' Ade goes on. 'Quick, girl. Heal. *Heal*.'

But it's hard to remember how. She tries to feel with her mind for the exact location of the injury, but her mind is slow and sickening, blackening at the edges like burning paper.

'Joomia. We need you,' says a different voice. Aula's, this time.

Mentally, Joomia frowns. Something is very wrong.

'Heal,' Ade whispers.

Healing herself seems to require a different level of consciousness – something that, in the privacy of her own head, she's been calling her tree-self. A knowledge that limbs may be regrown, that sap will clot like blood, that scores in bark will heal tougher. Slowly, very slowly, her scalp – and the cranial bones beneath it – harden and reform as she scrapes her blurry thoughts and powers together and directs them at the pain. She is vaguely aware of time passing, but it is hard to say how much. Sap feels potent on her tongue as the magic does its work.

The loud noises seem to have stopped, and now Joomia

335

can hear only the billowing sound of sail canvas filling with wind and water rushing beneath her.

From a long way off, she feels Ade gently tipping water into her mouth and feeding her scraps. Her body drinks, chews, swallows, but she feels more like she's watching from a distance.

Sunlight burns her face, and then rain, and then the cooler breezes of what must be night. At last she falls into a dreamless sleep.

When she wakes, it is to a bloody-orange sky above her, and wind and water singing in her ears. When, slowly, she levers herself on to her elbows, she sees she's on the trimaran, facing backwards. Two ships are following them. She frowns and looks at the figure holding the steering oar tight to her left. Aula. There is something taut and grim in her face. With a feeling of unease, Joomia shifts, numb from lying so long on the uneven wood.

Aula glances down at her. 'You miraculous idiot,' she breathes. 'We were so worried.'

What . . . what happened?

Joomia looks around and sees Sol in position at the sail, Karragan on the safety lines, Ade sitting right at the front. Taurus is next to her, Etain's head in his lap. Her unease shifts to dread. Something's wrong. She crawls over to them. She feels her stomach turn over.

'She's not dead,' Taurus says, unable even to smile in relief at the sight of Joomia. 'She needs Phythia. She needs healers.'

Joomia stares. **Her hands . . .**

'She needs Phythia,' Taurus says again. Joomia gets the

impression he's been chanting it to himself. 'Unless, Joomia . . . you can . . .'

Joomia looks hopelessly at the burns. The largest stretches right across Etain's abdomen, the dark skin left around it turned purplish and swollen. Even with the breeze, Joomia can smell necrotising flesh.

'I can't get her to drink,' Taurus murmurs. 'She's too hot.'

Joomia can't think of anything to say to him. **How far away are we?** she asks at last, turning to Sol.

'Not far,' he answers grimly. He looks utterly exhausted.

Joomia can't bear to look a second more. She makes her way unsteadily back over to Aula and holds her breath for a few seconds, so she won't cry.

How did – how did it happen?

'The ant queen exploded when Etain killed it. All the ants under Vulcan's power sparked when they were killed, but she was so much bigger – it was like a mini-detonation.' Aula swallows and goes on, stony-faced, like she's only working on autopilot. 'It set Etain on fire.

'Vulcan's dead. He was strangling Taurus, trying to stop them from killing the ant queen – and Etain managed to cut off his arm. We tried to stop the bleeding – one of the soldiers even tried to cauterise the stump with his fire powers – but he'd lost too much blood.'

Are his soldiers still chasing us?

Aula allows herself a crooked smile. 'No, they're following Sol. Well, under Domaga's captaincy. Turns out they weren't so loyal to Vulcan with the ant queen gone. They've already started getting the parasite ants out of their

337

necks.' She pauses, looking nauseated. Then she says, 'Oh, and it helps that Sol had Kreywar's powers all along.'

Joomia scrambles to make sense of this. **You mean . . . Sol can make land?**

Aula nods. 'Didn't even need the bones after all. Taurus figured it out, managed to get Sol to start something, distract Vulcan and his men while we got at the ant queen.' She takes a shaky breath and lifts her finger to point. 'There it is. Home.'

Taurus

Vulcan's soldiers come tumbling out of the forest beyond the beach as we approach. Aula jumps off the back of the trimaran and shoves it on to the sand with us balancing inside.

They pause when they see us: the Chosen Ones of Chloris, two accomplices, a prophet and their leader's miscreant siblings. I see their hands going to their weapons and, for a moment, I'm terrified we're going to have to fight our way through them.

But then Karragan stands up and, with as much authority as he can muster on the amount of sleep he's had, yells: 'Stand down! Move out of the way!'

They hesitate.

'Go,' he hisses at us. 'Go, go, *go*!'

There's a split-second hesitation. Everyone looks at me. But I'm not the leader: I'm holding *her* in my arms. Finally, sucking her lip, Joomia takes the reins.

Aula, go and get Phythia. We'll meet you at the Cave of the Ancestors.

I lift Etain off the trimaran as carefully as I can. Aula disappears into the trees, while we hurry through the ranks of Govindan soldiers, not looking at any of them.

I slow almost as soon as we're out of sight. I might've managed on a normal day, but I've barely slept for three, and Etain's heavy. I grit my teeth and continue, but when my arms start to shake, I let Sol take over.

He's barely said a word since he ordered that Vulcan be buried in the molten centre of the new island he'd raised from the sea. Nothing seems to have sunk in for him yet. His only words to me have been, *I made a promise to her*.

Sol only makes it a little further before Joomia has to help him. We pass a clearing that wasn't there before, the trees cut down at the roots. My heart waits expectantly for a reaction to this scene, but the only thing I'm able to dredge is a kind of dull horror. I'm already in a nightmare. Even Ade only manages a single grieving keen. By the time we make it to the Cave of the Ancestors, I can feel every one of us waiting to give out.

Aula's there though, and she's brought Phythia.

Etain's trembling as we lay her down. Her feverish skin has gone grey. I hold my breath as the healer looks her over, unreadable. Phythia seems to be holding hers too as she checks Etain's pulse, peels back her eyelids. She opens her mouth and closes it.

She looks up at me.

And she shakes her head.

Silence.

Ringing in my ears.

My breath comes out in a strangled moan.

'How long?' Aula asks.

'Hours, I'd guess,' Phythia says.

'You can't do anything?' Aula presses.

Phythia points to Etain's blackened fingers, and the blistered, stippled skin on her stomach. 'Sepsis. It's too far gone, Aula. I'm . . . I'm sorry.'

I put my head in my hands. Sol takes my shoulder and shakes me gently. 'Is there nothing that will save her?' he whispers urgently. 'Nothing?'

I look up at him. 'If there was, don't you think I would have—'

I stand up, suddenly understanding what he means. I close my eyes and feel for the compass point. This sleep-deprived, it's shaky and fragile, but it's there. It spins.

It spins.

And finally it stops.

'Aula,' I say. 'Pick her up. Follow me.'

The Chosen

The largest vishaal tree where Vulcan split Nine hasn't stopped bleeding, and the coagulated sap has formed runnels and clots among the roots. The vines have, if possible, grown higher and thicker, nearly blocking the trunk from view. Taurus approaches it in a sleepwalker's daze, and for a moment he wonders if he's asked the right thing. When Aula stops beside him, Etain's breathing is no more than a whispering candle flame, ready to snuff at any moment.

'What now?' Aula asks.

'I don't know,' Taurus mumbles. 'I just followed—'

But Ade interrupts him. 'This is right,' she says. 'This is right.' She ushers Aula forward, and Aula fights her way, teeth tearing, hands ripping, through the tangled ropes of vine until there's a way free to the trunk; the wound Vulcan made in it is visible here.

Joomia doesn't hesitate: she clambers up the root and pulls at the wound in the bark, widening it just at the bottom. It creaks open for her and more pale sap curls out, viscous as tears.

Then Aula steps forward and folds Etain's curled-up body into the opening. They look at Ade, who nods.

This is right.

Joomia claps her hands together as if she's slamming a book shut.

And the wound in the vishaal tree closes, with Etain inside it.

Etain

I am floating, or sitting or swimming. I can't tell which. The smell of tree sap is so strong I can taste it – slightly bitter, slightly sweet – on the back of my tongue.

I understand intuitively that this is a place of calm; the red chaos of flames and Vulcan's laughing face can't haunt me here. It feels like finding a cool, shady hollow to shelter from the glare of a midsummer sun. There's still something bad eating away at me, but it's slowed; it doesn't have the same energy here.

There's a shift in the darkness, and I find I'm looking at someone. I can't see her exactly: there's no light, wherever we are, and therefore no sight, but I know she's there. Perhaps it's just my mind sketching her into place.

I remember the clink and chime of her bangles. I can hear them.

I can hear her chatting in the prophet house, surrounded by other prophets, drinking wine until their lips and teeth would be stained red. She never laughed: she cackled, loud as a blackbird, snorting with mirth. Aula and me would wander in when we were tots and try to make them notice us and she'd get off her chair and come back with two small glasses filled with pomegranate juice. 'Wine, ladies?' she'd say, with a smile. I remember that smile. I'd do anything for it. I'd study from dawn until dusk. I'd tidy my afro into braids; I'd dress my bulky smith body into neat linen lines. I'd change my accent, tuck secrets down my throat, train with a man I hated.

I sniff. I can smell the thyme oil she used to drop on my bedsheets.

'Ma?' I ask.

She's holding me as I sleep, her arms tucked around me like a harness. It feels like a memory, but something tells me that it's not. There's a small part of me that knows this is only happening inside my head, but just now it doesn't seem to matter. I feel so safe.

Etain, she whispers. It's her voice, but there's a strange echo to it, as if there were other voices woven in. I move backwards on the bed, into her, to feel the press of her body better.

So, she says, *how was your week?* Just as if it were any other morning, maybe the day after I'd been studying late or doing extra duties with Nadrik, and this was the first time in a while we'd seen each other.

I tell her everything that's happened. I tell her about the other island. Vulcan, Sol, Domaga. I tell her about the ant queen, and the explosion – the last thing I remember. I tell her how angry I've been with Ade, what a relief it is to have Aula back. I tell her about kissing Joomia.

And I tell her about Taurus. About all the things I didn't see, all the strange and wonderful ways I need him without realising. I tell her about every moment he's held me up, every moment he's guided me. I tell her I think he's in love with Aula.

She sighs with happiness, and reaches for my hand. *And you?* she says.

I shuffle around on the bed to look at her. I could tell her how hard it's been to live up to everything she's expected of me. I could tell her how much I've damaged myself – and other people – by striving to meet a destiny I could never totally succeed at. I could tell her I don't think her lessons were always fair.

But I just say the only thing that matters. 'I miss you. Wise One, I miss you.'

The taste of sap in my mouth grows stronger, and I have the strangest sense of something poisonous being drawn out of me, through every vein, every cell.

She touches my cheek, and smiles. And it's enough just to look at her again.

343

So what now?

I don't have to ask what she means. I know I can stay here, and feel her arms around me for ever. Or I can go back.

'I want to stay with you for a little longer,' I say. And I bury my nose in her tunic. My mind conjures up the familiar smell of her. It makes it worse. I never want to let go.

You still have a family, Etain, she says. *They're waiting*.

'Not yet,' I say. 'Just not yet.'

It's because she doesn't protest, she doesn't tell me to buck up my ideas, that I know what I have to do. Because, really, I'm the only one who can choose.

'They need me,' I say.

Who need you, my darling?

'All of them. My people. They need a leader. And I think . . . I think I'm the right person to take them the next step. Maybe not for ever, but for a while longer.'

She smiles and I feel the ghost of her lips on my forehead. *Damn right. I don't make mistakes*.

I laugh. I forgive her.

And the bed is gone. She's gone. But it hurts a little less. I feel a solidity sinking back into me, right down to my bones. My skin is sticky and thick – like I'm covered in syrup – and when I open my lips I end up disgorging a mouthful of pungent-smelling sap.

I realise I can see a strip of light in the dark and then, out of nowhere, Joomia and Taurus and Aula are leaning in towards me, pulling me towards that narrow slit of brightness. I struggle, crawling in the dark, closer and closer to their faces. They reach out and I find their hands. They're holding me, pulling me gently out of the tree. They lift me out. I'm born again. I look up at the sky, at the forest around me, and I blink away tears.

Etain?

I feel like a leader. I feel like a queen.

Epilogue

Six months later

Etain

It's late enough that it's early, and I'm walking through the woods. There's an urgency in the way the ferns snap under my feet; a taste in the night air which feels like change.

High above me, in the cradle of branches of what used to be two cities – branches high enough for clouds – my people are asleep. It's so much darker down here than anything I ever was used to in Athenas, but there is enough watery moonlight tonight to see by and I find it restful.

I come to the roots of the Trees. There are still traces of Ade's thorns against the trunks: constriction marks and lacerations. The worst mark goes right down the middle of the bark of High Tree: an ugly, bulging scar.

But it has not harmed the tree. I know about that. I know about scars. The one on my stomach has a refracting, translucent kind of sheen, like amber. Hardened sap. It's taken a while, but my hands have mostly recovered too: covered in a shiny, tough skin that's stiffer than I'd like, but still deft enough to have helped make and set up the steps into High Tree at last.

There are fifty steps now, attached by *oluwaseyi* and *serpil* magic, carved from wood and forged metal. They go all the way up to the first branch, to the first new living-wood platform.

I wait there, at the foot of High Tree for a while, and as the sky pales toward dawn, I hear people climbing down the steps. Joomia smiles when she sees me, and jumps the last few steps into my arms. I run my hands through her hair; feel the ever-so-slight dent on the side of her skull, where Vulcan cracked her head against the floor of the ship.

Behind Joomia comes Karragan.

I asked Vulcan's soldiers to stay here. But some of them grew really sick, their control by the ants meaningless without Vulcan to direct them.

We managed to cut some of the ants out of them immediately, as Joomia had tried to do for Astor. Some of the ants had really worked their way in though, and we lost quite a few of the soldiers in the first few days.

It didn't exactly make my coming back easy.

Most of my people were glad enough to see us return and be relieved of their slavery. They were free to mourn the parts of the forest they'd been forced to cut down. Some of them just assumed I was their leader again, and that now that I'd returned we could try to go on as we had before. Einar didn't like that much, but then again, he hadn't done much to rally them while they were under the Govindan men's control.

But things were—

Things *are*—

Different.

We're not the last island on Erthe any more. We're not alone.

And *not alone* often also means conflict. Not many of my people were even slightly interested in continuing any kind of relationship with Govinda, and were horrified when they found out I thought we should give it a try.

It was a hard battle, and I only won it really because of Sol and Domaga, Aula and Joomia, Ade and Taurus.

Sol explained about his own people and how their origin story lay close to ours.

And Domaga told them how badly they needed a chance, like we'd had when Lore brought us here.

Aula stood by me, and let me have my time, and went on being Aula, and the Athenasians liked that because at least she was something they recognised. When Joomia got better, the Metisians felt better too.

It turned out no one had much expectation of them becoming one again.

'Well,' Sabine said, 'their becoming one might have united the vishaal trees, but it didn't exactly *unite* us as a people like the prophecy said it would, did it?'

But I think Sabine missed the point of it, as I had too. But I think I understood now. Aula and Joomia becoming one didn't end the story. Aula and Joomia becoming one *began* the story. Just like it was up to me to decide whether I was going to carry on living in the prophecy made about me. Just like Taurus was going to have to decide whether he wanted to be my compass. Or his own.

Karragan bows shyly to me and Joomia as he approaches. There's a small curl of amusement in the corner of his mouth, and I can tell he still en't sure what to make of a female leader. Actually, he en't sure what to make of anything to do with me. Not my size nor muscles from the forge, not my relationship with another woman, not the loose clothes I wear when it's hot.

But he's getting there. He's learned to watch rather than to comment, and allow himself to be corrected, and laugh at himself when he gets it wrong.

'Your people are very lazy,' he says to me. 'Still asleep when the sun comes up? And on a day like this?'

I laugh. That kind of judgement I can live with.

'Where did you say the celebration would be?'

'The north-western beach. The one with all the pine trees. But, Karragan, no one will be there for a couple of hours.'

He nods. 'Yes. Yes. I know. I just like the quiet. It is very different on Govinda.'

I smile. 'I like the quiet too.'

'Not as much as your silent friend there. She still won't talk to me,' he says.

I've explained about the limits of Joomia's voice, but he still doesn't understand why she can't extend her silent speech to other people. I hear a little hurt in Karragan.

'Would you like to join me?' he asks. This too is a learned courtesy – he just *told* women where to be before, but I can tell he prefers this new, unbinding option.

'We've got to meet someone. But we'll see you there.'

He nods and walks off in the other direction, and Joomia takes my hand and kisses it.

He's funny.

350

'I hope we still *get* to be quiet, once today's happened.'

We will. I don't think the Govindans are going to think much of the trees, she says. **And if they *don't*, and want to stay down here – Sol can always make us more land.**

I laugh, but there's sadness already in my chest at what we're about to do.

There are goodbyes to say, and I've never had to say them before.

It's going to be all right.

'Yeah, I know that really. I'm just trying to get used to the idea.'

The good thing about leaving, Joomia says, **is you can always come back.**

Taurus

I've gotten pretty good at getting lost lately.

It's definitely a recent thing, what with this woman named Lore predicting, oh so long ago, that I would be my sister's compass, but when I start to think about it, it all adds up. I'm not quite finished getting unlost though, and I'm not sure where I'm supposed to go from here.

But Etain is. And she doesn't mind giving me a bit of direction.

The question is whether Aula will let her give it to her too.

'Ready, boy?' Ade says.

We're on the beach – *our* beach – the one that's nearest the Cave of the Ancestors.

'No,' I say. 'No, definitely not.'

'Be brave, T,' says Etain, strolling down on to the sand, hand in hand with Joomia. Both of them are glowing. I roll my eyes at them and pretend I don't love it. They know I do, anyway.

'It's not going to work,' I say. 'She *said* she wanted to do this on her own.'

Just wait and see, Taurus, Joomia says. **She's coming now.**

A few minutes later, I spot Aula on the trimaran, sweeping round to the bay. She's really got a handle on it now, steering herself with confidence. She looks kind of serene, but there's tight anticipation there too. I didn't really start to see it – the desperation to explore gnawing at her – until we'd finished building the steps up High Tree, and it became obvious no one was expecting her and Joomia to join again.

The trimaran's in a lot better shape now that Joomia's worked it over. Most of it is now living wood thanks to her etheling powers, but she had every kind of magi put something into it.

Looks good, Joomia says, as the edge of the trimaran shifts the sand.

Aula eyes it up. 'Probably the safest boat on the sea, thanks to you.'

Yeah, well. I gotta take care of my other half.

Aula snorts. 'Thanks for coming to see me off.'

'Oh, we're not yet,' Etain says. 'I'm here as Anassa to tell you – *order* you – to come to the ceremony on the north-western beach.'

'*No*, Etain. I already said. I'll watch from the water.

I want to be gone before anyone knows it.'

Etain makes an exasperated noise, but it's easy to see the fear, the worry, the understanding beneath it. 'OK, fine,' she says. 'But let me give you one more leaving gift.'

'I'm gonna be weighed down as it is . . .'

'*One more* and no complaining.'

Aula rolls her eyes. 'Wait — where are you going?' she says as Etain and Joomia skip off.

'Well, it's a *surprise gift*,' Etain says. 'So we hid it in the bushes.'

Aula gives me a grumpy look. 'Did you have anything to do with this?'

I can't look at her. 'Kind of.'

'OK, I'm worried.'

'You should be,' Ade cackles.

They carry it between them. A canoe: beautifully crafted, shaped like a thin leaf, curved at both ends like an Old World shoe. Etain carved it herself from one of the fallen trees Vulcan's ants harvested. She says it was nearly as enjoyable as working in the forge, but I wasn't fooled. I think she's done with fire these days.

'It's . . . it's *beautiful*,' Aula says. 'But I don't understand . . . do you want me to row away in that instead?'

'No,' Etain says. 'Not exactly.' She looks at me.

'Look, three months ago,' Etain continues, 'Taurus told me he wanted to go away. He said he wanted to make a boat, and put it in the water, and see what was out there. He knew you were going, but he didn't want to follow you or for you to think he was just copying you. He said he had stuff to figure out too, and I believe him. We all know you want to

353

be alone out there. And I get that, Aula. I get that you need to do some searching. And I get that you need to do that by yourself sometimes. So Joomia and me . . . and Ade . . . we came up with a compromise.'

The canoe replaces the middle hull, if you want it to, Aula, Joomia says. It means one of you can row away and do some thinking on your own if you need to. It has space for food and water. You could separate for days at a time if you wanted to.

'But *only* if you want it,' I say. It's time for me to be brave and say my piece. 'I know it's your thing, and if you say no, I'll do this some other way. I'll stay and make my own boat and . . .'

I chance a glance at Aula. She's frowning slightly. I don't know what that means, so I just carry on.

'But if you let me, I could come with you. We could do at least *some* of this together. We could see what there is to see.'

I let out a long breath. I don't have anything more.

Aula sighs and winds her hair up on to her head. And then she takes my hand and looks round at all of us. 'This en't fair. If you wanted to say all this, you should have said it a month ago, not on the day I'm supposed to leave.'

We all look appropriately chastened.

'But,' she says, 'it's a big ocean. Bigger than it used to be.'

There's a smile tugging at the corners of her mouth. My heart beats out hope in double rhythm.

She looks seriously at Etain and Joomia. 'So if I drown him when he gets on my nerves, you're never gonna know where his body is. Are you all right with having that on your conscience?'

Joomia laughs.

Etain looks at me and smiles. 'Are you, Taurus?'

But I think we all know the answer to that.

The Chosen

Etain, Joomia and Ade join their people on the north-western beach as the sky turns rose, heralding the sun.

'Is he close, Ade?' Etain asks. 'When did Domaga say they'd be here?'

'Patience, girl,' Ade says. 'Spiders don't tell me exacts.'

'Nor do you,' Etain points out, but there's no heat in it.

When true dawn comes, the people of Chloris are gathered, waiting in excited silence. They don't know *what's* about to happen – Etain has been hazy with the details – only that something momentous will take place this morning.

As the sun floods the skyline, they see it: a ship.

It's heading for the north-western shore, and as it comes, the ocean boils behind it, leaving a dark path of hardened rock in its wake. Taurus and Aula watch from a safe distance on the trimaran.

As he sees the shore, as he gets closer, Sol feels light in his heart. He has been preparing for this for a long time, and his journey has been difficult. He's exhausted. But he'll rest soon. First he's just enough strength to show how far he's come in half a year.

The people of Chloris speculate loudly. 'Is it a path?'

'But where does it lead?'

'It's a bridge,' Etain says as Sol pulls into shore, behind

him the narrow strip of land he's just formed.

Einar sneers, 'And what's the point of this bridge, *Anassa*?'

'To make the space between us – between Govinda and Chloris – a little easier to cross,' Etain replies, not rising to him. 'To open our islands up to each other.'

Einar looks appalled.

But Karragan doesn't. 'It's the start of something,' he says, smiling as Sol climbs down from his ship. 'A new chapter for my people. And yours.'

What comes after? Joomia asks, a smile in her voice.

Etain takes Joomia's hand. 'I was thinking we'd rebuild the world,' she says.

Acknowledgements

Thank you, Silvia Molteni, for continuing to support and encourage me, as well as for getting me hyped up about future projects. I'm so glad to have you as my agent.

Thank you, Leo Nickolls and Michelle Brackenborough, for not one but two stunning covers. I've stared at them both for hours.

A million thank yous to the wonderful Emma Goldhawk – especially for being Anassa's big sister and pointing out the shipwreck sites so Etain and Taurus could avoid them. You talked me through all my stresses with patience, even extending my deadlines. I won't ask again, I promise!

Thank you, Sue Cook, for your eagle eye during copy edits.

Thank you to Sarah Lambert, Steph Allen, Sarah Jeffcoate, and the genius Hachette team, especially at YALC this year, when they passed around seed packets featuring the Ariadnis cover! You all do amazing things at Hachette and you've been so helpful, but mostly, I just think you're great people.

Speaking of YALC, thank you to all the authors I've had the chance to meet this year and bribe to be my friend: Patrice Lawrence, Alice Broadway, Gemma Fowler, Hayley Barker, Carlie Sorosiak, Vic James and Taran Matharu have been especially friendly and encouraging. If you're a new author, go and offer them ALL THE BISCUITS, or in the case of Alice Broadway, all the tea.

Thank you to everyone who came to the launches of Ariadnis in London and Somerset – it meant so very much to have everyone turn up for my brainchild. Particular thanks to Claire and James Brooker, Emma Craigie and Mum, not only for cooking afterwards but for forcing copies of Ariadnis onto your friends (and for the book shelf dedicated to it in your house). Dad, Daile, Tild and Phoeb: I love you! Thank you for showing me every copy you found in Oz.

All the Gores – it is really quite good to have you as a second family. JK, it's amazeballs.

I have heard that Oliver Lee (also known as Caravan Lee) has done some impressive Ariadnis pushing over in Oz too, while the indomitable Jenny Byfleet has had New Zealand covered. You're angels, I miss you.

Yael, my magical friend. Thank you for all your wise words, your nudges in the right direction, your tireless cheerleading and smiles. Also, fearlessly fighting the good fight for libraries and librarians everywhere, thank you, Lucinda Murray, sorry I'm terrible at calling.

Thank you early readers and hard core enthusiasts, Rosey, Katie, Yael, Cerise, Aimee, Izzy and everyone on the vast network of diversity websites who gave me tips about trans representation and things to avoid.

I am lucky to have so many wonderful pals who read the first book, did not hate it, and continued to be my friend, so please continue doing that.

Seb: Zoen! Bisous! Knuffel!